Subscribe to my newsletter!

Sign up for my monthly emails for all sorts of goodies, including:

- My free short story, *The Spinster*
- Deleted scenes and excerpts
- Discount to my bookstore
- And more!

Sign up at www.katherinegrantromance.com

Copyright © 2021 by Katie Flanagan

First ebook and paperback edition March 2021

Cover design by Julia Gerbach
Interior design by Asya Blue

ISBN (paperback) 978-1-7343813-5-1
ISBN (ebook) 978-1-7343813-6-8

www.katherinegrantromance.com

Also by Katherine Grant

Check out the full Countess Chronicles series:

The Ideal Countess

In this National Indie Excellence Award finalist, an eager debutante is caught between the notorious Duke of Cornwall and her childhood friend, the Earl of Windemere.

Alice never dreamed her Season would go this well. She has beautiful dresses, new friends, and she's caught the eye of the most dashing bachelor in London, the Duke of Cornwall.

But her friend, Hugh Osborne, the Earl of Windemere, is concerned the duke's attentions towards Alice aren't completely honorable. While she dreams of marrying the impossible duke, Hugh scrambles to find a way to protect her - and win her heart - before Alice's reputation is dashed to pieces.

New Year's Masquerade

New Year's Eve, 1810

Bernard Talbot, Earl of Gresham, is ready to take the next step: make Miss Lisbeth Dawes his countess and continue the Gresham legacy.

Then, just in time for the New Year's masquerade ball, Annabelle returns. Annabelle is Bernard's first and only love, lost to the Duke of Surrey seven years ago. Now she is widowed and hoping to step back into Bernard's life.

With just one night left before his wedding, Bernard must decide whether to honor duty or follow his heart.

The Duchess Wager

The duke accepts a wager

Fitz, the Duke of Harrodshire, views marriage as a business arrangement, not a question of the heart. Especially once he bets his friends that he won't marry the next woman he fancies. He knows it will be an easy win - until they take refuge from a snowstorm at Bleneccle Manor and he meets Lady Margot Wickham.

A widow in mourning

At her parents' home in Northern England to recover from her husband's sudden death, Lady Margot Wickham isn't sure she'll ever be ready to face the duties of being a Dowager Countess. When unexpected travelers show up in a snowstorm, Margot is grateful for the distraction.

Until she realizes she might be too distracted by a certain duke.

Duty calls

When Margot gets notice of unrest at her husband's cotton mill, she realizes she can put off duty no longer. Alarmed, Fitz volunteers to accompany her south. He plans to help her resolve the issue - but the road trip is a convenient excuse to stay close, too.

Plus, a free short story, *The Spinster*, available exclusively at www.katherinegrantromance.com

Countess Chronicles #3

The Husband Plot

Katherine Grant

Chapter One

March 1811

On the morning of her second wedding, Miss Lisbeth Dawes knew several universal facts to be true: the world was unfair to women, wedding days did not always result in marriage, and she was likely making a mistake.

She comforted herself with the fact that at least it wasn't the *same* mistake she had made three months prior in January. Then, she had woken to her wedding dawn knowing she didn't love her fiancé and that she would be bored to tears before their honeymoon even started. To marry Lord Gresham, she knew deep down in her bones, would be the greatest mistake of her lifetime. She'd snuck out at morning light in her drab old day dress to settle her thoughts. To talk herself into the marriage. To remind herself that a married woman was a much freer woman.

She had ended up talking her fiancé out of marrying her.

Oh, it wasn't as bad as all that. Lord Gresham's heart belonged to another, a woman whom they'd all discovered just before the masquerade was a widow free to marry. He would be an idiot *not* to marry beautiful Annabelle. And Lisbeth would be an idiot to wed a man who was head over heels in love with someone else.

Lisbeth absolutely without a doubt was *not* hurt that no secret man harbored similar feelings for her.

This wedding morning, Lisbeth wasn't quite as clear-eyed on how she felt. Her bones still jangled, but she wasn't sure whether it was with terror or anticipation. After all, she was making a different mistake this time.

She was marrying a man she had never met.

It was an unusual arrangement, to be sure, and one whose circumstances were quite by accident. Lisbeth hadn't set out to marry a man sight unseen. She simply didn't want to make the same mistake twice. After the failure of her New Year's wedding, Lisbeth told her father, Lord James Dawes, the Marquess of Ipswich, that she was afraid she would talk herself out of marrying *any* man in her acquaintance. Lord Dawes interpreted this to mean she must meet new men, and when he heard the Duke of Berkwell's grandson needed a wife, he started a correspondence.

It was all very businesslike. Mr. Adrian Hathorne, son of the duke's second son, stood to inherit a substantial West Indian sugar plantation, if he married an Englishwoman of good breeding. Once they were married, he would return to Kingston to take over the plantation, leaving Lisbeth in London – almost as if she were a spinster, except with all the privileges of a married woman.

It was the perfect arrangement for Lisbeth. For she planned to live a full, grand life, and one could really only do that if one married. She would set up her own household, where she could eat supper in the library and crowd the walls with French paintings. She would become a patroness of the arts, with a retinue of playwrights, poets, sculptors, portraitists, composers, and musicians who gathered at her invitation and filled her rooms with thundering debates. She would have wild, passionate affairs. And she would funnel her pin money – stolen from slave labor – into abolitionist organizations and relief for the poor and crime reform and every other cause that made her cry.

After all, her husband would never know. He would be in the West Indies.

It was a grand plan, as long as Lisbeth could go through with it. At the moment, however, with her maid Hannah changing necklaces for the third time and her mother fussing around the dressing room, Lisbeth only felt sure she was making a mistake all over again.

"At least we've gotten you into your wedding dress this time," her mother, Lady Cecilia Dawes, said as she smoothed the fabric around Lisbeth's shoulders. "You look lovely, Lisbeth."

It was a bit of a mother's fib. Lisbeth could see plainly in the mirror that "lovely" was a stretch. The gown was lovely, to be sure, a white muslin with silver thread embroidery, but its long, column design only accentuated how short Lisbeth was, how broad her shoulders, how scant her bosom. Her brown hair was the only feature that Lisbeth felt deserved a compliment, curled nicely around her face and decorated with a dyed ostrich plume soaring high to the ceiling.

She hoped Mr. Adrian Hathorne wasn't too disappointed when he finally laid his eyes on her.

Although she didn't think a gentleman who agreed to a bride sight unseen should have the right to disappointment as to how she looked. Lisbeth certainly wasn't expecting Mr. Hathorne to set her heart racing. From what she knew about him – the twenty-four-year-old son of a Hathorne and a free Jamaican woman, who desperately needed a wife to claim his inheritance – Lisbeth imagined a groom with a dark face, oversized paunch, and perhaps bad breath. Why else wouldn't he be able to find a wife, with hundreds of thousands of pounds awaiting him.

She wondered what he expected her to be.

Her mother dismissed Hannah and turned Lisbeth from the mirror, two strong hands gripping Lisbeth's shoulders.

"Are you sure this is what you want to do? It's not too late to cry off. I wouldn't blame you. We could take a tour of the Lake District and come back next year to try the Season again."

Lisbeth smiled into her mother's question. Lady Cecilia had known such a different life than Lisbeth. Tall, lithe, witty, charming, there wasn't a person in the world who didn't love Lady Cecilia. She'd had her pick of suitors. She had gotten to fall in love.

A year ago, Lisbeth had dreamed of falling in love. One season of courting rituals in London's ballrooms had cured her of that; she wasn't sure there was a single man of peerage that was worthy of her conversation. If there was, he wasn't interested in *her*.

No, Lisbeth had had enough of the plotting and dreaming and talking and thinking about marriage. She would get it over with, claim her status as a Married Lady, and move on with her plans.

"I'm sure," she reassured her mother. "I'm grateful to you and Papa for arranging this so neatly."

Her parents had encouraged the match but not the means. They would have preferred to have Mr. Hathorne court Lisbeth throughout the Season, or at least stay at their home for a week or two to establish a connection. But Lisbeth had insisted: if she met the man, she might not marry him.

This way, she would be a married lady after all when she returned to the dreary Almack's ballroom. Better, as a married lady, she could choose to avoid Almack's for the rest of her life.

"It is perfectly fine to change your mind," her mother prodded. "You have strong ideas, but no one will think the less of you for thinking better of them."

"No, they will think the less of me for twice failing to make it to the altar. In any case, *they* don't matter." Lisbeth touched her hands to the ostrich feather, making sure it had not fallen crooked. She smiled at her mother, mustering a lie. "All that matters is that I am completely sure with every fiber of my being that I am right to marry

5

Mr. Hathorne."

Lady Cecilia still set her lips in a flat, skeptic line. She hooked her arm through Lisbeth's anyway. "Then let's make sure we aren't late to the church. And if you change your mind on the way, no harm done."

The ride to St. George's at Hanover Square was not long. Perhaps twenty minutes at most, if one counted waiting in the sitting room for the carriage to pull around from the mews, the fuss as the housekeeper pressed good-luck kisses to Lisbeth's cheeks, and the delay at the intersection of New Bond Street. It shouldn't have been enough time for Lisbeth's stomach to turn to acid.

But it was.

By the time the carriage pulled to a stop, Lisbeth was quite sure she would be sick. Her skin was clammy, her ears hot. Her stomach cramped.

This had to be absolutely the worst idea she'd ever had. More foolish than her scheme to house a brood of puppies in her bedchamber as a twelve-year-old. More damning than her stolen kiss from a stranger at Vauxhall Gardens last summer. More damaging than talking Lord Gresham out of the wedding.

She was marrying a complete and total stranger.

"Lisbeth?" Her mother peered up at her from the church steps. The footman still stood at attention, hand out to help the bride down from the carriage. "Do you want to go home?"

Oh, she did. She wanted to flee to their house in the

country and lock herself in her rooms and never come out. No, that wasn't quite right. She wanted to return to their townhouse on Frampton Square and live a brilliant life in London, full of parties and sparkling conversation and healthy debate on topics that mattered, without the specter of spinsterhood shadowing her every move. She wanted to crave somebody's company and have them yearn for her in return. She wanted to feel things more deeply than she ought and think more thoroughly than she should and die with more friends than could fit in a church.

"Lisbeth?" This from her father now, his usually calm face pinched in concern.

Her parents were nothing but concerned for her these days. Ever since Lord Gresham had rushed off to Gretna Green to elope with the Duchess of Surrey. And if she fled now, they would be nothing but concerned for the rest of her life.

The rest of her long, quiet spinster life.

"I'm fine. Only savoring the moment." Summoning a smile, she stepped from the carriage, taking first the footman's hand and then her father's arm. Only one more man to go before she was free.

Her father waited with her in the church's nave while Lady Cecilia slipped forward to the pews. Lisbeth distracted herself from panic by reviewing who she would soon see. It was a fashionably small ceremony, with only close family on either side in attendance. Her grandparents were in town for the occasion, as were her two elder brothers and her Aunt Vivienne, which was a treat. From the groom's side, Lisbeth expected his grandparents the Duke and Duchess of Berkwell, his half-sister, and perhaps a cousin or two.

And then of course there was the groom.

The church organ groaned. Lisbeth's father placed a palm over her hand. "Are you sure, my dear?"

She nodded. She couldn't quite smile, but she tried to be witty, at least. "Let's find out what my husband looks like, then."

The sanctuary doors opened.

The room was dim enough that at first, all Lisbeth saw were outlines. The silhouettes of their guests in the pews. The stone pulpit. The priest in his billowing robes.

Then her eyes adjusted, and she got her first real look at him.

Mr. Hathorne.

The most handsome man Lisbeth had ever seen in her life.

He stood proudly at the altar, shoulders squared, arms tucked patiently behind his back. He was slim and fit, the body of a man who enjoyed regular exercise. His broad face, squared by a firm jaw and thick black eyebrows, watched her approach with a blank kindness.

But what really did it for Lisbeth – what sucked the air from her gut and made her miss the next step – were his eyes. The most brilliant green glittered at her, so unexpected from his brown West Indian complexion.

They arrested her. They mesmerized her.

They electrified her.

Those eyes were on her now, taking in her full bridal glory as she and her father reached the altar. Lisbeth's cheeks heated, knowing what he saw. A dumpy little woman compared to his sleek physique. Pale cheeks that refused to bloom beside his glowing brown skin. Dull chicory eyes to meet his unforgettable gaze.

The priest asked who gave away the bride, and Lord Dawes hesitated, squeezing Lisbeth's hand one last time. This was her final chance. She could walk away.

She probably should. She had no business marrying a man with bewitching eyes. No doubt he was praying that she would come to her senses just now and beg off.

Lisbeth peeked at Mr. Hathorne. He hadn't moved, his eyes steady on her, except that his lips had twitched a little. The corners were pulling upwards.

Almost into a smile.

She squeezed her father's hand in affirmation.

There was no going back now.

Chapter Two

At least it was all over. The wedding, the celebration, the well-wishes from his family, the reserved congratulations from hers, the toasts, the smiles, the small talk – it was all behind him now. Adrian had successfully married Miss Lisbeth Dawes, sight unseen.

Now the only tribulation left was the wedding night.

He glanced down to Miss Dawes – *Mrs. Hathorne,* he corrected himself – as the footman handed her into the carriage. How strange it was to suddenly have a wife. A beautiful, compact, glimmering wife. She was the epitome of an English lady, down to the ostrich plume nodding above her head.

Adrian didn't know what she expected from him as a husband. He hoped he could live up to it. He knew theirs would be a distant marriage – geographically and emotionally – but he hoped in the few months they had together, he could earn her respect, so that once he left for Inglewilde Plantation she would speak kindly of him.

They turned as one before the carriage door shut, raising their hands in a final wave to the wedding guests. His wife's family had spilled onto the front steps, while his party crushed into the grand threshold of Lord Dawes's townhouse. His grandfather and grandmother – the Duke and Duchess of Berkwell – looked somberly on, while his half-sister Mary managed a pale smile. Behind Mary, his cousin Robert laughed at something said by Lord Brabourne – the only guest not related to the Hathornes that his family had invited.

It was the picture of a farce. Two families, pretending to congratulate each other on a match well made, when in reality everyone wondered in whispers why any grandson of a duke and daughter of a marquess would need stoop to marry as strangers.

Or perhaps they were whispering about what a shame it was that Miss Dawes had not managed to marry a man with a title. Or how tragic it was such a pretty English rose was wedded to an *African.*

The footman closed the carriage door, and Adrian turned away. Back to the new Mrs. Hathorne, perched perfectly on the bench opposite.

He had never expected to marry. His father had shipped him and Mary to England to be raised properly, but Adrian had always understood himself to be destined to inherit Hathorne Shipping and Inglewilde Plantation. He hadn't imagined that included marriage, especially not to the daughter of a proper English lord. He had nearly fainted when he read his father's letter in January: the doctors said his father had only six months to live, and his father wanted Adrian married before he died.

It was hard to picture his father bedridden for months from fever. It was harder still to picture himself a husband.

That letter still sat heavy in his breast pocket.

Without it as a physical talisman, Adrian wasn't certain he would have made it to the church this morning.

He looked to his bride as their carriage rumbled over Mayfair cobblestones, transporting them from the safety of her father's opulent townhouse to his less-fashionable quarters at No. 73, Upper Norton Street. Adrian hadn't known what to expect from the London lady who would marry him without introduction. He knew she had been jilted at the altar earlier that year, but he had assumed there was some other reason why she would agree to so drastic a measure. He'd imagined someone too powerfully shy to brave the *ton's* ballrooms, but Miss Dawes had chatted easily with everyone at the wedding breakfast. Neither had she said anything vulgar, inappropriate, or stupid – all reasons a family might shield their daughter from good society.

By every measure he had seen so far, Lisbeth was a charming, intelligent lady. The perfect English wife for the perfect English son.

She met his gaze with a pretty smile. She did that often – smile. Already, Adrian had witnessed a palette of variations: the close-lipped, the surprised cry of delight, the sympathetic upturn accompanied by a nod, the laughing grin. This one was a little nervous, the sparkle not quite reaching her eyes.

Adrian didn't blame her. He was nervous, too.

"I'm afraid my house is not as fine as Lord Dawes's," Adrian said by way of conversation. "You will, of course, have carte blanche to fix it up to your desires."

"I'm sure it's lovely. I don't have strong opinions on houses, you see, as long as they have a large library and a healthy helping of sunshine."

"In the case of books, my collection doesn't come close to Lord Dawes's." Her father's library was famous in London, for it sat where the ballroom should have been and housed over three hundred titles. Adrian wondered how many of them Lisbeth had read. "We shall have to aspire to rival his."

It was the first marital "we" either of them had uttered. Lisbeth smiled again, but Adrian only felt vaguely nauseous.

After all, there wasn't going to be very much "we" in their marriage. Now that he was married to an English lady – connected at last both by birth and by marriage to aristocracy – his father would add it to the petition to the Jamaican assembly as evidence why they should grant him privileges to be sole heir to the sugar plantation. Which meant Adrian could finally return to the West Indies. And Lisbeth would stay behind.

She was merely a pawn. A willing pawn, but the adjective did not change the noun.

He wondered again why she had agreed to such an arrangement.

Number 73, Upper Norton Street was quiet compared to the Dawes townhouse. It was a narrow, four-story house with black-and-white tiles on its front steps as its major claim to fashion. The servants lined up in the parlor to greet their new mistress: the butler Ford, the housekeeper and cook Mrs. Siswell, his valet Mr. Adkins, the two footmen, and the three maids. Lisbeth greeted them with her cordial smile, which made her look so stately for a woman no more than five feet tall.

Mrs. Siswell offered Lisbeth a tour of the house. Adrian followed along. He could easily have excused himself to his study on the pretense of business, but he was growing more nervous by the minute, and it seemed the best remedy was to stay close at hand. If he retreated, he might find endless excuses *not* to return to Lisbeth that evening, and he did not want to fail her so soon.

Lisbeth was an active participant on the tour, exclaiming over the cleanliness of the kitchen, commiserating on the fight against mice, asking after how often the carpets were cleaned and how many candles the chandeliers required. Every now and then, she included Adrian, too, casting him glances or asking his opinion or simply offering him a compliment.

He didn't mind it. The attention. In fact, when they crossed the whole of the dining room without a single glance directed his way, Adrian felt a little left out.

He would, perhaps, enjoy having a wife.

Assuming that he could get through the wedding night.

The tour ended on the third story, in the creaky old corridor. Mrs. Siswell pointed towards one door and then the other. "This is your apartment, ma'am, and that is Sir's. I expect your Hannah has everything settled for you in there. May I get you anything? Perhaps a cup of tea or some sherry?"

Lisbeth's eyes drifted across Adrian as she answered the housekeeper. His stomach flipped. She looked nervous again, which meant he absolutely could not be nervous. He was the husband.

He was supposed to know what he was doing.

"No, thank you, Mrs. Siswell. You may retire for the evening." Lisbeth turned as she said this, offering a curtsey to him. "Good night."

Adrian bowed, watching her retreat behind the oak door. She would need some time to retire. A woman had things she must do, though he didn't know what they were. Change out of her dress, undo her hair, he supposed. It took them long enough to get ready that it must take at least as long to undo all that work.

He was aware that he was trying to distract himself. Or trying to delay himself. It would not do. He had *duties* to attend to. And Adrian never shirked his duties.

He retreated to his own suite, which included a bed-chamber and a dressing room. Mr. Adkins was already there, nightshirt and dressing robe hanging freshly pressed.

"Many congratulations, sir," Mr. Adkins bustled. "I'm sure one could not have asked for a more suitable bride."

Adrian tried to smile in reply, though his inside was

so knotted he imagined it came out as a grimace.

Mr. Adkins undid Adrian's tie and helped him shrug out of his wedding suit. "I thought perhaps you would want a shave tonight, sir?"

"A shave?" Adrian had never been in the habit of a nighttime shave, especially since he'd just been under Mr. Adkins's knife that morning. Though when he ran a palm across his jaw, he had to admit it was a little prickly.

"In consideration for Mrs. Hathorne." Mr. Adkins winked. "I also took the liberty of pulling out your cologne."

Adrian blushed. These were the types of considerations a gentleman should already know by the time of his wedding night. "Of course. Good thinking, Mr. Adkins."

So he found himself sitting back, getting slathered with shaving cream. At least it was another delay. It would give Lisbeth more time to do whatever she needed to do to prepare.

He turned his thoughts away from her. It made him too nervous.

Mr. Adkins babbled away, as he usually did, filling Adrian's silent room with cheerful chatter. Normally, Adrian enjoyed it, but he couldn't even bring himself to pay attention to the distraction. The moment loomed too close. The truth loomed too large.

Adrian was a virgin, and he didn't have the first idea how to go about a wedding night.

The average gentleman would have solved this problem years ago. Some of his schoolmates started lessons early with willing lasses around Eton grounds. Others went through a rite of passage with expensive London courtesans on landmark birthdays. They set up actresses as mistresses or wooed widows with lonely beds.

By the time the average gentleman got to his wedding night, he was a veritable expert in sex. It was necessary, in order to ease his wife's suffering as she surrendered to marital duties.

But Adrian had never dared join his peers in their extracurricular schooling. He had too much to prove. He wasn't from England, after all, no matter that his blood ran thick with dukes and earls. He was West Indian; he was Black. From the moment he stepped foot on English soil at the age of seven and a dockhand tried to press him into hauling freight, Adrian had known: he needed to behave *better* than everyone to prove his nobility.

So he had kept his head down and come out as top of his class. He had sailed the Hathorne Shipping line without picking up any of the sailors' sins. He studied the trends of horses, racing vehicles, even fashion to stay in vogue with his friends, but he stayed far from vice, scandal, or anything else that might bring shame.

The scheme had seemed an excellent idea until tonight.

Finished with the shave, Mr. Adkins helped Adrian into his nightshirt and dressing robe. "I'll retire now unless you need anything else from me, Sir."

Adrian wanted to grab the man by the coattails and

beg him not to leave. Instead, he shook his head. "Any last words of advice?"

The valet grinned as if it were a joke. "I daresay you don't need advice from *me*."

And so the moment had come. There were no more excuses. No more reasons to delay. There was only the door that stood between Adrian and his biggest fear.

He decided a knock was polite. After a moment, Lisbeth squeaked, "Enter." She cleared her throat as Adrian crossed the threshold, so that by the time he turned from closing the door, her voice was lower, huskier. "I trust you are well."

Lisbeth stood by the fire wearing nothing but a lace shift, whose pattern he was fairly certain did *not* cover her most private areas. Her hair fell softly around her face and past her shoulders with a smooth brown shine. She glowed in the firelight like a woman in a Vermeer painting.

Adrian gulped. His mouth was dry, his stomach was turning, and his cock – he didn't dare pay it any attention. He had no idea what came between now and the bed.

"Thank you," he responded from knee-jerk scripting. "And you are well?"

She smiled. This one was brave. Adrian could see how it took effort for her to summon it, how her eyes danced across his face, as if trying to read him. She was waiting for him to make the next move. To show her how it was done.

Adrian cleared his throat. He was a smart man. He could figure this out. He knew it started with kissing. From there, surely, biology would kick in.

Crossing the room to join her by the fire, Adrian stepped right in front of her. Closer than he'd ever been to a woman. Now he saw her pink nipples thrusting wantonly through the lace pattern. He didn't know nipples could be so erect. He felt his own erection swell at the observation.

Lisbeth stared up at him. She was so short. He wasn't sure the mechanics of the kiss, considering she only came up to his shoulders. Adrian brought a trembling hand – he ordered it still before he touched her – to cup her neck, his thumb resting just before her ear. Her skin was soft, the kind of soft he could wish to caress forever. Her eyes closed at his touch. That was good; Adrian didn't feel her hopes quite so much without her bright gaze watching him. Stooping, he closed his own eyes and pursed his lips, as he supposed one must for a kiss. He leaned in.

And kept leaning, until suddenly he found himself breathing hair.

He'd missed.

He'd missed her lips.

For god's sake, he couldn't even figure out how to *kiss* her. How was he ever going to figure out the rest of it?

Lisbeth let out a little gasp at finding her husband rooting around her hair. Adrian tried to pass it off as intentional, burying his face further in the brown coiffure. "Your hair smells so good."

"Thank you." After a moment, she added, "You smell divine, too."

Divine. That was a much better word for complimenting. And thank god Mr. Adkins had suggested the cologne.

Withdrawing from the safety of her hair, Adrian beheld his wife's face again. She still had her eyes closed, her chin upturned as she awaited her kiss.

He had not disgusted her entirely yet, then.

Holding her face in both his hands now, Adrian kept his eyes open as he leaned in. He watched her lips as he grew closer and closer. They were pink, thin, nicely shaped with a cupid's bow at the top. And they were right there. Not moving. Hard to miss.

This time, he didn't miss. This time, his lips touched hers.

It was softer than he expected. Stranger than he expected. Lovelier than he expected.

She tasted of white wine. She felt like fire. His whole body – from his toes to his fingertips to his eager, throbbing cock – connected to her lips as one. He was nothing but this kiss. He wanted nothing but this kiss.

Then Lisbeth's hands reached up to his shoulders. The touch was light but so heavenly. She ran her fingers under the lapels of his dressing robe, drawing little lines across his chest that stoked the fire raging under his skin. Adrian dropped his own hands, tracing them down her neck, her shoulders, skipping down to her waist. And then, before he could overthink it, up to those pert nipples awaiting him under the wide lace loops.

Lisbeth gasped again. Her eyes flew open as her

mouth withdrew from his. Alarm flooded her irises.

He dropped his hands. Clearly, that was *not* the thing. He stepped back.

"Mr. Hathorne," she said, her voice back to that high-pitched squeal.

He'd done it wrong. He had offended her. Perhaps he had even hurt her.

Adrian should have known he couldn't do this.

He gave her a little bow. "Madam. Sleep well."

And with that, he beat a hasty retreat back to the safety of his own rooms. Where he could spend the rest of the night wishing himself any fate but this.

Chapter Three

The morning sun was different in No. 73, Upper Norton Street than in her father's townhouse. Lisbeth watched it rise through the narrow window afforded her bedchamber, which faced the common gardens behind the house. The sun was high in the sky before it could reach through her window, and even then, it was so pale and weak that Lisbeth felt no warmth. The whole courtyard had a pall of gloom, with sickly hedge bushes protecting barren brown earth that might one day yield kitchen herbs.

It matched her mood. Lisbeth didn't know the exact details of a wedding night, but she knew that her evening had not included the most crucial element.

Her cheeks burned as she remembered it. Of all things she'd feared about her marriage, the wedding night was not one of them. She was eager to understand what happened between man and woman, that act which seemed to obsess the entire population. She could not have love, but Lisbeth had thought she would at least have physical excitement.

Instead, she had humiliation.

Oh, Adrian had tried to be kind about it. But it was clear from the moment he crossed the threshold and looked at her with those glittering green eyes that she wasn't what he wanted. How he stared at her. How he hesitated to come close. Before he entered the room, Lisbeth had felt bold and wanton in her lace negligee, a delicious, scandalous feeling that made her skin tingle in anticipation. He kissed her, and she thought perhaps she'd misinterpreted his eyes.

Then he touched her. His fingers on her breasts – oh, it had been the most wicked feeling in the world. Lisbeth felt as if he had unlocked her. She thought her knees might buckle. She had nearly whimpered in desire – indeed, she was afraid she had rather moaned his name to beseech him to continue.

But the touch that unleashed her finished the whole affair for him. He'd thanked her, as if they had completed their duty, and fled.

She repulsed him.

She knew that hadn't been the sum of marital relations. He hadn't even touched her between the legs. Lisbeth had explored that region herself enough to know it was key to pleasure between man and a woman. Adrian hadn't even come near it.

Sighing, Lisbeth turned from the window and rang for Hannah. There was no use moping about it. She should have expected it, really. Adrian was the kind of handsome that stopped women in their tracks. He must be used to the same type of beauty. The breasts he cupped must usually be supple and overflowing. The faces he admired must be those of perfectly-sculpted goddesses. He could hardly be expected to celebrate a wife who was at best "lovely."

But that kiss. Oh, it had been a million times better

than the one she'd stolen at Vauxhall Gardens last summer. That had been just a week before Lord Gresham formalized his offer for her. Lisbeth had snuck out to a public masquerade, with no one but Hannah as her chaperone. The world had been closing in around her, and she wanted one night where she had complete romance, before agreeing to a life with a man who she could at best call a friend. She had danced three waltzes, then accepted the arm of a tall, mustachioed man dressed as a pirate for a walk down a dark little path. He had said sweet nothings, clichés that Lisbeth would normally have scoffed at, and then he'd kissed her.

That had been exciting for how forbidden it was, no matter that his mustachio prickled her skin and his lips tasted foully of tobacco.

Adrian's kiss, though, had been soft and sweet and perfect. Lisbeth could have kissed him all night.

Well, you didn't. She shook herself. No, there was no use dwelling in that which she couldn't change. Lisbeth had never spent much time worrying that her looks weren't enough, not until the matter with Lord Gresham, and she did not intend to make it a permanent feature of her personality.

She would treasure the delicious kiss as an adventure, and she wouldn't worry about whether there would be another. She had plans to carry out, and one day they would include a passionate love affair with a man who couldn't take his hands off her. For now, she was content to begin establishing her household.

Her chin-up philosophy carried her cheerfully for the entirety of half an hour, until she entered the breakfast room and discovered her husband at the other end of the table.

Her devastatingly handsome husband.

Just the smell of his cologne – a warm spice that spread across the room – heated her skin. Swallowing against her physical reaction, Lisbeth assembled a breakfast plate and took her seat. "Good morning, Mr. Hathorne."

Adrian looked up from the broadside he'd been reading. "Good morning, Mrs. Hathorne."

Lisbeth almost asked him how he had slept, but she stopped before the words left her lips. She didn't want to know that he had slept soundly, when she'd been up all night with humiliation, nor did she want to hear that he had tossed and turned in regret of his choice in wife.

"What are your plans for today?" Adrian asked.

Lisbeth wondered if he inquired only for the sake of conversation, or if he was truly curious how his wife would spend her time. "This morning I would like to sit down with Mrs. Siswell to understand the housekeeping accounts. Then this afternoon, a friend of mine is hosting a tea, which I should like to attend. As for this evening, shall I plan on dining with you here, or will you be supping elsewhere?"

Adrian blinked at her with those long, dashing lashes. She almost forgot what she had just asked, remembering how he had lowered his eyes to her right before their kiss.

"We will eat at home tonight," he responded. "Who are you having tea with this afternoon?"

"Lady Gresham." Lisbeth tossed it out, curious if he would react. The lady – who insisted Lisbeth call her Annabelle – had sent a note around when she first got to town a month ago, apologizing again for the scandal and inviting Lisbeth to join her weekly salon. Lady Cecilia had refused on Lisbeth's behalf, but Annabelle's teas were quickly earning a reputation among the ladies for being highly political, and Lisbeth was eager to go.

Adrian swallowed his bite of toast, then regarded Lisbeth with the blankest of expressions. "You are friends with Lady Gresham?"

Lisbeth smiled. "I must be grateful to her, mustn't I? If not for her, I would be married to Lord Gresham, and not you."

For the briefest of moments, his expression changed, into the same wide-eyed horror he'd worn after touching her breasts. Then it smoothed back into a careful canvas that revealed nothing.

But Lisbeth had seen it. And her stomach dropped. For it was true: he regretted their marriage. Already.

"I have heard of Lady Gresham's teas," Adrian said, picking up his knife to slather jam on toast. "She encourages political talk."

"Yes, precisely why I want to go. Today's topic is the use of transportation as punishment. I'm quite eager to learn more about it."

When he looked up at her from his toast, Adrian's gaze did not feel blank or friendly at all. There was suddenly a cold anger in his green eyes. "You misunderstand me. The fact that I have heard of Lady Gresham's teas is not an endorsement. It is the exact opposite. They are no place for you, my wife, to go."

For a moment, all Lisbeth could do was stare at him. This was an unwelcome surprise. Her father had assured her autonomy: he had all but shown her the marriage contract, which he promised guaranteed her full control of her own whereabouts and activities. He had inserted that clause so that Adrian would not whisk her off to Jamaica. Oh, she should have insisted on reading it, instead of trusting her father. Or perhaps she should have insisted Adrian read it before committing himself in vows.

Lisbeth forced herself to cycle through an inhale and exhale. This was simply a little matter of miscommunication. It was to be expected at the outset of a marriage. "You misunderstand *me*, sir. I was not asking for your permission."

His reaction was not satisfactory. Instead of apologizing, Adrian set intense, angry eyes on her. In fact, Lisbeth rather felt he glared at her.

Ford interrupted with a letter neatly folded on a silver tray. Adrian read the note, then stood. He glared at her again. "I'm called away on business. I shall see you tonight for supper. I expect to hear that you were at home all afternoon."

He strode off without another word or look or bow. Lisbeth, stunned, stared after him.

She had been this way her whole life. Willful. Curious. Bending the limits others set for her. Her father had promised he would make it clear to the Hathornes. He had promised this husband wouldn't care what Lisbeth did with her days. He had promised Adrian wouldn't stand in her way.

Lisbeth had no appetite now. She had no desire for anything, except to turn back the clock and choose *not* to go to the church yesterday morning.

However, that option was unavailable. Lisbeth forced a bite of cake. She would simply have to shake off her skirts. Better to know from the outset what kind of husband she had ended up with. One who thought he could order her around. Who found her disgusting. Who couldn't possibly be her friend, let alone lover.

There was no use moping. Lisbeth would simply have to make the best of it.

Chapter Four

*S*o *this is marriage*, Adrian thought to himself as he hopped into a hackney cab. Awkward encounters in the bedroom and battleground conversations at breakfast.

He was grateful to be headed to the docks. Mr. Adrian Hathorne, merchant, was a much more comfortable role for him to assume than Mr. Adrian Hathorne, husband.

He was still embarrassed about their wedding night, or lack thereof, but Adrian refused to let it hang over him like some sort of great shame. Their marriage would never be conventional; perhaps it was for the best that he simply let Lisbeth believe her duties over. They could begin their separate lives that very day, with him off to the shipyards and her seeing to the household. As long as she didn't completely drag his name through the gutter – at least, not until he was safely in control of the Hathorne fortunes – Adrian didn't mind one bit what this wife of his did.

He turned his focus to the streets beyond his cab window. They quickly descended from the clean calm of Soho to dirty chaos. The character of faces changed, too, as they approached the wharves, with Lascars and Chinamen and even lasses with skin like Adrian's elbowing through the crowds. The faces blended together, though, into the bedlam of the streets. Vendors hawked wares from carts or tables or bags; street urchins darted back and forth; men leered and women jeered. All around him was a battle, the average Londoner's desperate fight for existence, and somehow, Adrian was lucky enough to be settled above it all.

It was enough to remind him *why* he had married in the first place. Why he was headed to the docks, too, and why he would continue plying the *ton* with complacent bows.

He had a mission to lift two hundred and thirteen souls from misery, and he couldn't do it until he had secured his place as his father's heir.

The hackney pulled to a stop in front of the West India Docks, where it was quickly assaulted by a new set of vendors eager to offer Adrian everything from a shoeshine to a tup in the nearby pub. Adrian remained in the safety of the cab for a moment, taking a fortifying breath of soupy London air, before jumping out and shouldering his way to the safety of the docks.

The whole complex had been carefully designed by Adrian's father's friends to protect profits. A red-brick wall protected the wharves, keeping undesirables out and preventing underhanded sailors from slipping away with even an ounce of precious cargo. Lining the street behind Adrian was the great warehouse, ready to store the sugar and coffee and cotton unloaded from the masted ships every day. The docks themselves were designed so a ship could arrive, unload, and then turn around at the export docks to pick up new cargo and depart, all in a day if the company so desired.

Adrian always thought the place gleamed smugly at the rest of London, daring an ordinary man to think better than beings so powerful as the trading lobby.

If only one could help what kind of dynasty one was born into.

The Crawler was docked in the Hathorne Shipping preferred berth. She was one of the oldest ships in the Hathorne Shipping line, purchased from the Navy after a healthy life fighting the American colonies. Now she knew no end of problems, from leaks in the hull to deck floorboards prone to giving way under a man's weight. She had just arrived that morning, according to the note Adrian had received, yet already she teemed with activity. Adrian had to jump out of the way of five barrels of sugar before he could climb the gangplank.

His cousin Robert had beaten him to the main deck and was conversing with Captain Bertram, making the old salty sailor throw his head back with a laugh.

Robert and Adrian shared paternal lineage: the former's father was heir to the Duke of Berkwell, while Adrian's father was the second son shipped off to the West Indies to make a fortune independent of the family. Only a year younger, Adrian had followed Robert to school. And Robert, grand old goat that he was, took Adrian under his wing. Adrian had dozens of schoolfriends because Robert had dozens of schoolfriends.

Adrian would suspect he hadn't earned anything himself, all inherited from goodwill towards Robert, except for his reputation as teachers' pet. Robert was too busy having a good time to win over his instructors, while Adrian applied himself so well that three separate tutors took it upon themselves to write letters of compliments to his grandfather, the Duke of Berkwell.

"Hathorne, what are you doing here?" Robert barked when he saw Adrian climbing the gangplank. To Captain Bertram, he added, "I saw my cousin married yesterday morning. I thought he would be at home, wooing his lovely bride, not seeing to business already."

Captain Bertram raised his eyebrows, thick bushy monstrosities that had been bleached by so many hours in the sun. "Indeed, sir, if I were lucky enough to have a bride, I daresay I shouldn't leave her side."

Adrian grimaced at them both. "On the contrary, it is fashionable for a husband and wife to spend time apart. Now, Captain, how was the voyage?"

They kindly let the subject drop in favor of a tour of the vessel. Captain Bertram summarized the cargo, a misadventure with an almost-hurricane, and the ship's state of disrepair as they went. They'd lost ten percent of the sugar due to the storm and three crew members to yellow fever. As for the ship, there were patches nearly every three feet, broken steps between decks, and the glass window in the captain's quarters had shattered during the storm.

Adrian tried to keep his focus on the matters at hand. These were all serious issues, ones which would require their insurance firm and likely a new ship altogether.

But even in the hold of the ship, he could hear seamen on the wharves shouting lewd jokes. Singing bawdy tunes. Discussing how soon it would be that they could reunite with their favorite ladies.

It only served to remind him of last night. When he missed her lips. When he grasped at her breasts. When he ran away.

They were back on the main deck when Adrian realized Captain Bertram was waiting for him to say something. He'd missed a question.

"I'm sorry, Captain, what was that?"

"I suppose your head is in the clouds dreaming of your bride." The captain shared a smile with Robert at Adrian's expense. "I only asked if you're taking a honeymoon, sir."

Adrian tried not to grimace again. "No, Mrs. Hathorne and I are remaining in London through the spring."

He didn't add that he would be returning to Kingston as soon as possible, without her. For a groom to say that the day after the wedding wouldn't be the thing, even though they had agreed to it as part of the marriage settlement. He was supposed to be in love, or at least in lust, not wishing himself half a world away from his wife.

Taking their leave from *The Crawler*, Adrian and Robert retired to Carroway's, their favorite coffee shop a few winding streets away. It was their preferred locale for passing an afternoon, rubbing elbows with sailors and merchants rather than shutting themselves in a dreary study. Most of the men there didn't look twice at Adrian's complexion; more often than not, they were Lascars or West Indian sailors of even darker complexion. Robert ordered them coffee and meat pies while Adrian claimed a table at the window, where they could see the bustle of Poplar High Street.

Their first order of business, as always, was to review the correspondence carried from Kingston to London by the captain. Rather, it was *Adrian's* first order of business. Robert's was to shake hands with their acquaintances, flirt with the coffee girl, and generally chatter with people until he had no option other than to focus on the letters before him.

Adrian split the pile in two. He handed Robert the notes from assemblymen who wanted support from the West Indies lobby and kept for himself the letters about the Hathorne estate, including one from his father. The family was lucky to have ships arriving every six weeks or so, making it easy to stay in touch though they hadn't seen each other since Bartholomew had put Adrian and Mary on the ship to England seventeen years ago.

But Adrian could hardly settle into the letter before Robert started pestering him.

"So how does it feel to be a married man?" Robert asked. "Should I continue putting it off as long as possible?"

"It is divine, of course." Adrian tried to smile before directing his attention back to the letter. His father's handwriting was one of the most comforting things in the world, all the more so because Adrian couldn't remember the sound of his voice. He knew he should save the letter for later, when he could savor it in the quiet of his study, but first he wanted to glance through it, as if to steal a hug from a long-lost visitor before settling down at the fire to hear their stories.

And as always, with that yearning came a prick of guilt. Because he waited just as eagerly to inherit at his father's death. Because he couldn't compel his father to action now. Because in more important ways than a little boy wishing to see his papa, Adrian hated everything his father stood for.

"She's pretty enough," Robert continued, not caring that Adrian's attention was elsewhere. "I was worried what your sight-unseen agreement would net you, but she has a good fire behind her eyes."

Adrian didn't want to think of that fire in her eyes, or the one she had lit inside his skin the night before.

By the time you receive this, you will likely be married to Miss Dawes – that was how his father's letter opened. *I congratulate you on achieving this final step in my dream, with a daughter of the peerage, no less. I have always had such faith in you, and you have never disappointed me.*

"She is witty, too. She said the funniest thing yesterday. I don't remember it now, since I was a bit in my cups, but I do know I got the stink-eye from Grandmama for laughing too loud."

Adrian remembered that moment, too. He'd been on the opposite side of the room, discussing curricles with

Lisbeth's brother, when Robert laughed, the kind of unbridled guffaw one simply didn't hear in a drawing room. And there had been Lisbeth, bright with a smile of delight, watching her great triumph.

Adrian didn't care to admit he'd felt a spike of jealousy. It wasn't unusual for him to be envious of his cousin, who had grown up at Adrian's side yet had such an easier life. But Lisbeth was *Adrian's* wife. Robert was the one who should be jealous of *him*.

He set his attention to the letter again. His father waxed on about how glad he was Adrian would return soon, and how sure he was news of the marriage would secure the privilege bill. They were waiting for that final approval before Adrian could return to Jamaica, and they both hoped that would pass before Bartholomew succumbed to the disease in his lungs.

Then Adrian's eyes settled on one last sentence, one that seared him so badly that he folded the letter and put it away.

Fanny Mae had her child – a boy – and we purchased five more hands, so we are building a new set of shacks in the back forty.

That brought it to two hundred and nineteen souls in misery, waiting for him.

"I think it is time we sell *The Crawler*, if we even can," Adrian said, as much to redirect his own thoughts as Robert's. "She might be so bad that she must be sold for scraps."

"Yes, yes, that much is obvious." Robert waved an

impatient hand in the air. "But what of your wife? Are you pleased with your wife, now that you've actually met her?"

Adrian considered telling Robert the truth. That Lisbeth was lovely, if a little headstrong. That *he* was the problem. That he was an embarrassment to mankind.

But the trouble with Robert was that he couldn't possibly understand. He was a dashing heir with skin so white that it peeled red if he sat too long in the sun. He assumed Adrian had lived the same easy life he had, that Adrian had lost his virginity somewhere between Eton and London. That Adrian was as much of a gentleman as he was.

Adrian took the coward's way out, slapping on the perfect smile that always appeased his peers. "Of course. She is the perfect lady. Now, about *The Crawler*, I think it would be wise to dispose of her and purchase a new ship before we formalize the partnership with Brabourne."

"Blast *The Crawler*! You don't fool me, Adrian. Something is wrong with Mrs. Hathorne. I won't let this drop until you tell me, so forget trying to distract me."

Sometimes, Adrian wanted nothing more than to throttle his cousin. Was it unreasonable for a man to want to keep certain issues close to the vest? What gave Robert the right to insist on information?

But Robert being Robert, Adrian had no choice except to give in.

"There's nothing wrong with Mrs. Hathorne," Adrian hissed. "There's something wrong with me."

Robert took a sip of coffee, waiting.

Adrian supposed he had to keep going. "I can't consummate the marriage."

Now Robert's eyes widened. He visibly tried to keep a curl of distaste from his lips as he whispered, "Can't get it up, or can't keep it up?"

Adrian couldn't believe they were discussing this. In public, no less. His whole body flashed hot with embarrassment. "No, it's not that. I don't know how even to get that far. I'm a virgin."

Lifting his gaze from the oak tabletop, Adrian tried to gauge his cousin's reaction. Robert had wiped his face of all expression, which meant he didn't want Adrian to see how he felt. Which probably meant Robert was disgusted with him.

As well he should be. Not only was Adrian incompetent, but he'd let his cousin believe otherwise all this time.

"What about…" Robert started, but he didn't even try to finish his own sentence. Adrian had never spun a lie about a dalliance. He had simply let his cousin assume that he got into such activities.

Robert cleared his throat. "Well, that's not so bad. All you have to do is…*do* it. It's easy. Did you give it a try last night?"

This was too excruciating. Adrian could barely handle living the humiliation. He wasn't sure he could survive telling Robert about it, too.

"Look, plenty of gents mess it up the first time," Robert

said. "The problem is when you're in your head. You can't overthink it. You've just got to let nature take over."

Groaning, Adrian let his head fall to the table. He couldn't take this. How could he possibly explain that he'd *tried* to let nature take over, only to completely offend Lisbeth and humiliate himself in the process?

"To be completely honest – and I wouldn't tell just anyone this – I myself don't enjoy it when I don't know the woman," Robert pressed on. "Maybe that's your problem, too. Maybe you simply need to get to know her more."

"Get to know her?" Adrian flashed back to their disastrous breakfast. He'd been so focused on not letting his embarrassment show that he'd ended up snapping at her like some heavy-handed lord. He should have stayed calm, no matter what she said, but Lisbeth had stared at him with that same alarmed expression as she had the previous night, and Adrian had lost control of his emotions.

No, he was as inept at conversation as he was with intercourse.

"Yes, that's the thing. Squire her around town. Take her to a dance or two. Make her laugh. Steal a kiss in a garden. You've missed the courtship, that's your problem. Well, now make up for it."

He had skipped the courtship on purpose. His wedding was a calculation in his father's bid to place the Hathorne estates firmly in Adrian's hands. He would abandon whomever he married within months. Adrian didn't want to fall in love with her.

He had two hundred and nineteen souls waiting for him in Kingston. He didn't want to leave one here in London, tugging his heart in distraction.

But even as Adrian thought this, he remembered Lisbeth at the fireplace last night. Hair down, skin gleaming, eyes glowing.

All around him, people were struggling, and somehow, he had the luck to be married to a woman whose hair smelled of cinnamon.

Robert clapped him on the shoulder. "So you're a few years behind on the race. You'll catch up. You always do."

Adrian wasn't sure he believed his cousin. He wasn't entirely convinced he should even try, with his father's letter burning heavy in his pocket.

Yet he had a sinking sensation that Lisbeth was not a person he could ignore.

Chapter Five

Lisbeth's palms left damp handprints on the muslin folds of her skirt as the carriage drew near to Lady Gresham's townhouse. The idea of the afternoon tea was growing less and less appealing, though she couldn't say whether it was the fact that Adrian had so clearly forbidden it or that it was hosted by the woman Lisbeth was supposed to be.

In any case, she wiped the fear away. If she was nervous on Adrian's behalf, that was plain silly. The marriage contract was on her side. Let him bluster at her about it – *if* he found out. She should like to see him try to stop her from doing anything.

And if this ridiculous sweating was on Annabelle's behalf, well, Lisbeth had no interest in comparing herself to the woman. Lord Gresham had fallen in love with Annabelle well before he ever met Lisbeth. It was *she* who had no claim to him, nor any wish to claim him. She wanted nothing but his happiness with Annabelle.

The Gresham townhouse stood behind a fine wrought-iron gate tipped with gold-painted spears. A liveried footman ushered her through, up the marble steps, and into an upper story drawing room. A murmur of voices pervaded the whole corridor, so that Lisbeth was expecting – rather than surprised by – the large group already assembled.

There must have been nearly a dozen women in the drawing room. Lisbeth recognized most of them. Some had even been part of the disastrous house party for her Wedding That Didn't Happen. When the footman announced her – boomed "Mrs. Hathorne" so the whole house could hear – all eyes turned to Lisbeth.

She summoned her most polite expression of boredom and sought out her hostess. Annabelle practically glowed, like an angel in a Caravaggio painting bestowed with the light of God. She was a famed beauty of their generation, with hair so gold Rumpelstiltskin might have spun it, and skin that was creamy and pale, and a tall figure that suggested perfect curves beneath her gown.

At least, that was what Lisbeth had heard gentlemen whisper to each other about her.

Today, Annabelle wore a pink dress with gold trimming and a matching turban twisted about her head. Everything about her was so much more elegant and pretty than Lisbeth, whose ostrich feather had caught in the door of the carriage and she feared was looking a little rumpled. Surely Annabelle had never even thought of the humiliation of a husband who wouldn't kiss her properly.

"Mrs. Hathorne, how good of you to come!" Annabelle took up Lisbeth's hands in greeting. "I believe you know everyone here, but let me reintroduce you as you have the pleasure of a new name."

Lisbeth smiled and curtsied as Annabelle introduced the guests one by one. They all tried very hard to keep emotion out of their expressions, but she could still read it: confusion that she would be so friendly with Annabelle, horror that she would show up at Lord Gresham's house the day after her marriage, pity that she was not the hostess, or perhaps pity that her new name did not carry a title with it.

Lisbeth let it all wash over her shoulders. She did not need the *ton*'s sympathies. They couldn't understand that she hadn't wanted to marry Lord Gresham, nor could they fathom the arrangement she had now. They would find comfort in their own situations by judging hers.

Let them. As long as she could keep on doing whatever it was she wanted to do.

"Do take a seat. May I pour you a cup of tea?" Annabelle ushered her to a vacant chair while a footman materialized to offer a plate of refreshments. Lisbeth helped herself to a watercress sandwich and cheese puff, then accepted the tea Annabelle handed her.

"Now then," Annabelle said, seating herself beside Lisbeth, "shall we get started, ladies?"

The group quieted. Annabelle introduced the topic by reading a recent article from *The Times* on transportation; then she asked whether it was a cruel and unusual punishment to send a man to a new land with no means of returning.

Lisbeth spent a few minutes watching the discussion. Most of the ladies seemed to have attended before, for while a few looked a little alarmed at the topic, no one balked at the idea of discussing such a thing. Still, they danced around opinions, instead quoting their husbands or fathers or vicars.

When no one had said anything of particular interest, Lisbeth cleared her throat and leaned forward. "What about when it is children? I have read reports that children as young as seven have been torn from their mother's arms and sent to Australia. Is that not cruel and unusual?"

"But they are criminals, Mrs. Hathorne," one of the ladies – an older woman, with silver hair beneath her cap – objected. "If a mother can let her child become a criminal by the age of seven, she has no business being with it."

The woman beside her – likely her daughter – concurred. "Is it not better to deport the criminals early, when they are harmless children, than to let them grow to be strong men who can rape and kill us?"

Lisbeth tried to remember the duo's names. She had met them during her previous Season, but they had hardly crossed paths more than twice. The elder was a baroness, she believed, the younger still on the marriage mart.

Yet their identities escaped her. So she had to launch her attack without the pleasure of lashing their names to her words. "When was the last time a woman of good birth was raped by one of these criminals?"

At this, more ladies than just the duo gasped.

"I cannot remember such a case," Lisbeth pressed on, "yet you use it as evidence in favor of sending children across the world."

"You make a fair point, Mrs. Hathorne," Annabelle said, calmly raising her rose-painted teacup to her lips. "I often feel the points our newspapermen make are based in fear rather than rational, fact-based arguments. In the case of children, I wonder, Lady Pemberly, if you consider there to be a threshold at which point they should be transported? Is it a suitable sentence for any level of crime, or is there a severity of the trespass that would lead to the sentence?"

The hour allotted for the salon quickly disappeared in debate. As carriages started arriving to take the ladies home, the conversation returned from the benefits of a sliding scale of justice to regular civilities, asking who would be at that evening's ball, trading little pieces of gossip, and promising to call on each other in the morning. A few of the ladies had kind words for Lisbeth, but she felt for the most part they held themselves away, still wary of the scandal tainting her name.

Lisbeth knew it would have been much worse, had she not married Adrian.

Annabelle turned from paying farewells to grasp Lisbeth's hands again. "Must you rush away like everyone else, Mrs. Hathorne? If not, I should love to steal a few minutes of your time."

The name was still so strange. Lisbeth winced inwardly every time she heard it, as if someone had mistaken her identity. She couldn't possibly be Mrs. Hathorne. That person must be old and tired of kisses and ready to spread gossip in broad whispers.

"I should be delighted, and please call me Lisbeth. As you said in your note, we are much too familiar to be formal with one another."

Annabelle sparkled at this. "You make me a happy woman, Lisbeth. Let me finish my farewells, and then we shall sit down to chat."

The drawing room was fast feeling cavernous as it emptied of ladies. When the last guest had left, Annabelle led Lisbeth to a smaller sitting room on the ground floor, overlooking the back garden. As she went, she described the rooms they passed through, noting the family portraits and French mirrors and Ottoman carpets.

Lisbeth had been to the house before, of course. She had been given a tour by Lord Gresham himself, with her mother as chaperon, just after their engagement was announced. Luckily, she wasn't a woman who enjoyed decorating, otherwise she likely would have had the color of the curtains chosen – perhaps even ordered – by the day of their wedding.

Seeing it all again now, Lisbeth was surprised by how disinterested she felt. She really couldn't care less that the wall was covered with ugly old portraits, or that the hallway was so dark one needed lamps on at all hours of the day. It felt exactly like visiting anyone else's house: she could admire and appreciate it, but she certainly didn't want to live there.

Annabelle led her to an elegant little table overlooking

the garden, which boasted a few evergreen hedgerows among the brown of March. "I am so glad you came this afternoon, Lisbeth. I wasn't sure you would. After all, you have every right to hate me until the day you die."

From another woman, the words may have come off as insincere, or perhaps obsequious. Yet Annabelle matched them with such an earnest smile that Lisbeth couldn't help but respond in kind.

"That would be rather unsporting of me, considering I am now a married woman myself."

"Lucky Mr. Hathorne. I only heard the good news of your engagement last week. I have to say, I was a little disappointed, as I was hoping to prove myself your friend this Season. We had the Duke of Harrodshire ready to dance your first set, you know."

Lisbeth smiled. She had heard about the Duke of Harrodshire's offer, as well as his *tendre* for a certain widow in Wickhamshire, from her friend Alice, and she was heartily glad not to have to rely on such a trick to earn the esteem of society.

"Tell me about Mr. Hathorne. I understand he is the heir of the Duke of Berkwell's second son?"

"Yes, Mr. Bartholomew Hathorne, his father, owns a number of interests in the West Indies. Mr. Adrian Hathorne and his elder half-sister, Miss Mary, were born there, but they have been raised in His Grace's household since they were young." It was all she knew about Adrian. She didn't know when Mary's mother had died, nor whether their father had actually married Adrian's. He was claimed as the legitimate son, which was the primary concern of society, and Lisbeth had no intention of inquiring further.

Annabelle smiled in encouragement. "When did you meet him? Was it romantic? I understand he is only recently come to town."

"Actually, we did not meet until yesterday at the wedding ceremony." Lisbeth paused, flickering her eyes across Annabelle's perfect face to gauge her response. Perhaps Annabelle had assumed Lisbeth and Adrian were a love match, given Lisbeth had surrendered Lord Gresham on account of love. The lady's brow furrowed in confusion, but otherwise, Lisbeth could find no hint of judgment. Yet.

"It was my preference," Lisbeth continued. "He could not come to London before this week, so either we could meet a few days before the wedding or wait until the day-of."

"It certainly adds excitement to the day," Annabelle murmured. "How do you find him? Are you glad you waited until the wedding day to meet him?"

This was, perhaps, the question Lisbeth had avoided asking herself all day. Had she known that Adrian was so handsome, would she have been able to marry him? Had she had a conversation with him, would she have wanted to marry him?

Was she glad that she had married him, now that she had done both those things?

"He is very handsome," Lisbeth answered Annabelle. "On a superficial level, I'm very glad I didn't know that beforehand, for I'm not sure I would have had the courage to marry him."

"Courage to marry a handsome man?" Annabelle laughed. She sobered, however, when she realized Lisbeth hadn't said it as a jest. "I suppose beauty can be intimidating. Still, I'm sure he was just as intimidated by you when he saw you under your veil."

Lisbeth couldn't help raising a skeptical eyebrow. "I do not pretend to be beautiful, and now that I am a married woman, I suspect it is of little issue, either way."

Annabelle blinked at this. Then she pressed on, "What of his character? Are you happy with what you find in that quarter?"

"We have only had limited conversation thus far," Lisbeth admitted. She wasn't sure whether to disclose he hadn't wanted her to attend the salon. It was an argument they hadn't yet settled, and somehow it felt disloyal to air such a disagreement when Adrian hadn't had a chance to apologize to her for his obtuseness.

"Ah yes, I suppose you had other activities last evening." Annabelle's lips spread as if with a secret. "It is wicked of me to ask, so tell me to mind my own business if you like, but how did you find your wedding night?"

Lisbeth might as well have stepped into a winter wind, so thoroughly chilled was she by this question. It was terribly familiar, for two women who only had in common a discarded fiancé. Lisbeth should set Annabelle down and return the conversation to something safe, like sharing news of dear Alice, shut up in confinement in Cumbria. For surely Annabelle would never understand how Lisbeth had found the wedding night. Surely no man had ever gasped in dismay after kissing Annabelle's lips, or run away in horror after touching her body. She likely never stood still, either, getting lost in her own hopes and dreams while the man mustered the courage to do his duty.

Lisbeth opened her mouth to change the subject. But Annabelle looked so friendly and kind – and, after all, must know a fair amount about a husband's activities, since she was twice married – that what Lisbeth ended up saying was, "I found it disappointing and confusing, if I may be honest."

Annabelle reached out and took her hand again. Even though Lisbeth's palm was clammy, she didn't withdraw. "You are not the first bride to feel that way. Was it very painful?"

Lisbeth understood what she was asking. Her mother had now twice given her the speech on what to expect: her husband would guide her through it, there would be a moment or two of pain, and then from there it would improve into an experience that she would learn to enjoy. She had stolen copies of bawdy books from her father's library, too, studying illustrations of various positions men and women (and sometimes men with men or women with women or men with two women) found themselves in.

Which meant she couldn't answer without admitting the truth.

"It wasn't painful," she said, her voice evaporating to some high-pitched whisper. "For it didn't happen."

From there, the truth tumbled out, without Lisbeth quite hearing her own words. Annabelle's gentle fingers strengthened their grip on her hand, a friendly presence until Lisbeth had finished with Adrian fleeing the room.

"I see what you mean. Dreadfully disappointing and confusing."

Hot tears stung Lisbeth's eyes, which she refused to let spill. She raised her chin as high as she could. "I can only conclude that my husband is not interested in his marital duties, for I literally repulse him."

Annabelle offered her a delicate muslin handkerchief. "Dear Lisbeth, I cannot conclude the same. We do not have enough information. There are a hundred reasons why Mr. Hathorne may have behaved as he did. You may be right that the reason is damning: for example, he may have a mistress who had slaked his needs earlier in the day. But let us be generous for a moment. Perhaps he had a sudden upset stomach and wanted to protect your eyes. Perhaps he had drunk too much and realized he could not perform as expected. Perhaps he was simply overtired from a momentous day. We cannot know *why* he behaved as he did, so we must not draw conclusions based on such speculations."

Lisbeth tried to remember how Adrian had looked at her just before he fled. His green eyes had been sharp, but with what? She had assumed disgust. Could he have been sick? Or drunk?

She wasn't sure anymore. She only knew it was just after he touched her breasts that he ran. And he hadn't come back.

"You are a gorgeous, delightful woman," Annabelle said. "I have every confidence that Mr. Hathorne will return tonight ready to enjoy all you have to offer. Just be sure he sees to making it an enjoyable experience for you as well as himself."

Lisbeth returned the handkerchief. "You are kind, Annabelle."

"May I call on you this week to find out how it goes?"

"I would be delighted." Lisbeth was a little surprised to discover it was true. Already, she felt she and Annabelle would be close friends, no matter how strangely their relationship had started.

The thought reminded Lisbeth who Annabelle's bedfellow was.

"You won't share this conversation with Lord Gresham, will you?"

Annabelle drew a cross over her heart. "I will mention only that you attended my salon and we have made friends. Anything specific you say is always secret with me."

"Thank you." Lisbeth couldn't quite make the words mean all that she was grateful for: the afternoon discussion, which was stimulating and illuminating and thrilling in all the ways Lisbeth loved; the friendship, which was unexpected and wonderful; and for somehow knowing that Lisbeth had needed to share her story, humiliating though it was.

Annabelle glowed again. "Of course."

Returning to her carriage, Lisbeth felt weary but lighter. She didn't know what to expect from the evening, but she didn't feel quite so frightened when she pictured facing Adrian again.

Chapter Six

Adrian returned to Number 73 for supper. Everything about the meal felt a little stilted, a little performed. They ate in the dining room, whose formal eight-foot table stretched too long between the two of them. The meal was an interminable six courses, all served on the fine china and silver that came as a gift by way of his grandmother. Even Lisbeth – though beautifully elegant in her silk gown and pearls set in her chestnut hair – would have been better suited in a ballroom than a quiet supper with her husband.

Adrian had no objection to a well-appointed outfit, but he would prefer they settle into their reality rather than pretend to be something they weren't.

He resolved not to let it rattle him, however. His goal that evening was to better acquaint himself with this wife of his, and hopefully consummate the marriage. The last thing he needed when he returned to Kingston was a wife in England claiming their marriage was a farce.

"Mrs. Siswell told me she is still new to your household, so she and I both have to learn what your favorite meals are," Lisbeth said as a footman served him a plate of meat and potatoes. "I thought we might as well start with my favorites and see which you and I have in common."

Adrian nodded. He wasn't particularly picky about

English food. He'd never met a meal he couldn't eat.

"Do you like roast pheasant?" Lisbeth prodded.

He took a bite. The meat was well-prepared: tender, juicy, and flavorful – perhaps even beyond the standard English seasoning of pepper. He gave Lisbeth another nod. "This is quite good."

She smiled, though Adrian couldn't help but notice it was a tight-lipped affair. It was more that she closed her mouth into a firm line than twitched it into a smile. He remembered how Robert had made her laugh at their wedding breakfast. He wondered if he would ever be able to do the same.

He dismissed that as a silly thought. He had no need to woo his wife or to make her into a pet whom he enjoyed teasing. He'd be leaving her behind in a handful of months; he needed only to make sure she was left well-appointed in household, wardrobe, and bank account. As long as Lisbeth supported him in name on this side of the Atlantic, Adrian would consider it a successful marriage.

"I spent some time this morning acquainting myself with the library," Lisbeth said from far down at her end of the table. "Your collection has great variety, though it is smaller than I anticipated. Are there any other books tucked away that belong with our library?"

For a moment, Adrian's pulse spiked at the thought that she may have discovered the stack of books in his bedroom. They were his personal collection, ranging from the ragged copy of *Robinson Crusoe* that had been his comfort on that first Atlantic crossing to the abolitionist writings of Ignatius Sancho.

He had no intention of letting his wife discover his secret intentions.

But he calmed an instant later when Lisbeth continued, "I mean, of course, amongst the Berkwell estates. I understand you have spent most of your time in the country as of late, so perhaps your larger library is still hidden away in the hedges of Kent."

"I'm afraid this is the whole of it," Adrian said. "You have my encouragement to widen it at your discretion, and you may direct any bills to me rather than pay them from your pin money."

"How kind." Her smile was a little bigger now, but it did not quite feel genuine.

Adrian chastised himself. He was supposed to be making conversation and developing a connection with her, not holding himself aloft out of fear. Setting down his fork, he asked, "Who is your favorite author?"

At last, Lisbeth's face flamed with an expression of something that felt real. "It is impossible for me to choose only one. Would you have me choose between a poet and an essayist? A painter of words and a speaker of truth? No, I cannot do it."

He couldn't help his own little smile of amusement at her ardor. "What of novels? Do you subscribe to their reputation as rubbish sentimentality, or do you include them in your list of great works?"

"I contend that novels, like all other forms, can be brilliant, or they can be a waste of print. It depends on their content and execution." Lisbeth raised a daring eyebrow at him. Adrian couldn't help but notice how perfectly slender it was, as if painted by an artist to highlight her luminous eyes. "What of you? Do you forbid yourself the pleasure of stories?"

"I wouldn't say I forbid myself." Adrian was surprised to find himself straightening in defense. "I simply don't see why I would waste my time on make-believe when there are so many subjects to learn about."

"Do you not think the imagination is necessary in order to make room for the theories you read?"

Something in the way Lisbeth said this, her eyes settling firmly on his, not wavering despite the distance between them and the rising candle smoke, made Adrian wonder if she sensed he had a dream for the future. One that certainly did require the use of an imagination.

He shook his head to clear himself of the idea. She was simply a pretty girl with a good tongue for debating. She couldn't see into his soul any more than he could properly kiss her.

"If you make a recommendation, I would be happy to try a novel," Adrian conceded.

Lisbeth looked a little shy now, smiling down at her food. Adrian sipped his wine in triumph.

After dinner, he retired to his study for an hour or two, until the sun had set on Upper Norton Street and the servants started turning down the house for the night. He waited to hear Lisbeth bid Ford goodnight, listened to her soft footfalls on the carpeted stairs, before ascending himself.

Tonight would be different. Robert had coached him through the motions. First, he let Mr. Adkins follow the same routine as last night, including the shave and cologne. Second, he ordered a tray of sherry delivered to Lisbeth's room. Finally, he brought a gift, the better to start a conversation before embarking on the physical journey.

This time when he knocked, he found Lisbeth waiting for him at her little table by the window, the sherry tray already set out. With relief, he noted a Chinese print silk robe tied tightly around her body, with only her ankles and wrists and a little bit of her wide collarbone peeking out as bare skin. She rose at his entrance and gestured to the chair opposite her, inviting him to sit.

Adrian had spent all day trying not to think of Lisbeth's reaction to the night before. Did she cringe now, to receive him again, when yesterday had been such a disaster? Or was she such a Miss that she didn't even know he had failed the evening before?

He covered his anxiety by handing her the gift, wrapped in a soft fold of velvet. Lisbeth took it with a cautious smile, which widened to a grin when she discovered it to be a first edition of a Jonathan Swift.

"To begin your library expansion," Adrian said, taking his seat.

Lisbeth caressed her fingertips across the cover and spine. "Somehow you guessed that Mr. Swift is one of my favorites, even though I wouldn't admit so at supper."

He had chosen the book based on price, not the content. Adrian decided he didn't need to admit that. "Would you read me a passage?"

He poured sherry while she lovingly turned the pages, finally selecting a section towards the middle. She held the book delicately in one hand, the other smoothing flat the open page.

> *Some persons of a desponding spirit are in great concern about that vast number of poor people, who are aged, diseased, or maimed; and I have been desired to imploy my thoughts what course may be taken, to ease the Nation of so grievous an Incumbrance...*

Lisbeth's voice took on a new quality as she read; while clear, she suddenly spoke low and husky. She took her time with each word, as if tasting it with her tongue before letting it loose. Adrian's eyes were drawn to her lips, how gracefully they formed each syllable, how lovingly they reached for the next. Occasionally, she paused, her tongue darting forward.

Adrian wondered if his had been her first kiss. Last night, he had been too consumed by his own horror to think of it. But she had been engaged before; had Lord Gresham taken physical liberties? And had she enjoyed it? Lord Gresham was surely a man of experience, the type of fiancé who could teach a woman how to kiss properly.

This was a dangerous train of thought. Adrian tried to shake himself from it. Yet now he was convinced Lisbeth likely knew a thing or two about being physically loved, which meant she knew just how badly he had bungled it last night. Had she been sitting in judgment all day? Ruing the day she agreed to marry the West Indian grandson of the Duke of Berkwell?

He marveled that she hadn't locked the bedroom door to him entirely.

Coming to the end of her selection, Lisbeth raised her eyes from the page to meet Adrian's. She looked so happy, ensconced in the glow of her favorite words. Perhaps he was overreacting. Perhaps she was simply trying to make the best of the situation, just like he.

"What do you think of Mr. Swift's proposal?" she asked Adrian.

Adrian blinked. Lout that he was, he hadn't paid attention to even one word she had read.

"It reminds me of the discussion on transportation this afternoon," Lisbeth continued, when he didn't respond. "Everyone is so scared of the poor man, as if not having enough food is a sin, and so the government conjures up policies to remove him from our sight, when the worst crime he may be guilty of is stealing an apple."

Now Adrian's stomach tightened for a completely different reason. "What discussion on transportation this afternoon?"

It was almost imperceptible, how Lisbeth froze. But he saw it, before she batted her eyelashes with a guileless smile. "Why, tea at Lady Gresham's, of course. I told you about it this morning."

"Yes, and I told you not to go."

"Did you?" Lisbeth raised her eyebrows, as if in surprise. "I don't remember you saying anything like that at all."

Adrian studied her. The innocent expression was a disguise, one she knew how to pull on at a moment's whim. She must have learned it to hoodwink her parents; he wondered how often it worked for her.

He wondered if she really thought it would work on him.

"You are an intelligent woman," he said, squaring his elbows on the table. It was so small that leaning forward just this much put him practically in her face. "Let us not play games. I told you not to go, yet you went anyway. Does my word as husband mean that little to you?"

That, at least, wiped the ruse off her face. Now Lisbeth's eyes lit with fury. "You signed a marriage contract, Mr. Hathorne, that guarantees me the freedom to come and go as I please. Perhaps you should have read it more carefully. I can assure you, I have no intention of being commanded around by a man who will leave me in a matter of months."

He *had* read the marriage contract, but he had never imagined that clause was intended for something so small as her afternoon activities. After all, a husband had to trust his wife would not sully his name. "I don't intend to command you, but suppose for one moment that I know better than you on this subject. Suppose I know how you attending a scandalous tea salon will bring ruin to my name. Will you permit me to exercise my good judgment to tell you not to go?"

Lisbeth scoffed. "My attending a tea with other respectable ladies of peerage cannot possibly bring ruin to your name."

That she could dismiss it so easily – dismiss *him* so easily – lit Adrian with anger. "You are a silly little girl to think so. Do you not see the complexion of my skin? Do you not hear the whispers that follow my every move? The *ton* is just waiting for me to do something scandalous to rip me from my family, to brandish me a stupid Blackamoor. My wife, attend a tea where they discuss transportation? It could jeopardize our very status in society."

Lisbeth glared out the window. "You are the grandson of the Duke of Berkwell with an annual income of fifty thousand pounds. They would not dare."

They would dare when they heard what he would do with Inglewilde Plantation. But he couldn't tell her about it. He couldn't explain why he needed every single alliance in perfect balance, why he needed a sterling reputation, why he wanted a wife without reproach. Not without revealing his secret intentions, and he wouldn't ever trust Lisbeth with such a truth.

"You will not return to Lady Gresham's salons."

"Or what?" Lisbeth practically spat venom at him. "What will you do when you hear I have attended next week's tea? Will you lock me up? Beat me into submission? Have me whipped like one of your slaves?"

Adrian didn't let his fury show. If they argued much longer – if she said one more inflammatory word – he might never want to speak to her again.

He did not offer a bow in goodbye. He simply turned on his heel. It was at the door between their rooms that he decided to say one last thing. Not to win the final word in the argument, but to keep her from making the same mistake again.

"Do not speak to me of slavery. You do not know the ground you trod on."

She glared at him, but Adrian felt better for having said it. Perhaps he would have one less nightmare because of it.

Chapter Seven

Somehow, Lisbeth slept that night. She didn't think she would, not with rage consuming every fiber of her being, but she must have, because the next thing she knew, pale daylight filtered into the bedchamber as her maid relit the fire in the hearth.

"Did you sleep well, ma'am?" Hannah asked, seeing Lisbeth's eyes open. "Would you like me to bring you up a tray?"

Lisbeth considered. She could take that route: eat in her room, avoid Adrian all day, lock her door at night. She could freeze him out before he even left for the West Indies, so that last night's were the last words they ever exchanged, save perhaps for a few conversations around logistics.

But Lisbeth couldn't sustain such a campaign. She knew that even as her pulse quickened at the memory of last night's argument. She hadn't expected this marriage to be one based on love or friendship, but she had assumed there would be a modicum of respect.

Instead, she had heavy-handed commands and no physical relationship whatsoever. Adrian might have returned last night, robed and perfumed and looking every bit the fallen angel there to seduce her, but he hadn't touched her. The way his eyes had flared, then frozen, when she compared herself to a slave; from that alone, Lisbeth could sense that he would never approach her again.

She had spoiled herself in his eyes, with words she wasn't even sure that she meant. She had only wanted to remind him how little strength he had over her. Somehow, it had instead leeched her of her own power.

Yesterday morning, Lisbeth had thought she could survive the few months until Adrian left. She had thought she could brave his disinterest and scorn, in the interest of the life she had always wanted. But already, she was weary. Dreading her husband, second-guessing herself, regretting things she said – it was no way to live.

"Perhaps some coffee?" Hannah prodded.

"No thank you," Lisbeth said, sliding out of bed. "I'll eat with Mr. Hathorne. Would you help me dress? The yellow muslin should do."

It was one of her favorite day gowns, soft and loose with pretty white flowers embroidered down the sleeves. She had worn it the day her father first suggested a marriage to Adrian Hathorne, so it was only fitting that she wear it this morning, the day that she ended said marriage.

Adrian was not at the breakfast table when she descended. Ford assured her he had not yet eaten, so she fixed a plate of food – though she couldn't find even the tiniest of appetites – and waited. She considered the household as she did. Ford, at his post just outside the door, ready for her next request. Mrs. Siswell, no doubt bustling below stairs putting out some sort of emergency. They set a good atmosphere for the rest of the staff: they took their duties seriously, managed everything with good diligence, yet always had a kind word for both master and servant. Lisbeth would miss them, though she had only been with them two days. She would miss the experience of being mistress of the house.

Still, she knew she must do it. She could not live shackled to a man who scorned her. Even if he were all the way in Kingston, she would know how he felt about her. She would wonder how quickly he'd forgotten her. She would imagine all the women he chased after and envy them for it. She would fear his letters, which would surely censure her. And she would never know if he was going to come back, claim his right as husband to ruin the life she built for herself, just to punish her.

Lisbeth was shuddering at this scenario when Adrian entered. He read a newspaper while he walked, even as he collected – one-handed – a plateful of cakes, eggs, and sausage, so that he didn't notice her until he sat down and looked up to reach for the salt cellar.

Incidentally, the salt cellar was a wedding gift from Lisbeth's cousin, porcelain hand-painted with Eve frolicking in the garden. The pepper, naturally, had the partner illustration of Adam. Lisbeth supposed she would have to wrap the gifts back up and return them to the sender.

Adrian's whole being darkened when he saw Lisbeth. His eyes had been glittering with thought, but after connecting to hers descended with quick, decisive gloom to his plate. "Good morning."

"Good morning." Lisbeth tried to keep her tone impersonal. She was, after all, negotiating a business transaction. There were no feelings of the heart involved whatsoever.

Still, she wasn't quite sure how to start a conversation so important. She tried to think of an opener that would angle towards the state of their marriage, but in the end, she had to rely on the weather. "I think it will rain this afternoon. What say you?"

Adrian did not look up from his portion. He was quiet for so long that Lisbeth thought he wouldn't respond, that he had decided to ignore her completely. Then he said, "It is England, after all."

"Yes." Lisbeth had read about the West Indies – particularly in the last few weeks, when she knew she would marry a West Indian planter – and knew there, the sun always shone and the heat was enough to kill an Englishwoman. She supposed Adrian must miss the good weather.

He cleared his throat. "I should like to apologize for my behavior last night. It was overly harsh."

Lisbeth had supposed he blamed her for disobeying him and saying unforgivable things. She was so surprised, it spurred her to admit, "I got carried away in anger, too."

He raised one of his black eyebrows, but he still didn't look up. "As husband, I must model better behavior."

His words pricked her as surely as a blade in her ribs. She'd heard men speak this way her whole life, and it had never made one iota of sense. As if she were a child who needed a better nurse, or a mare that needed a new groom. As if as a grown, married woman, she was helpless in behavior unless her husband showed her the way.

She couldn't believe she had married a man who would speak to her that way.

"About that." Straightening her shoulders, Lisbeth summoned a calm energy for what she had to say. "Given our disinclination towards each other, Mr. Hathorne, I think it best to annul this marriage."

Now, at last, he looked up. His startling green eyes clung to her. "Annul?"

"Yes. It is the only logical conclusion to this situation. You and I don't like each other. You want to order me about, and I won't follow your orders. Then there is the question of our physical relationship…"

Adrian launched out of his chair, the feet scraping in protest against the wood floor. "Out," he growled to the footman entering with a fresh pot of coffee. He shut the door that connected the room to the kitchen, then stalked to the hall entrance, barking something at Ford before shutting those doors too.

He turned to Lisbeth.

"You should know better than to discuss sensitive matters where walls have ears, Madam."

There was an elegance to his ferocity that Lisbeth had

to consciously not admire. His every movement might have been choreographed, he was so sure of himself.

"I'm sure they've already been discussing it. After all, there has been no evidence of a deflowering. The maids will have noticed."

She knew her face flamed red at these words, even though she worked so hard to say them as if listing the menu for supper. Adrian tore a hand across his scalp, turning to the window.

"We do not suit," Lisbeth said. "Surely you agree."

"That is something one concludes *before* marriage, not after."

"Everyone knows we married without meeting each other. They'll understand if we conclude this experiment failed. I'm sure there are bets on at White's about how long our marriage will last."

Adrian still stared out the window at Upper Norton Street. "The scandal would ruin us."

"It would ruin me," Lisbeth corrected. "A failed engagement followed by a failed marriage. I will have to retire to the country, resign myself to life as a spinster, and return to *ton* only when I am so old and gray that no one remembers. You will be fine. I should expect you to be remarried by June."

He was shaking his head. "They do not provide annulments on grounds of consummation. We shall have to provide reasons. Your father's solicitors will handle it, of course, which means they will give the reason that you didn't realize what I was when you married me. You didn't realize you were marrying an octaroon. You didn't want to sully your bloodline with the tar brush."

Lisbeth flinched. "That's not true."

"If you want an annulment, that's what you will have to say. They will leap at the chance to defend a fair English lady from a man such as me."

Lisbeth didn't like what he said, or the way his voice had grown deep and distant. He still wasn't looking at her, but she could read the anger in his neck and shoulders.

"It's not true," Lisbeth repeated. "I knew..." she couldn't say the word herself "...about your ancestry. I don't see how it is any different than being descended from a Frenchman or Spaniard. I should not like to ruin you with an annulment. But sir, I cannot stay married to a man who so abhors both my person and my actions."

Adrian frowned at her. "I don't abhor either your person or your actions."

Lisbeth wished his eyes weren't so intense. She wanted to be able to meet his gaze without getting mesmerized by it. "You object to my friends and my opinions so much so that you forbid me from doing things, and you cannot bring yourself to consummate the marriage. What else am I to conclude?"

"That I don't know what I'm doing!" This came out in a shout, almost a plea, and immediately, Adrian covered his face with his hands. "I've never been a husband before, you know. It seems I am exceptionally bad at it."

Lisbeth had never seen a man come undone like this before. Her first instinct was to run to him, wrap her arms around him, tell him that it didn't matter after all.

But it did matter. This was her life, her sense of self-worth. She could not melt in sympathy simply because Adrian was at loose ends.

His dismay lasted only a few moments. Then he knelt before her, his hands resting on the arm of her chair. "You are unhappy, and it is my fault. I apologize. Sincerely."

Lisbeth couldn't quite breathe with him so close. "Thank you."

"Would you give me a week? Let me court you, without the pressure of the bedroom. Let us get to know each other. Let us see if we can make this better. If at the end of the week, you still feel we do not suit, then we will notify your father's solicitors of an annulment."

Lisbeth couldn't choose between watching his eyes – so green, so enthralling, so intimate – or his mouth – so lush, so soft – as he spoke. She couldn't choose between feeling hot frustration at being penned in or a sweet balloon of hope.

"One week," she said, edging her words with steel. She felt the shame of surrender until Adrian smiled, and then –

Then she thought perhaps she had made the right choice.

Chapter Eight

Adrian locked himself in his study for the morning, the better to plan a spontaneous week of wooing. He had never courted a girl, had never even stolen wildflowers from the path for a pretty governess. He didn't know the first thing about how to win over Lisbeth. But he knew that he must.

He still couldn't believe she had suggested an annulment. That she had lain their problems so bare on the table, with less interest than their discussion on novels. That she told him so easily he had failed her.

In only two days, too.

An annulment would be a disaster for a hundred reasons. There were the obvious ones: it would ruin his privilege bill, give Robert ownership since Adrian would be the laughingstock of every White man who read the London gossip rags, and if Adrian were to marry again, it would be to a woman so desperate for money that she could look past a failed marriage.

The only reason he cared about was the one he couldn't voice. If the privilege bill failed, then he wouldn't inherit Inglewilde Plantation and the 219 souls waiting for him. If he lost Lisbeth, he lost all hope of righting his father's wrongs.

He stared into the fireplace, a new kind of despair

gripping his heart. He had failed. He had failed his people, and his wife, too. In the course of two days, he had horrified her, stormed at her, and abandoned her. No wonder Lisbeth wanted an escape.

That she had horrified him, too, did not lessen his guilt.

Besides, Adrian believed Lisbeth that for her, this had nothing to do with his African heritage. After all, her father had met Adrian before marriage was even proposed. It had all been disclosed in the discreet, proper way these things were handled. And when Lisbeth had finally seen him at the altar at St. George's, she hadn't grown pale or trembly or anything like that. Adrian had spent his wedding morning anticipating his bride's reaction, bracing for her to faint in horror. But Lisbeth never took her eyes off him. Even before her father placed her hand in Adrian's, she smiled – Adrian's first smile from her. Pretty and happy and hopeful.

Compare that to the expression she wore at breakfast when she said that he abhorred her. Bleak. Helpless. Desperate.

Adrian never wanted to be responsible for an expression like that again.

He shook himself of all morose thoughts. He had spent enough time feeling sorry for himself. Now he had to figure out how to save his marriage.

Adrian did not know much about courting a woman, but he did know a few small things about Lisbeth. She loved books. She disliked decorating. From the dresses he had observed so far, she didn't have a particular interest in fashion.

He decided to begin where most of London did their courting: a ride in Hyde Park followed by ices at Gunter's. He invited Lisbeth by way of note served on Ford's silver tray, and she accepted the same way. Adrian could hear her murmuring with her maid in her bedchamber as he dressed for the occasion. He wondered if she was putting the same care into her ensemble as he was.

Adrian had learned even before he came to England that the outfit made the man. He paid particular attention to what other gentlemen wore and hired Mr. Adkins because the man had previously worked for the leader of the pack, Beau Brummell. For that afternoon, Adrian selected his green waistcoat, pale yellow trousers, and silvery necktie. It was one of his favorite outfits, understated but not without personality.

He awaited Lisbeth in the sitting room, opposite the hall from the breakfast room, which he could hardly look at. Adrian's skin hummed with anxiety, so he tried to focus on the small things he could control. He could be polite. He could solicit Lisbeth's opinions. A gentleman didn't mention a lady's coiffure or apparel, but he could compliment her general appearance.

He would *not* mention anything about Lady Gresham's salons, nor would he try telling Lisbeth to do anything.

She joined him a few minutes after their appointed

time. She wore a pretty blue ensemble with a ruffled jacket over top to protect her from the March wind. She came to a pause just inside the door, yards away from him. Usually, Lisbeth carried herself so proudly that Adrian forgot she only came up to his elbow. Now her eyes were guarded, her shoulders pinched. She looked small.

Because of him.

Adrian bowed to her, then put on a smile, if only to make the whole afternoon feel less like a funeral march. "Are you ready for a drive?"

"Yes, thank you."

The curricle was already pulled up to the house, a groom holding the horses still until Adrian could take the leads. The vehicle was designed for a gentleman to drive, the better to show off his companion. Lisbeth arranged herself beside him so that her hands were folded demurely in her lap, her chin pointed away from him.

"Off we go," Adrian found himself saying. "This should be good fun. I've never been driving in Hyde Park before."

Lisbeth turned to him obligingly. "Have you not? How curious."

"I haven't spent much time in London, except for business." Adrian remembered he was supposed to be asking her questions about herself. "Have you gone driving in Hyde Park often?"

"Almost every week last Season."

"Ah yes, with Lord Gresham, I imagine." He kept forgetting that she had been promised to someone else before.

He wondered if he would ever encounter the bounder, and what he would say if he did.

Lisbeth raised an eyebrow. "Yes, once with Lord Gresham. Another time with the Marquess of Asbury. Twice with a Mr. Lansdell. But mostly with my family."

So her Season had been healthy with suitors. Adrian wondered that she had thrown away the chance at a second one by marrying him. A man she had never met. A man who would abandon her for Jamaica in a handful of months.

The clouds overhead began to spit a cold drizzle. Adrian hadn't considered the weather when he came up with this plan. Yet another failure. The groom, at least, had pulled up the curricle cover so they were protected from most precipitation.

"Why have you limited your experience in London?" Lisbeth asked. "If you have been in town for business, then surely you could have gone driving in Hyde Park or secured an invitation to a ball. I remember your cousin Robert from last Season. Why did you not accompany him, knowing you needed to marry?"

Adrian didn't think it needed explaining. Robert could go anywhere and do anything; he was the White heir to a duchy. Adrian was only the mixed-race son of a second son. He commanded thousands of pounds, to be sure, but that did not erase who he was.

Lisbeth seemed to read his thoughts. "Did you never give it a try, to see how people would react? Or did you simply assume the worst of us?"

"It is important to me to be without reproach," Adrian said. "It is easier to remain so when no one has met me."

"So you would rather hide than discover whether you could make real connections? That's a shame. Just think: you could have met a woman you truly loved, had you only gone to Almack's one night. Instead, you are stuck with me."

She bit her lower lip after saying this. Adrian watched her work at it, her gaze casting desperately out the side of the carriage. He didn't know how to respond to such a statement. There were so many insults in it, as much to herself as to him.

The drizzle was growing steadier, heavier, closer to a proper rain than afternoon spittle. Soon, it was going to start blowing sideways into the curricle, and then Adrian would be guilty of endangering his wife as well as enraging her.

He turned his attention back to the horses. "You are stuck with me more than I am stuck with you."

For a moment, the only sound was the rain spitting against the curricle's roof. Then, Lisbeth said, "Perhaps. However, there is no comparison between my situation and that of a slave. You are not cruel. I am sorry for saying such a thing. My words have been ringing shamefully in my ears."

It had been the one thing he could hold against her. Now she looked up at him with wide, sincere eyes, and he knew she meant the apology. They had been words thrown in fury.

He forgave her. It was surprising, how easily it came to him.

Afraid of what he might let slip, Adrian said nothing in response, and they rode in silence for a few minutes. Hyde Park was empty – everyone else in London had enough sense to stay inside on such a miserable day – and Adrian was growing so chilled beneath his coat that he couldn't imagine eating an ice. So much for his perfect afternoon of wooing.

Adrian tried to think what Robert would do, were he ever to have such a disastrous courting session. Likely he would say something charming to win a laugh. Adrian could think of nothing. Except, "You look very beautiful this afternoon."

Lisbeth did not laugh at this. She looked at him as if he had declared his allegiance to the French cause.

"The blue complements your eyes," Adrian continued. "They are such a dark, deep brown. Like coffee I could drink all day."

Lisbeth drew her eyebrows together in a serious, concentrated frown. "Why did you want to marry me?"

He wished he could take back the poetry. He had been trying to salvage something, not dig them into deeper trouble than ever.

The truthful answer to her question was that he needed to marry any English woman of good breeding.

He didn't care whom, as long as she would consent to being left behind in England for the foreseeable future. Lisbeth had been the first daughter offered up to him.

Adrian knew better than to say that.

He thought instead of what he admired about her. What made him glad to have married her. "You are beautiful, caring, easy to have a conversation with. You are a natural hostess. You ask interesting questions. What man wouldn't want to marry you?"

Lisbeth still looked skeptical, until a gust of wind pushed the rain horizontally into the curricle directly onto her right half. In what seemed like a matter of seconds, her side was completely drenched. Adrian spurred the horses forward, towards a canopy of trees that would hopefully protect them from the worst of the rain.

She was shivering so badly that even her legs shook. Pulling the horses to a stop, Adrian wrapped her against him, rubbing her arms and back to try to warm her. Lisbeth was so small compared to him. She fit against him like a nesting shell. There was something intimate in feeling he could hold her whole being in his two hands.

Lisbeth looked up at him, teeth chattering, eyes fierce. "If you think I'm beautiful, why haven't you *had* me?"

Adrian's groin tightened at the same time as his shame. She was in his arms, after all, her lips so close to his. If he were only the kind of man who knew how, he could *have* her right there.

He shut his eyes for a moment. He needed to find the

right answer to her question. He wished there were any but the truth, but he couldn't see a way out of it. He had to admit it.

"I've lived my life without reproach. Where most gentlemen would have an education in…marital relations…I don't." Adrian peeked open his eyes to see Lisbeth frowning in confusion. "You are the first woman I've kissed. I'm not sure I know what comes next."

There. He'd said it. He had shared his most humiliating truth with the woman who could most humiliate him.

Let the consequences fly.

He still held Lisbeth wrapped against him, so that he could feel her ribs expanding with each breath. For a long moment, she only kept frowning at him. Then she lifted a gloved hand to his cheek. She arched upward until her lips touched his. They were soft and sweet. She kissed with her fingertips as much as her mouth, feathering wet touches across his jaw and down his neck. Adrian had never been both cold and hot at the same time before, had never lost all thought in favor of his nerves.

He could kiss his wife forever.

Lisbeth withdrew sooner than he wanted, his hands gripping either side of her waist. She smiled one of her pink grins, cheeky and delicious. "Perhaps next week we'll figure out what comes next together."

Adrian had never so badly needed a single week to go well.

Chapter Nine

They were to go to the theater that night.

Lisbeth's head spun with how quickly the day had reversed itself. She had been so sure she would be back on the feather mattress in her father's townhouse that night, yet here she was, arguing with Hannah about what to wear to Covent Garden.

She didn't know how to feel about heading to the play that night. She didn't even know what they were seeing – and Lisbeth *always* knew what was playing at the theaters. That was how off-kilter she was from just one drive in the park.

One drive, in which so much happened. Adrian called her beautiful - twice. He held her in his strong, warm arms. He bloomed with embarrassment. Lisbeth had never imagined a man wouldn't know how to have marital relations. She'd loved how innocent he looked as his skin heated, transforming that mask of indifference into something human.

Lisbeth wanted to transform him again. She wanted Adrian to never look so buttoned up around her. She wanted him to always be just a moment away from kissing her.

Which was why she revolted when Hannah insisted she wear one of the silk dresses from her trousseau. Those were designed by a French modiste for some tall slender figure, pretending it was redesigned to flatter Lisbeth, but in truth simply extended with some extra cloth at the shoulders and hacked into a hem at the skirts. Lisbeth wanted to go in one of the creations her Aunt Vivienne had bestowed upon her. Aunt Vivienne's gowns were never intended for willowy debutantes. Instead of demanding that Lisbeth's boxy frame hide in billows of extra silk, they proudly displayed her shoulders as her crowning feature.

They made her feel pretty.

Hannah wanted Lisbeth to show up in the height of fashion for her first appearance as a married lady at Covent Garden. Lisbeth wanted only to see Adrian's eyes widen again.

After all, Adrian had invited her to the theater on the heels of their kiss. The one that she had initiated. The one that had left her thoroughly wet and breathless.

He had called her beautiful.

She didn't want him to see her next as a potato in a silk sack.

In the battle of the dresses, Lisbeth – of course – won. She wore the golden yellow gown made of a shocking velvet and even went so far as to have Hannah powder her shoulders along with her face. Hannah had her little victory too, though, convincing Lisbeth to forego her usual ostrich feather cap in favor of a matching yellow turban coiled over her curled hair.

All in all, Lisbeth felt daring and exotic in her outfit,

quite unlike the dumpy insecurity her clothes usually bestowed upon her.

Adrian, awaiting her in the sitting room, looked impeccable, as always. His jacket and breeches were perfectly tailored, his formal white stockings displaying deliciously muscled calves. A buttery golden waistcoat added just enough color to give the impression he glowed. Lisbeth felt she had seen him in a fashion plate, only she hadn't believed a man so perfect could truly exist.

Then he greeted her with a smile. She hadn't seen many of those on him. His smiles took over his whole face, transforming him from a somber man to someone young and joyful. One could almost believe he was carefree, seeing a smile like that.

Lisbeth tried not to get swept up in it. She knew it was momentary, that soon enough he would be serious again. She knew he was only trying to save the marriage to prevent a scandal. She redirected their attention by saying something inane. "What luck – we are matching."

Adrian looked down at his waistcoat and smiled – again! "Not quite luck. My man consulted with your maid on what color would be appropriate."

Lisbeth didn't know what to say to this. She had never heard of such a thing: a husband and wife coordinating their outfits. She wasn't sure if it spoke to vanity or affection. Or both. Or neither.

They took a closed carriage to the theater. Since they didn't have the livery of a great house, they were in the

queue for what felt like hours, waiting their turn to disembark at the entrance doors. Lisbeth filled the time with
chatter. She wondered if Adrian could tell her prattle was
nervous, or if he thought she actually considered a catalog
of all plays she had previously seen good conversation.
Surely she was speaking too quickly to sound natural.

"Have you been to the theater before?" Lisbeth asked,
when she felt she couldn't listen to herself babble any
longer.

Adrian nodded. "I went quite often at Eton and
occasionally to the travelling troupes that stopped near
Maidenheath House in Kent."

That was good news. Lisbeth adored arts of all kinds,
and theater had a special place in her heart. It was nothing
short of magic that she could believe a painted set piece
was the ocean, or that her nerves could stand on end in fear
that Macbeth would murder Duncan. It was when she had
discovered Lord Gresham couldn't rub two words together
about art that she had known she couldn't marry him.

"What is your favorite play?" Lisbeth asked. "Or if
you cannot choose only one – for I'm sure I couldn't – who
is your favorite playwright?"

Adrian raised an eyebrow. "Would I be an Englishman
if I didn't answer Shakespeare?"

A boring answer, if it was true. Lisbeth had nothing
against Shakespeare, except for that one could easily claim
to favor the bard without knowing the first thing about
his plays. "I promise not to have your English citizenship

revoked if you favor someone else. Even if it is Marlowe."

Adrian's lips twitched in amusement. Not quite a smile, but an expression that leaked into his eyes with a sparkle. "Very well. My true favorite is Monk Lewis."

Lisbeth had only heard of Monk Lewis, who wrote both salacious Gothic novels and plays. His drama, *The Captive*, had supposedly sent audience members into hysterics for its portrayal of a woman wrongfully imprisoned in an asylum.

Now she wanted to see one of his plays even more.

"Have you been to Covent Garden before?" Lisbeth asked.

"Once, when I was seventeen or eighteen, in town with my grandfather. I don't remember the name of the play, but it starred Mrs. Westin."

He looked out the window as he said this, his eyes cast far away with recollection. Lisbeth had heard more than one gentleman sigh over the name of Mrs. Westin, remembering her as the beauty they first lost their hearts to. Lisbeth imagined a woman like Annabelle, with golden tresses and a perfect figure and sultry eyes that beckoned a man closer.

She could easily imagine Adrian falling in love with someone so magnificent.

The carriage tugged forward.

"What are we seeing tonight?" Lisbeth asked. She had been so caught up in the invitation – its proximity to the kiss, its meaning within their week of courtship, its implications on her wardrobe – that she had forgotten to ask earlier.

"I'm not sure of the name." Adrian turned his gaze back to her, and it was so intense, she had to look away. "I confess I only wanted to take you to the theater, and I didn't think to ask what the features are. However, I believe the drama stars Mr. Edwin Clarke."

The famous Blackamoor actor. The newspapers were in a flurry about him. There were some who didn't want a Black man on stage, displaying human emotions alongside White actors. There were others who said Mr. Clarke was the best actor they had ever seen tread the boards.

Lisbeth felt Adrian's eyes on her still, weighing her reaction. She decided on a playful smile. "How daring. What will people say when they hear we have seen the infamous Mr. Edwin Clarke?"

She could tell it wasn't quite the right reaction when he slid his gaze out the window again.

The carriage finally pulled to a stop at the theater doors, and their footman opened the door to hand Lisbeth down. She lifted her skirts to protect them from mud until she was inside the theater.

There was so much to love about attending the theater. The energy as everyone assembled, chattering about nothing, judging about everything. The anticipation of waiting for the curtain to rise, knowing one was about to be transformed by a special kind of magic. The unity that everyone there, regardless of birth, was about to experience the same thing.

Lisbeth was a little too nervous to enjoy the ascent to their box, however. Behind her, Adrian was silent, her misspoken words hanging heavy between them. Ahead awaited his family to welcome them into the private Hathorne box.

She had met his family at the wedding, of course, but Lisbeth had been so overwhelmed by the nerves of the day that she hardly remembered what she said. She had kept stealing glances at Adrian, wondering how her new husband felt about his wife. Now she would find out what kind of impression she had made.

Lisbeth didn't usually concern herself with how others perceived her. She knew she generally made a favorable introduction, for her wit was fashionable and she was not so uncomely that she would offend anyone. Adrian's family, however, was different. If he ended up granting her the annulment, they would likely be her sworn enemies beginning about one week from that night. If Adrian didn't annul the marriage, then his family was now *hers*. When he left for the West Indies, they would still call on her. She might celebrate holidays with them. If there was a child – quite unthinkable at the moment – they would lay claim to its attention and love.

His cousin Robert was laughing when they walked into the box. Robert had the same broad forehead as Adrian, but his hair fell flat against his head where Adrian's stood in tight, proud curls. She already knew Robert by his laugh, a carefree guffaw that other gentlemen, who didn't stand to inherit a dukedom, might try to curtail.

At the moment, he was entertained by Adrian's half-sister Mary. The daughter of Mr. Bartholomew Hathorne's first marriage, Mary looked almost nothing like her brother. Everything about her was pale to the point of sickly: wispy white-blond hair, skin so translucent one could see trails of blue veins on her wrists and neck and temple, and eyes the faded blue of dusk. She was slender, too, and narrow-faced. The only family resemblance was in expression, for she and Adrian wore the same careful mask of indifference whenever emotion wasn't called for.

It was Adrian's grandmother, the Duchess of Berkwell, who greeted them. "Mrs. Hathorne, what a treat it is for me to call you that." She clasped one of Lisbeth's hands in affection, then turned to press a kiss on Adrian's cheek. "You two are going to be the talk of the evening. Everyone is anxious to greet the new couple."

Lisbeth did like the duchess. She was not much taller than Lisbeth, though she wore her stature with much more grace, perhaps because her shoulders and hips were within fashionable reason. That night, she wore a green gown and a string of matching emeralds at her neck, which set her brown eyes glittering in almost the same way Adrian's did. People respected her simply because she was a duchess, and so she did whatever suited her, whenever it suited her. Including running her fingers against Adrian's side to tickle him. "A smile would not be out of place, you know."

Adrian obliged, though what he mustered up barely broke his careful mask. "I should hope there are more interesting people here than a mere gentleman and his wife."

"A mere gentleman with fifty thousand pounds per year and a connection to the Duke of Berkwell," the duchess corrected. "The *ton* is foaming at the mouth to get in your good graces."

Lisbeth resisted the urge to raise an I-told-you-so eyebrow at Adrian. He was quite incorrect about how he would be received. Money and family were all one needed to win the heart of the peerage, and he had both.

"Grandmama, you are hogging them," Mary said. "I want to get to know my new sister."

"But then I shall be stuck with Adrian," Robert objected, "and I already see him too much."

Lisbeth did love a good fight for her attention. "There is no reason I can't speak to both of you at the same time." She joined them at the balustrade, overlooking the theater house.

Her nerves fading away, Lisbeth could almost hum with the energy of the Covent Garden Theater Royale. The boxes were practically full, men of all classes milled about the ground floor, and the whole place thrummed with excited conversation. In that very moment, Lisbeth imagined, someone was being introduced to their future spouse; someone else was discovering her husband's affair; some lords were discussing tomorrow's vote; and behind the curtain, in a bowel of the building, the magical actors were dressing to bind every single person with the same spell.

Mary was busy pointing out her acquaintances, most of them lords and ladies Lisbeth had also met the previous year at the Season.

"Oh, and there is Lord Brabourne with his uncle, Lord Everly, the Marquess of Verne." Mary asked, discreetly signaling to a box across the theater, "Have you been introduced? They are close to the family."

"I met Lord Brabourne at the wedding." In her fever of nerves, Lisbeth had barely noticed the man other than to note he was not a blood relation to the Hathornes. She did remember him snaking a thin-lipped smile at her upon introduction. Now, she took a closer look from across the way. Lord Brabourne was perhaps a decade older than she, with thinning blond hair and a curled moustache shining with wax.

"He is the more persistent visitor of the two," Mary said, with a soft expression that Lisbeth couldn't interpret. She wondered if Mary mentioned Lord Brabourne as a potential suitor. A year older than Adrian, Mary must have been almost twenty-five and still unmarried. Lisbeth understood she'd been affianced to a man who was killed with Nelson at the Battle of Trafalgar; she supposed it must have been a love match, else Mary would have made another connection by now.

"You are lucky you haven't been introduced to the uncle yet," Robert drawled. "All Lord Everly talks of are his daughters and his horses."

"He only speaks of his daughters because he hopes

you'll marry one of them," Mary rejoined. Lisbeth was a little surprised at how easily she poked fun at her cousin; given her wan pallor, Lisbeth had expected Mary to be careful and reserved.

"Everyone hopes I'll marry one of their daughters. Yet I have no plans to tie my neck in that noose until I am well into the next decade, so they should all start speaking of something more interesting than how well Miss Such-and-Such embroiders."

Lisbeth began to fan herself in imitation of an innocent lady. "Do you not find women interesting by their own merit, Lord Eusford? Or must they be under consideration for the singular position as your wife to deserve your attention?"

"You wound me, dear cousin." Robert clamped a palm across his heart. "That you would think so lowly of me, and that you would call me by so formal a name. Please say that you will call me Robert from this moment forward."

She rolled her eyes at him. "You miss the point, Robert. You offend my sex when you so thoroughly dismiss us as a topic. Perhaps Lord Everly has been trying to impress upon you the brilliance of his daughters' embroidery skills because they are truly inventive. Are you not interested in how the other half spends our time?"

"I think the trouble is that Robert has never sewed a stitch in his life," Mary chimed in. "You would not dismiss such accomplishments if you knew how hard it is to do successfully."

Robert leaned against the balustrade with a game smile. "Why, is it harder than horseback riding?"

"By miles," Mary nodded.

"Than country dancing?"

"By a hundred allemandes," Mary said.

"Than sword fighting?"

"By a thousand tiny pricks to your finger," Lisbeth exclaimed, leaning in to join the game.

A hand landed on hers, and Lisbeth suddenly realized Adrian stood beside her. He watched them with that mask of indifference, but his fingers were cold against her skin. She turned her smile to him. "Your sister is showing me how to torment Robert when he says something thoughtless."

"Lisbeth is a natural at it," Mary laughed.

Adrian nodded. "I can imagine." His eyes drifted to Lisbeth's. "Shall we take our seats?"

"Of course." Lisbeth wasn't sure, but she was fairly certain she was supposed to understand *something* he wasn't saying from the way he looked at her.

She had never imagined a husband could be such an enigma.

Nor had she imagined she would want to sneak out of the box with said enigma and plant another kiss on his delicious lips.

The family let Adrian and Lisbeth sit in the front row, with Mary on Adrian's other side and the duchess and Robert behind in a second row of seats. The curtain rolled open on applause, and the first attraction of the evening began – a recital by a soprano visiting from Hanover. As a rule, Lisbeth preferred orchestral music to the piercing tones of song, yet when she closed her eyes in the theater, she could feel the full-bodied trills slide across her soul. And when she thought about the miracle of a human body creating such a perfect sound, Lisbeth's eyes stung with tears.

She wasn't ready for the music to end when the audience erupted in applause and the soprano retreated. Lisbeth stayed in her seat, letting the beauty settle into her bones. She peeked at Adrian, who stood in ovation. He wasn't quite smiling, but he did glow.

"What did you think?" she asked when he sat back down.

"Exquisite." His words came fast, with a heat Lisbeth hadn't heard from him before. "She paired such power with feeling. The lyrics were so moving. It made my hair stand on end."

"You speak German?" Lisbeth hadn't understood the lyrics, except for one word she recognized as black. "What was she singing about?"

"I know enough to understand." Adrian looked almost shy, drawing his shoulders and arms within the frame of his body. "It was a song of homesickness. She longed to go back to her childhood, to her mother, and to the land she knew."

Lisbeth closed her eyes again to remember the music. She had felt longing, but she hadn't thought of it as homesickness. For her, the song had been a wish, a dream for a beautiful future that could never be.

She didn't dare say so to Adrian. Not here, at least, in public, where a personal conversation was impossible.

They were interrupted, anyway, by the arrival of none other than the Lords Everly and Brabourne. The latter hung a step or two behind his uncle, as if a lackey waiting for his superior's orders. As for Lord Everly, he was even bigger than he'd appeared across the theater, both in height and girth, obviously following the fashion of the Prince Regent. His cheeks jostled as he bowed to the duchess. Then he turned to peer at Adrian.

"Hathorne, I see you have made good on your father's promise and found yourself a wife."

Adrian bowed his head. "Lord Everly, may I present to you Mrs. Hathorne. I believe you are acquainted with her father, Lord Dawes."

Lord Everly flicked his eyes over her, and Lisbeth suddenly felt woefully inadequate in her velvet dress displaying so much shoulder.

"A pleasure to meet you." But he didn't bow to her or ask any further polite questions. He returned his attention to Adrian. "I shall write to the assembly in favor of your privilege bill. In a few months, we can finalize all the other paperwork."

Adrian bowed his head again. Behind his uncle, Lord Brabourne watched the exchange with a gleam in his eye that set Lisbeth's hair on end.

"Come now, Everly," the duchess cried, "the theater is no place to discuss business. What did you think of Miss Stienburg's performance?"

"I cannot lie to you, Your Grace. Brabourne and I talked through the whole thing. Lady Everly has decried us as utterly hopeless."

They were supposed to titter along with his laughter, excusing the man his artlessness simply because he owned up to it. Lisbeth could only manage a small smile.

"Why come to the theater if you don't enjoy it?" the duchess asked. "Surely you and Brabourne could have the same conversation at White's if you so choose."

"We are here for the second act," Lord Everly said.

"Ah yes, the famed Mr. Clarke. He is supposed to be the most talented actor London has ever seen." The duchess beamed. "I am here for him, too."

"Your Grace will forgive me if I don't believe that abolitionist propaganda. How could an ape be more talented than Edmund Keane? Eh, Hathorne?"

Lisbeth's whole body cringed at the word. She wanted to slap Lord Everly. She wanted to spit at him and chase him and his nephew out of the theater and leave them to the mercy of the Covent Garden guttersnipes.

Instead, all eyes were on Adrian. Poor Adrian, who wore that mask of indifference, although Lisbeth was close enough to see a little, momentary quiver at his jaw.

He didn't smile for the lords. But he did bow his head, a third time.

Robert was the one who spoke. "As the ladies are always reminding me, most of us men are nothing but apes. Either way, I'm looking forward to the performance."

Everly and Brabourne finally left, though with such a glow of satisfaction about them that Lisbeth's stomach churned. She looked to the duchess, then Mary, for a sign of how she was supposed to react; Mary started a monologue on how much she admired the soprano's gown, and the duchess seemed happy to listen, as if nothing untoward had just happened.

For his part, Adrian stood silently, his eyes focusing so hard on his sister that Lisbeth suspected he wasn't seeing Mary at all.

The interval finally ended, and they all resumed their seats a little too eagerly. Across the way, Lisbeth could see Lord Everly sitting smugly in his box, hands clasped across his chest like a proud little king. Behind him, Lord Brabourne ran two fingers along the curl of his moustache.

She slipped her arm through Adrian's. She leaned into him, so close that, if she grew tired, she could rest her head on his shoulder. Maybe she would, indecent as it was, to show the whole theater exactly how Adrian fit into her world.

The curtain raised to considerably more applause than the first act. The scene began with English actors, and Lisbeth let herself get caught up in the story of two courtiers plotting to win the affections of the queen.

Then Mr. Clarke entered. He wore a resplendent

costume, with gold piping across his jacket that gleamed in candlelight. His very step told the story of his character, the honest courtier who was torn between loyalty to his friends and to his king. Lisbeth leaned forward, ready to be lost in the magic of a master actor.

But where usually she could dismiss her surroundings – once, she had even attended the theater despite monthly cramps that felt like knives stabbing her womb – Lisbeth found herself thinking too hard about who Mr. Clarke was. She analyzed each syllable of his perfect accent trying to detect if he was hiding a Jamaican flair. She watched his skin glow darkly in the candlelight and wondered if he felt it as a brand, proclaiming him to everyone that he was as an Other. She saw his eyes rake across the audience and wondered if he was seeking reactions, if he was measuring them for acceptance or rebuke.

She was aware the whole time of Adrian beside her, hands clasped carefully across his lap.

The audience applauded Mr. Clarke thrice: once after his first monologue, again when he killed one of the scheming courtiers, and the third time when he leapt from the tower set piece to his character's tragic suicide. Lisbeth clapped along, though she barely felt the energy of the play, and saw both Lord Everly and Lord Brabourne across the way sitting conspicuously still.

When the play ended, the general audience stamped their feet on the floor to show appreciation, and Mr. Clarke was greeted with a wolf whistle as he bowed. Lisbeth beat her hands together gratefully. The newspapers had made a show of decrying his performance, at best saying he couldn't distinguish himself from the rest of the players in the company, but it was clear from the audience that Mr. Clarke was a talent. If only she had been able to relax and enjoy the performance.

"That's what I call tragedy," Robert said, leaning forward and slapping a hand on Adrian's shoulder. "I need nothing else in an evening but a good suicide scene."

Adrian shrugged off his cousin's grasp. "You have always had a greater appetite for melodrama than I have."

"What did you think, Cousin Lisbeth?" Robert's face pivoted towards her, so close that she could smell tobacco on his breath. He did it in a friendly manner, with the non-threatening nonchalance of a man who could occupy any space he desired. Still, Lisbeth resented it.

She stepped back as much as she could as she answered, though that meant backing into the wall that divided her from the next box. "The actors were excellent. The play itself was mediocre."

"She has a discerning eye, your wife," Robert said to Adrian. "What do you say, shall we go find out what their lordships thought of Mr. Clarke after all?"

Adrian's eyes betrayed no emotion, neither humor nor ire nor sorrow. He almost looked like he would acquiesce.

Lisbeth couldn't let him shuttle over to submit to more of those silent nods. She seized his arm in supplication. "Oh no, please, can't we go meet Mr. Clarke backstage? I should so like to praise him in person."

Adrian looked down at her in surprise. His eyes flicked to her grip. Lowering her fingers to wrap around his, she fluttered her eyelashes as prettily as she could.

"There's an idea," Robert said, a heartless little laugh ending his words. "That will certainly show Everly what you think of the whole issue."

Resisting the urge to glare at Robert – or roll her eyes at him – Lisbeth focused her energy on Adrian. She willed him to ignore whatever strange hold the lords had over him, to instead set those green eyes on her and see her. She could help him change how he navigated London; she knew it in her core. If only he would let her, Lisbeth could free Adrian to smile whenever he wanted, not only when it was safe.

Adrian folded his hand around hers and drew her knuckles to his lips. "It's best we retire for the evening. After all, it has been a long day, and you must be tired."

Lisbeth almost reared back in anger. Almost. Had he said it the day before, she would have let loose her tongue, for no husband of hers had the right to decide when she was too tired to do anything.

But in that moment, Lisbeth knew two things: Adrian was trying to win her over, and there was more to this situation than she understood.

She decided to give him the benefit of the doubt. For the sake of appearances, she even manufactured a grateful smile. "I'm not used to having so perceptive a husband. I shall work harder if I want to keep anything a secret from you."

Adrian's grip on her hand tightened. He tucked her close to his side, her palm resting on the ridge of his elbow, where she could feel the muscle and heat of his body. They bade goodbye to Mary and the duchess, then waded through the crowds on the stairwell. It was only when they were standing at the entrance, awaiting their carriage, that Adrian said in a murmur so low she almost missed it, "Thank you for going along with that."

Lisbeth had to tilt her head to an angle in order to see him. She was tempted to ask him to explain the dynamics she hadn't understood, but then she caught the expression in his eyes. The emotion written across his face.

He was smiling. He was grateful. He was human.

She decided she didn't need to understand the whys, not just now. For the moment, she would simply enjoy her husband unmasked.

Chapter Ten

Adrian couldn't believe what a day it had been. When he'd woken, still angry and lost from his argument with Lisbeth, Adrian had expected a quiet weekday. He had planned to meet Robert at Carraway's to discuss their insurance claims for *The Crawler* and put out word that they were in the market for a new ship.

Instead, he had been threatened with an annulment, kissed his wife in the rain, and withstood insults at the theater.

And somehow, after all that, he wasn't even tired.

He said goodnight to Lisbeth anyhow, since the clock struck one as their carriage returned them to Upper Norton Street. She had been quiet on their ride, twisting the fingers of her gloves rather than filling the air with chatter. Adrian imagined she was something more than exhausted, given all the excitement of the box. For a moment there at the end of the play, he had been afraid she would insist on meeting Mr. Clarke; he didn't know if he would have picked a fight with her there in front of all of London, or acquiesced and earned the ire of Lord Everly.

Having Everly as an ally was essential to inheriting Inglewilde Plantation.

But so, too, was having Lisbeth's good graces.

In any case, it had worked out. Lisbeth had

miraculously cooperated, and now she was safe in bed, where surely she was enjoying sweet dreams.

For his part, Adrian had retired straight to his bedchamber with a healthy serving of brandy. Mr. Adkins had pressed his best nightshirt again, but Adrian eschewed it for his oldest, a soft muslin that hugged his skin. Here, in the privacy of his chambers, with all the servants dismissed and his wife in her own rooms, Adrian could care for comfort over fashion. In the chair by his fire, he opened his mother's locket, staring at the curl of hair he kept inside as if it would provide him the comfort he needed.

Adrian had only select memories of either of his parents. His father hadn't often visited the nursery, but when he did, he was jovial and had presents for them and made them laugh. His mother, Rebecca, was more reserved, though Adrian remembered it as serene, always wearing the perfect clothes, not a hair out of place. She'd had black hair that tumbled softly around her shoulders when she let it out.

She had died a year after Adrian landed in England. She hadn't seen them to the wharf, instead pressing her final kiss to Adrian's cheek in the cool darkness of her bedroom. "Don't forget who you are," she'd said. Adrian wasn't sure if she had meant it as inspiration or as warning.

His father had loved her. Adrian knew that for sure, from his own memory of how they exchanged looks over the breakfast table as well as from what his father wrote about her in letters. Adrian believed she had returned that love, though men like Lord Everly whispered she had only married him for his Whiteness. After all, her own grand-mother had been a slave; she needed a White protector if she expected to stay a free, wealthy person.

Adrian wondered what his mother would make of his life now. How would she feel about him marrying the first Englishwoman who would have him? What of his plans for the Hathorne sugar plantation – would she applaud him, or scoff at the idealist who wanted to throw away a fortune?

A knock at the door roused him from his musings. At first, he thought it had come from the corridor, but then another, meeker knock sounded, and he realized it was Lisbeth from their private entrance.

"Just a moment," he called, scrambling to his feet. He couldn't greet her in the sack of a nightshirt, nor did he want her to see his mother's locket. Throwing the latter around his neck, he shrugged into his dressing robe and finally opened the door.

Lisbeth's smile was small and self-conscious. "I know we are in courting this week. However, I find that I'm feeling far too unsettled to sleep. I thought perhaps we could keep each other company with some conversation."

She wore a different night rail than the suggestive, revealing lace of their wedding night, but this one was so thin that he could see almost straight through it. Rosy nipples. The curve of her hips. A dark triangle at her legs. He lost all thought for a moment, relishing the sight of her.

Then he swallowed. "Perhaps we should keep the door

closed, for propriety's sake."

Lisbeth blinked, then nodded.

Adrian shut the door. He slid down to sit on the ground beside it. The back of his hand rested against the cool oak. He tried not to think of Lisbeth on the other side, practically naked. "Robert and I used to stay up all night doing this," he said. "We didn't dare leave our rooms for fear of waking the nurse, but we could hear each other clear as crystal through the walls, so we would sit up together, talking the night away."

"Ah, you did break some rules, now and then." He could hear the smile curling her words. She had smiled easily for Robert earlier, when she and Mary hung against the banister and laughed at whatever Robert was saying. Adrian supposed she had already discovered she had married the wrong cousin; she would never ask for an annulment from dashing, gregarious Rob.

He pushed away such ugly thoughts. "I paid the price for it the next day, for I don't function well without sleep. Robert can waltz around just as well on one hour as on eight, but I turn into an angry, useless mop if I don't get a proper slumber."

"The next time you are angry, then, I shall accuse you of sleeplessness."

Adrian had never focused on Lisbeth's voice before. He was always too busy watching her pretty lips for a smile or stealing glimpses of her dark brown irises. Now, though, her voice was all he had. She spoke a little lazily, sometimes speeding over the middle of words, and with a bit of a country lilt that made her sentences more melodic.

"Robert is so easy to agree with," she continued. "I imagine he led you into quite a bit of trouble in your life."

"I knew early on not to follow him. He can get away with pranks, but not me." Adrian had learned this the hard way the one and only time he joined Robert in mischief, when they poured vinegar in the communion wine. The vicar had caught them both in the act: Robert had been sent on his merry way while ten-year-old Adrian was forced to drink the vinegar as punishment.

That wasn't a story he needed to revisit.

"May I ask you a question?" Lisbeth shifted on her side; Adrian could hear some part of her body press against the door. He tried not to imagine her bare ankles, her soft arms, her round bottom.

"Of course," he said.

"My father told me that you were looking for a wife to claim your inheritance because of some Jamaican law. Tonight, Lord Everly mentioned a privilege bill. If you are your father's son by marriage, why do you need Lord Everly involved to claim your inheritance?"

Adrian took in a breath, holding it inside his lungs as he let the question wash over him. He should have known Lisbeth would pay attention to Everly's words.

The inquiry itself didn't pain him, nor did the answer. They were simply facts. Still, Adrian heard a trace of anger in his own voice as he explained, "In Jamaica, legitimacy does not matter so much as race. My mother was the daughter of a mulatto and a Scotsman. That makes me an octaroon. People like me, by which I mean people whose skin is not white as milk, do not have rights in Jamaica. If my father died, he could only leave me two thousand pounds as a legacy. No small sum, of course, but it is only a percentage of his fortune. However, since I am three generations away from an African, my father can apply for a privilege bill, which would make an exception for me and my descendants, to be treated with the privileges of White men."

He paused, trying to school his tone to be matter-of-fact. "I am not guaranteed any privileges. My father decided to bolster my claim by sending me to be raised by my grandparents, to go to school at Eton, and to marry an Englishwoman. All of this establishes me as English, invested in the interests of the kingdom, and not aligned with my mother's ancestry."

"In other words, they do not want to give wealth to an African man," Lisbeth said.

"If I considered myself African, I might do something heretical, like free my slaves." Adrian regretted it as soon as he said it. He knew better than to even joke about something like that. Lisbeth might actually believe him. "As it is, I know all too well how the Hathorne fortune relies on labor in the sugar fields. I need slavery just as much as Lord Everly and Lord Brabourne and the rest of the West Indian lobby does, if we are to maintain our fine lifestyles."

Lisbeth's voice dipped low in discouragement. "That's why you didn't want to offend Lord Everly. You need him to convince the rest of the Assembly to approve your privilege bill."

"Among other reasons. The West Indian lobby is incredibly powerful. Hathorne Shipping has a number of expansions planned that rely on their support." Adrian stretched his legs out so his slippered feet braced against the baseboards. His temple was beginning to ache from thinking too much of Everly. It was time to change the subject. "May I ask *you* a question?"

Lisbeth responded to the lightness in his tone with a smile; he could hear it again as she answered, "Yes, it's only fair."

"Did you love Lord Gresham?"

"*Love* him?" That she was shocked – and perhaps offended – was obvious in her tone. "No. Lord Gresham is a nice man. He didn't seem like he would be an overbearing husband, and I didn't have any other offers. But I didn't *love* him."

Adrian couldn't help grinning. "Then why did you decide to marry a man you had never met rather than try another Season? I'm sure you would have found a better option than me."

"You've clearly never been through a Season. It is an endless drone of people who think they are more interesting than they are, judging each other based on completely irrelevant attributes. They are all so bored, they jump at the whisper of a scandal. And here am I, jilted at the altar in favor of the most gorgeous woman of Quality. All people think when they see me is how unlucky I am in comparison to Annabelle. They pity me. The best I could hope for is some matron feeling so sorry for me that she would fob me off on a fortune hunter." This all came out as a string of fast, heated words. Lisbeth paused, inhaling so deeply that Adrian could almost feel her sucking his air from beneath the door. "Marrying you meant I didn't have to go to a single ball."

Adrian hadn't met this Annabelle. He had heard about her, from Lisbeth and Robert and even a few of the fellows at Carraway's. He couldn't see how any woman could be so beautiful that Lord Gresham would cast Lisbeth to the wolves.

"I hope at the end of this week, you don't regret that decision anymore," he said.

On her side, Lisbeth was quiet.

"Are you getting tired at last?" Adrian asked.

"A little. Are you?"

He didn't feel tired at all. His whole body hummed from the conversation, or perhaps from knowing that Lisbeth on the other side wore nothing except her translucent nightgown. "A little."

She turned the conversation to the theater, first asking what Adrian thought of Mr. Clarke's performance, then soliciting his opinion on the play in general. They had both seen enough theater that they could compare notes on favorite styles; Lisbeth adored a melodrama with huge set pieces, while Adrian preferred understated performances and subtle plots. This bled into their poetry tastes, too, with Lisbeth confessing adoration for Lord Byron while Adrian preferred William Cowper.

"I'm so glad you adore the arts as much as I do," Lisbeth sighed at one point. "The day before our wedding, Lord Gresham took me for a tour in his gallery, and he couldn't say one intelligent thing about any of the paintings. I thought I might die if I had to marry him."

Adrian smiled. "You're lucky, then, that Annabelle showed up to save you."

"Truly, I am. Look at me now. I can go to the theater whenever I want. I can be a patroness of the arts, with my own playwright and poet and painter to follow me around. I doubt Lord Gresham would have made room for such a lifestyle."

Her words were growing even more careless, a sign that she must be getting tired. Adrian prodded, "And you can do that now? I wasn't aware I had signed a cheque for any artists."

"Not yet. But you're leaving for Kingston in a matter of months. Then I shall be a married gentlewoman in London. I shall be able to do whatever I want."

What she said was true. Adrian couldn't explain why it made his stomach clench. Or why it made him say in a mulish, ugly tone, "That's assuming you don't sue to annul the marriage."

Lisbeth only sighed wistfully. "Yes, that's assuming you decide to stop ordering me about whenever I have a different opinion than you."

Adrian had a thousand responses in mind. He had only ordered her about when her actions were stupid, endangering his reputation and therefore his plan. But he had thought that was the way a husband handled a wife. His mother had certainly taken orders from his father, and he had never heard his grandmother balk when the duke told her not to do something. Though now that he thought of it, he couldn't recall a time when the duke admonished his grandmother for anything.

He didn't end up responding, though, for Lisbeth kept going. "I'm an abolitionist, you know. Slavery is evil, and ending the slave trade was not enough. Every human being should be free to decide how they live. I read all the pamphlets. I attend the lectures. I send my pin money to Sons of Africa. You can try forbidding me, but it won't work. I won't stop doing what I know to be the right, Christian thing to do."

As a rule, Adrian did not waste too much time wondering how the English around him thought about slavery. For the most part, he assumed they did not think hard on it; they rested easy knowing they had abolished the sale of humans in 1807 without worrying about the slaves who were already in bondage. At some point, he had lumped Lisbeth into this group, but knowing her as he did now, it was no surprise that she held strong opinions. Dangerous opinions.

Perfect opinions.

For a moment, he considered telling her his secret. That on his father's death, with the Hathorne properties securely nestled on his shoulders, Adrian meant to free every single soul and offer them a living wage instead.

But he hadn't told anyone his secret, not Robert – who stood to lose a fortune when Adrian cut the margins so drastically – and not even Mary, who was the one person that might understand without fear.

Adrian had never planned to tell his wife. And his plot was too dear to risk in the heat of a dark night moment, when what he truly wanted was to win her over.

So he stayed silent. He let her think he disagreed. He let the moment slip away, until he heard a soft, ladylike snore from the other side of the door.

Then he retrieved a pillow and a blanket, and he nestled in the threshold, falling asleep just inches away from a perfect wife.

Chapter Eleven

Lisbeth decided to take a walk that afternoon. It was a bright, warm day for March, with a strong sun that called to her to enjoy its beams. Before, she would have been obliged to be escorted at least by Hannah, though her parents had usually insisted on either accompanying her themselves or assigning the task to her brother.

Now, a married lady, Lisbeth could walk out the front door onto the street without anyone saying a bloody thing about it.

It was, perhaps, the most thrilling thing she had ever done.

Of course, Mayfair in the afternoon had only so many distractions. There were some acquaintances to greet, some street vendors to avoid, but all too soon, her thoughts outpaced her feet, and she found herself turning over the same old worries as she had all day.

She had told Adrian she was an abolitionist. And he hadn't said a single thing in response.

There was no point in regretting it. So her slave-owning husband now knew exactly how she felt about his business. If she truly wanted to bring an end to the evil practice, she would surely have to say the same words – or worse – to much more frightening men.

So she had confessed it after he explicitly forbade

her from mentioning slavery to him. Lisbeth had already demonstrated that she did not care for his unilateral commands. Let him see how well *forbidding* her to do anything worked.

Perhaps this was the last straw. Perhaps Adrian couldn't stomach the idea of a wife who opposed him so fundamentally. Perhaps she would return from her afternoon to find annulment papers awaiting her at the supper table.

Better to find that out now, before she wasted any more of her time daydreaming about rainy kisses.

Lisbeth was just turning away from New Bond Street – for she would rather be anywhere than on that shopping street – when a brougham pulled to a stop beside her and none other than Mary Hathorne stuck her head out the window.

"What luck running into you! I have just left my card at Upper Norton Street after stopping to see if you would come shopping with me. Will you join me now?"

Of course, Lisbeth couldn't refuse, especially not when Mary fairly bubbled with warmth, no trace of that Hathorne mask holding back her features. She climbed into the carriage and let Mary spirit her into the hellhole that was *ton* shopping during the Season.

They visited the glove maker, the haberdasher, and the *modiste*, all to fill various gaps in Mary's costumes. They walked the whole time, the carriage trailing them from store to store to collect Mary's packages. They talked of the previous night's play, of the fabulous soprano, of their shared horror at dancing with clumsy-footed Mr. Lansdell. Mary made a point of including her maid, Suzy, in conversation wherever possible, asking after her opinion in the best country dances and wondering who was wittiest below-stairs. It was a cozy chat, like three old friends enjoying an afternoon together, so much so that Lisbeth nearly forgot any shopping was being done.

"I was so afraid my brother would marry someone tedious, wasn't I, Suzy?" Mary drew her maid into the admission. "When Father wrote that Adrian should marry this Season, Suzy and I listed the different ladies who might accept, and each of them seemed worse and worse to have as a sister."

"Indeed, ma'am," Suzy said, a twinkle in her eye. She was a larger girl, tall as a man and with both wide hips and a large bosom. Lisbeth often wished she had that type of frame, rather than resembling a flat, squat box. "I daresay you were choosier than Mr. Hathorne himself."

"In many ways, I am more committed to the relationship than he is." Mary smiled at Lisbeth as she said this, as if to turn it into a joke in case Lisbeth didn't take it kindly. "After all, a husband only spends a sliver of the day with his wife. But sisters are much more tightly bonded. Why, we might see each other for tea and then in the ballroom the very same night."

Lisbeth clucked her tongue in agreement. "It would be quite shocking should a husband and wife do that, but I would be surprised if you and I did not spend every day in town together."

"Especially when I shrivel into an old maid and must rely on my brother's household for safekeeping."

Mary said this just as lightly as before, but it caught Lisbeth's attention. After all, Mary had to know that Adrian planned to decamp to Kingston before the year was out. And she didn't seem to be looking for a husband. What *was* her plan for the future?

"Surely an old maid doesn't shrivel," Lisbeth said. "Should you choose to do so, however, I shall be quite alone at Upper Norton Street when Adrian leaves for Inglewilde Plantation, and I will welcome your company whenever you choose to share it."

Mary tucked her hand through Lisbeth's elbow. It was not a comfortable angle, as Mary was at least half a head taller than Lisbeth, but Lisbeth appreciated the gesture. They were sisters, and there was no further question.

Unless, of course, Lisbeth or Adrian decided to annul the marriage.

"Do you plan to disappoint the men of London and remain single?" Lisbeth asked. They had turned down a side street, much narrower and quieter, which made the question feel less dangerous.

A little bit of the Hathorne mask drew across Mary's face; her eyes stilled, and her lips assumed a careful, neutral position. "Who can say, really," she said, in that same empty tone Adrian used when he spoke to Lord Everly. Then she warmed a little. "As long as I have a warm bed and Suzy to keep me civilized, I'm sure I shall be happy."

Lisbeth noted the look that mistress and maid exchanged, something slightly more than a smile. But before she could think too hard on it, her eye caught on the nearest shop window.

More specifically, her eye caught on a book in the nearest shop window.

It was perhaps the most splendid book she had ever seen, and she had grown up amidst the largest private library in London. It was not a large tome, perhaps as tall as a man's hand and not as wide, but it stood proudly splayed with gold-edged paper and a beautiful, perfect illustration of a ship at sea. A man stood at the prow, painted yellow as the sun, and behind him a girl whose purple skirts billowed in the wind.

Lisbeth's imagination unspooled at the image. Her heart galloped fast, knowing a story awaited her. It would be romantic and adventurous and melodramatic and perfect. It would keep her up all night. She would mourn all through the next day's breakfast, wishing she hadn't read it so fast.

She needed that book.

Mary and Suzy, of course, had noticed her interest. "Would you like to go in?" Mary asked.

"I didn't bring my purse," Lisbeth admitted. She never did; usually her maid or whoever escorted her around carried the money. Besides, she hadn't planned on shopping that afternoon.

"I'll pay for it. I derive great pleasure in collecting debts from Adrian." Mary tugged her elbow. "Come on, then, let me buy it for you."

It was not as if Lisbeth needed any further encouragement. Suzy entered the store first, holding the door open for them, and then Lisbeth hurried in.

The shop smelled of books. A perfume indescribable and irresistible. Dim candlelight revealed wall-to-wall shelves, all brimming with tomes. Lisbeth could spend the whole day there, breathing the air, fingering the books, letting her imagination run wild. But she was with friends, she reminded herself. She would keep herself in check and only indulge in the one book.

She was interrupted from turning to the window display by a gruff voice that fairly shouted, "No women in the shop!"

Lisbeth turned in surprise. The man in question was old and stooped, with scraggly gray hair escaping from a queue. He had sprung from a desk at the back of the shop and toddled forward on uneven legs. Yet his glare was fierce.

"Excuse me, sir," Lisbeth said, gathering her voice into as friendly a tone as she could manage. "I'm sure I didn't hear you correctly."

"No women in the shop," he repeated. "*Hartley's* is a gentleman's club only."

Lisbeth had never heard of such a rule – no women in a bookshop! But then, she had never heard of *Hartley's* either, and she thought she knew every bookstore in London.

She tried a smile. "I'm sure you can make an exception. You see, I am Mrs. Lisbeth Hathorne, previously Miss Lisbeth Dawes, daughter of the Marquess of Ipswich."

Usually when a bookseller found out who her father was, she received royal treatment. They offered her tea – once, even champagne! – and a cozy chair and a shop assistant to retrieve whichever titles she wanted. After all, her father never neglected to buy Lisbeth whichever books she preferred, and often he ended up buying half the shop's inventory in the same purchase.

Her words worked no magic here, however. The shop-keeper only advanced closer. "No women in the shop!"

Mary touched Lisbeth's shoulder. "Perhaps we should go."

But Lisbeth had begun to comprehend the situation at last. This man really wasn't going to sell her the book – he wasn't even going to let her *look* at it – all because she was a woman.

In fact, he was going to glare at her, to spew at her, like she was some kind of demon.

Because she was a *woman*.

"I have never heard of such an insulting policy, and I refuse to abide it. If you want me to go, sir, you'll have to sell me that book."

The man followed her pointed finger to the window display, and if possible, his eyes darkened with even deeper fury. "Leave at once, or I'll call the watch."

"Fine. I should like to see the watch remove two granddaughters of the Duke of Berkwell all because one lowly man was afraid to sell them a book."

Behind her, Mary gasped as Lisbeth invoked the duke's name. A little piece of her mind rang with alarm. This was *Adrian's* family, after all. They might not take kindly to being dragged into scandal.

But Lisbeth was too infuriated to care. This was pure prejudice. Worse, it was pure hatred. This man had something against women, and he would pursue it unchecked if she backed down now.

The shopkeeper surged past her, carefully not touching her, and let out a holler on the street for the watch to come. Lisbeth saw Mary nod at Suzy, who then fled the store. Out the window, Lisbeth saw the maid heft up her skirts and sprint towards New Bond Street.

Fine. Let Suzy do whatever she would do. Let the man call the watch. Let all of London know: this man had refused to sell a book to Mrs. Lisbeth Hathorne, and she would not stand for it.

At least if Adrian returned her to her father's house after this, her father would completely sympathize.

A clock somewhere deep in the store ticked away each second that they waited. The shopkeeper had positioned himself in the doorway, so his eyes could stay on Lisbeth while he continued yelling for help. It would only be a matter of minutes before the watch arrived, Lisbeth supposed. They might actually lay their hands on her when she refused to move. But surely they would do no worse than that.

She refused to shiver.

The shopkeeper was starting to holler again when movement flashed out the window. Only it wasn't the watch. It was Suzy, revealing striped petticoats as she dashed around the corner, and behind her, Adrian.

As with all things, he ran gracefully. His coat flapped behind him like a cape, and he showed no sign of physical exertion as he came to a stop beside Suzy.

Lisbeth could not tell whether her heart thumped because she was so glad to see Adrian, or so afraid.

He would surely hate her now.

The shopkeeper stopped yelling, eying Adrian suspiciously. Lisbeth heard her husband's soft, strong voice: "What is going on here?"

"Are you with the watch?" the shopkeeper asked at the same time as Suzy huffed, "Mrs. Hathorne, Miss Hathorne, inside."

"I don't allow women in the shop," the man barked.

Adrian had to duck to enter the warped shop door. Lisbeth saw his green eyes blink in the darkness of the store, and then they settled on her.

The watch may not have laid hands on a gentlewoman, but her husband had every right to. He might very well throw her over his shoulder and carry her all the way home to Upper Norton Street.

She checked that her posture, at least, was impeccable.

"Lisbeth." Adrian did not give any thought away as he flicked his eyes across her. "You look well. Suzy came running up to me on the street and I thought you were on fire or kidnapped or worse."

"This man has called the watch on me because he refuses to sell me a book."

The shopkeeper cleared his angry throat. "*Hartley's* is a gentleman's-only book club. No women in the shop."

Adrian looked from the man to Lisbeth to the walls of bookshelves. She still couldn't tell what he was thinking. "Which book is in question?"

Lisbeth gestured to the window. "I have not even been allowed close enough to discover the title."

"The women must leave, sir," the shopkeeper huffed, following Adrian as he stalked to the window display. Her husband picked up the book – gently – and examined the illustration before closing it to read the title.

"*The Harrowing Adventures of Captain Urselious Bigsby.*"

"A one-of-a-kind edition, sir," the shopkeeper said. "For men's eyes only."

Lisbeth scoffed. As if anything could be more insulting. But Adrian lifted his gaze to her at the noise, and she couldn't tell if he hated her or not. She bit her tongue.

"If it was for men's eyes only," Adrian said, "why was it on display on the window where anyone – man, woman, and child – could see it?"

The shopkeeper started to sputter a reply, but Adrian held up his hand.

"No matter. I don't care. My wife shall purchase it, and then we will leave you to the peaceful slumber of an empty club."

The man opened his mouth. Lisbeth knew what he was going to say. So did Adrian, who crossed to stand next to her, so close that his arm rested against hers. He placed a coin in her palm and raised an eyebrow at the shopkeeper.

"Unless you prefer for us to walk out without paying? You may always collect from my grandfather, the Duke of Berkwell. He is currently at court at St. James's Palace, if you do not find him in residence."

Lisbeth had never seen anything more glorious than Adrian – her husband! – staring down the small man with his beautifully ferocious green eyes. Trying not to smile *too* smugly, she dropped the coin into the shopkeeper's hand, then followed Adrian and Mary out of the store.

The sun washed the whole street in warm, rosy yellows. Adrian handed her the book as Mary's carriage rolled to a stop. "All this for a novel. I hope it is worth it."

Lisbeth hardly even cared about the book now. She had caused a shocking scene, and Adrian hadn't even scolded her for it. She couldn't do anything *but* throw herself at him, wrapping two arms squarely around his neck and hauling herself up to claim a wet kiss.

He exclaimed in surprise. His arms wrapped around

her waist, making her feel light and tiny and safe. For a moment or two, he kissed her back – perfect moments, where his lips were soft and warm and eager – before setting her back down on the cobblestone.

"Enough of that. One can only take so much spectacle in any given afternoon." But he was smiling. "May I trust you to return home without incident in Mary's company?"

Lisbeth wanted to steal him into the carriage with her. Then she noticed Mary was looking a little pale, and poor Suzy was red from her run, and Lisbeth supposed she had caused enough trouble.

"Thank you," she said, clasping the book to her heart. "Sincerely."

Adrian grinned again. "You're welcome, sincerely."

Chapter Twelve

Adrian had been on his way to White's when Suzy nearly bowled him over. She'd only been able to huff "Mrs. Hathorne," one tired hand pointing back the way she came, and shockingly, that was all it had taken for Adrian's heart to drop.

Lisbeth. Collapsed on the pavement with a turned ankle, perhaps. Caught in a building fire and crying out for help. Or worse – sliced by a footpad, or kidnapped for ransom, or squashed beneath the wheels of an errant carriage.

He had considered them all as he traced Suzy's steps, his mind tumbling faster than his feet, and his heart the whole time in the background squeezing with a cold, terrible fright.

In hindsight, the crisis had been much more in character of his wife.

He should be angry, Adrian admonished himself as he watched the brougham carry Lisbeth safely toward Upper Norton Street. Someone could have witnessed Lisbeth's tantrum. The watch could have come after all and trundled his wife through the shopping crowd like some sort of criminal. He should be seething, screaming, perhaps even annulling.

Instead, he was grinning. Still. Even as he turned back to New Bond Street, and from there onto St James's

Place. He was grinning like some silly love-struck fool.

Perhaps he should have taken a lover before marriage after all, so that he wouldn't fall into such helpless puppy love over the first woman to kiss him.

And now Lisbeth had kissed him twice.

Adrian arrived to White's all too soon. The gentleman's club was the bastion for most of London's fashionable men, their refuge from mothers, wives, and daughters. It frowned at the rest of the street with dark wood paneling and bowed, warped windows where dandies sat with their drinks, judging whoever passed by.

Not being a member, Adrian had to present his card to the butler, as if the man didn't recognize him, and then wait the requisite five minutes, designed to make a man contemplate his inferiority from every angle. Adrian steeled himself against it, turning his thoughts away from his own insecurities and onto the utter stupidity of the club.

A century ago, he would have looked forward to entering White's. It had been one of London's great coffeehouses, where servant and master alike could purchase a cup of Turkish coffee and talk as peers. Where great change was imagined and plotted. The reign of Charles II had been tempered by merchants rumbling for their rights within coffeehouses; the great works of Alexander Pope and Joseph Addison had been sharpened by criticism of their peers at Button's on Russell Street. Even White's, known primarily for attracting the fashionable set, must have made its mark.

But now it was just a club. An exclusive club that charged outrageous fees so one could hide from the world in smoky rooms and pretend that one had power.

Adrian corrected himself: the men in the club *did* have power. What they pretended was that they used it responsibly.

Adrian had never spent enough time in London to seriously consider petitioning for membership, and even then, he wasn't sure he would do it, knowing how easily he could be blackballed. He would surely never spend his time there, watching men who should be finding ways to lower the price of bread instead discuss how to spend their fortunes building *another* decorative folly on their country estates.

Robert, however, did keep a membership, and it was because of him that the butler finally escorted Adrian to a private room with only the barest disdain quivering on the man's lips.

"Hathorne, we had just about given up on you!" Robert exclaimed by way of greeting, rising to clap Adrian's shoulder and make room for him at the table.

Adrian executed short bows to the other men, Lords Everly and Brabourne. "I apologize for my tardiness. I was unexpectedly delayed on my way."

"London grows more unpredictable every day," Brabourne said, waving Adrian into a seat. He used an air of familiarity with Adrian, one that was both justified – because they had known each other their whole lives as neighboring Jamaican plantation families – and chilling.

Of all the people Adrian would disappoint upon inheriting, he felt the least guilty for deceiving Lord Brabourne. In his most honest moments, he might even admit to himself he looked forward to going from Brabourne's close ally to sworn enemy.

But now was not that time. Today, he had to stay on his father's mission to earn both Lord Everly and Lord Brabourne's investments in Hathorne Shipping so they could expand to South Sea trade, as well.

"We have all but settled everything," Lord Everly said, his dark eyes resting on Adrian as if expecting a reaction. As if savoring a reaction. "By the by, I sent a note to Mr. Ricketts this morning relaying my expectation that he will hear your privilege bill. Once this business arrangement is settled and you have returned to Kingston, I imagine you will be the designated heir to all the Jamaican Hathorne fortunes."

"Good thing I have my own fortune this side of the Atlantic," Robert joked.

Adrian sat between Robert and Brabourne and accepted a glass of brandy from a passing footman. They didn't require – no, they didn't even *desire* – a response from him, so he only bowed his head obsequiously and stayed silent.

The conversation descended into details of the partnership, derailed as always by Lord Everly pontificating on the best way to manage a brigade of ships and by Lord

Brabourne complaining of how the world had changed in the last four years and by Robert making jokes that no one really appreciated. Adrian took careful notes in his journal so he could faithfully report on the conversation to his father in his next letter and otherwise stayed as quiet as possible.

He had learned early on that Lords Everly and Brabourne considered Robert the only Hathorne necessary for negotiations.

"One last detail," Lord Brabourne said, when Robert started claiming another appointment. "In order to deliver our sugar commitment, we will need another ten hands. We cannot afford that investment at this point, so I would request that Inglewilde provide them."

Adrian's heart skipped, but he steeled his every muscle not to react. He had two hundred and nineteen souls awaiting him at Inglewilde; he would not let a single one slip away.

"Ah," Robert said, catching Adrian's stillness. "Does that need to be formalized? If you need extra men at harvest, surely neighbors lend each other a hand as necessary."

"It is not only at harvest time. We need ten more hands permanently." Brabourne's blue eyes fairly glittered as they landed on Adrian. "Do we have a deal?"

What was going unsaid was why Brabourne wanted them from Inglewilde; the Hathornes famously treated their slaves well, which meant they were healthier, happier, and lived longer. Adrian had always been proud of that, even bragged about it at school, until sometime around the age of twelve he realized they shouldn't be enslaved at all.

"I cannot commit to such an agreement without my father's approval," Adrian said slowly, spreading his lips in that odious complacent smile that these men seemed to expect. "I'm sure you can understand, my lord."

Brabourne flushed red to the top of his head. "It is not a large commitment. Only ten men of sound body."

"All the same, I am not at liberty to sell off even one man." Adrian could feel Robert watching him, could practically hear his cousin trying to read his thoughts, but he focused only on remaining pleasant and frozen and calm.

"Write to Hathorne, then," Lord Everly said, leaning forward to resolve the issue. "We'll hear back before you leave for Jamaica. Perhaps in the meantime, you'll reconsider how firm a grasp your father has on your balls."

This he accompanied with a loud laugh, which Brabourne was quick to join in. Adrian chuckled, too, as if he didn't understand that he was being admonished for even daring to speak at the meeting.

"Speaking of which," Everly continued, "Lady Everly is hosting a ball tomorrow night. Bring Mrs. Hathorne, won't you? We can all play a round of faro and whisper sweet nothings into pretty ears."

Adrian blinked. He had never been to a private ball in London before, and he didn't trust Lord Everly's invitation as far as he could throw it. Yet he couldn't see what trap the man was laying. He tried to measure his words, but it seemed the only answer was, "You are very kind. We shall look forward to it."

At least he could please Lisbeth with a night out.

They said facetious farewells, and then Robert and Adrian left together. Robert strode silently for all of three steps before demanding, "What was all that about? You've negotiated far larger terms than the cost of ten men without needing your father's approval."

Adrian glanced at his cousin. They had never discussed slavery, not once in all the years they had lived side by side. It had gotten to a point that Adrian was afraid to. There was nothing Robert could say that would not injure Adrian, not after they had both spent the last five years learning exactly how their family afforded fancy carriages and gilded windows.

"He doesn't need ten men," Adrian said. "He's lying to get a little bit more out of us. Maybe we'll give him three, in the end, but certainly not ten."

"Ah." For a moment, Robert glanced down, and Adrian almost thought he looked disappointed. Then he smiled, carefree and jovial again. "My cousin, the negotiator. Remind me never to be on the opposing side."

Adrian smiled, as best he could. But he was tired, and he felt a little singe of anger remaining across his skin.

He wished he could go back to the bookshop, if only to be Lisbeth's hero again.

Chapter Thirteen

L isbeth wished they weren't committed to dining with her parents.

She would far prefer to have a quiet evening with Adrian. They could order their supper served on trays in the upper sitting room by the fire and drink goblets of wine while laughing at the little man who had been so afraid to sell her a book. She could wear one of Aunt Vivienne's gowns and let the cloth droop past her shoulders, showing more skin than was decent. She could steal another kiss, or maybe two or three, and watch Adrian's eyes flare with a delicious sparkle.

Alas, her parents expected them at Frampton Square. The plans had been set since before the wedding, almost as soon as the betrothal had been suggested. The newlywed couple would have three days to get to know each other, and then Lisbeth's parents *would* see them to make sure their daughter was well.

Adrian dressed carefully for the occasion, though it was perhaps only obvious to Lisbeth, who was learning his patterns. His waistcoat was a pale, sky blue to match her evening gown; his boots gleamed; and his jacket looked new, closely fitted to show off the muscles rippling down his arms.

Lisbeth had never paid much attention to the muscles

of a gentleman's arm before. Now, however, all she could think was of those arms closing around her, making her feel as if she had the tiniest waist in the world.

Lady Cecilia fell upon them as soon as Hobbes admitted them into the parlor. Pulling Lisbeth into a decidedly indecorous embrace, she pressed a kiss to her daughter's ear and whispered, "Tell me you are happy."

When so ordered, it was easy to lie through the jumble that was Lisbeth's feelings. "I'm happy," Lisbeth whispered back.

Lady Cecilia moved on to Adrian, clasping his hands in hers and beaming. "What a pleasure to have a new son to welcome home."

To all the world, Adrian looked cool and calm, not a muscle twitching in response to her mother. But Lisbeth could see from a little spark in his eyes that he was happy and surprised by Lady Cecilia's greeting.

Let him see, then, that not all of London was out to shame him.

"I meant to keep this intimate among family," Lady Cecilia said, leading them into the sitting room, "however Lord Dawes does insist on bringing fascinating people home to dinner. Tonight we are joined by a pair of painters, Mr. Nadin and Mr. Levi."

They were quickly introduced to the guests. Mr. Levi was all soft, round shapes, with gray hair flopping over a friendly face and brown eyes that seemed in perpetual apology. Mr. Nadin, on the other hand, was young, slim, and sharp angles. He spoke with a slight accent that Lisbeth couldn't quite place until he explained he'd been raised in Calcutta. Suddenly both his speech and the faint brown hue of his skin made sense.

Lisbeth liked them both immediately.

Her eldest brother was there, too, and monopolized the conversation, asking after particulars of both men's biographies, as if it mattered whether they had gone to any grammar schools or not. Adrian asked after their travels, which had taken them both to the Continent. Lisbeth ached to ask what they painted, how they chose what to paint, how long it took them to complete a painting, who they worshipped as the great masters of the art, whether light was as powerful off the canvas as it was on it.

She waited her turn, which came when they moved to the table and she discovered her thoughtful mother had placed her between the two painters. Seeing her to the seat, Adrian smiled to the men, "I hope you are prepared for the delight of speaking to a true lover of fine art."

He might as well have stroked his finger across her bare neck; Lisbeth's every nerve lit up at his words.

Mr. Levi smiled. "There is no better dinner companion to have."

Adrian moved away, taking his seat between Lisbeth's parents, and she tried to tamp down her reaction. She could feel her heart trying to cling to his every gesture, as if to prove to herself that he was as excited by her as she was by him. He had been so perfect all evening, but that didn't mean anything other than that he was well-behaved at a dinner party.

Mr. Levi painted portraits for a living, so he had a whole host of amusing stories about lords and ladies who couldn't sit still. Mr. Nadin was more circumspect, but when he did speak, he spoke directly to Lisbeth's heart about how he moved through the world as an artist, always seeing opportunities for paintings in the smallest moments, like a little boy eating an apple off the street or an old woman bending over the washtub.

"You must tell me how I can buy your paintings," she said to the men as everyone stood to withdraw after the meal. "I aim to start a collection of my own, now that I'm married, and yours shall be my first purchases."

Her father raised an eyebrow. "I promised you gents a patroness, after all."

The gentlemen opted out of a full round of cigars on their own, so they soon rejoined Lisbeth and Lady Cecilia in the drawing room for after-dinner conversation. "The Marchioness of Leighstor told me she saw you shopping on New Bond Street today," Lady Cecilia said to Lisbeth. "You were with someone she didn't recognize."

"That was Miss Hathorne," Lisbeth replied, hoping the lady in question hadn't witnessed anything in the alleys off of New Bond Street. The Marchioness of Leighstor was an infamous gossip, especially when one dared to stray away from the strictest interpretations of polite behavior. "She was kind enough to invite me to join her."

"Ah. Are you quaking in your boots yet, Mr. Hathorne? Your sister and your wife are conspiring together." Lady Cecilia twinkled this joke at Adrian.

"It gives me great pleasure to see it," he replied.

"Did you stop in at Hatchard's?" Lord Dawes asked Lisbeth. "They have a new edition of *Ovid* that I asked them to set aside for you."

"No, we didn't get that far." Lisbeth stole a glance at Adrian, who had his emotionless mask on, before adding, "We did come across *Hartley's*. Have you heard of it?"

Her father frowned. "Isn't that a gentlemen's club?"

Her brother piped up, "A nasty one, at that. Full of the worst peers in England, if you ask me, all of them scheming how to get more money without doing a lick of good for anyone but themselves."

"*I* thought it was a bookstore, so I went in and tried to buy a book, but the man said he refused to sell to a woman. Can you believe such a thing?"

The looks around the room answered a resounding, depressing *yes*.

Mr. Nadin said, "I can believe such a thing, but I don't believe that you would let that stop you from buying the book."

Lisbeth grinned. How wonderful to create such a reputation for herself after just one dinner conversation. Across the room, she thought she detected a quiver of *something* in Adrian's expression, but she couldn't tell if it was chagrin or something better. To Mr. Nadin she responded, "You're

135

quite right. In the end, I prevailed, and I have one more book in my library."

"Shall I call there tomorrow to mop up the blood of the poor soul you vanquished?" Lord Dawes smiled.

"You may call there tomorrow to inform them of your displeasure, but I don't believe you'll find any souls within that store, living or not."

Lady Cecilia touched her fan to Adrian's arm. "Only three days in, and I'm afraid you've discovered our secret about Lisbeth: she is absolutely tenacious."

Lisbeth's heart tripped as all eyes turned to Adrian. Her tenacity was the one reason Adrian might *agree* to an annulment. And here her mother threw it in his face.

Of course, Lisbeth realized in the moment Adrian smiled at her mother, *he is performing as the perfect husband*. How long had it been before she saw his first smile, and now he had it on for the world to see? It was no different than the reserve he usually wore: a disguise so the world would only see what they wanted. His eyes even danced across the room, as if to laugh with his wife, when he responded, "I beg to disagree, Madam. It took me only one day to discover, not three."

Lisbeth tried to match his performance with a throaty titter as the rest of the room laughed. But suddenly, she couldn't focus on the people in front of her. Her mind got caught reliving every moment from the past day and night, guessing at what Adrian must have thought. When she declared herself an abolitionist; when he found her glaring down at the shopkeeper at *Hartley's*; when she lost herself in interrogating Mr. Nadin and Mr. Levi. She was the opposite of what Adrian could want in a wife. Rash, opinionated, and unafraid of scandal.

Surely he must be realizing in this moment, just as she was, that the annulment wasn't a solution for *her*. It was the only way he could live life the perfect, scandal-free way he wanted to.

Lisbeth's whole body went cold with the thought.

The party broke up soon after that. Lisbeth stretched out her farewells—extracting promises from Mr. Nadin and Mr. Levi that they would call on her soon, slipping in a final chat about books with her father, clinging to her mother in another indecorous embrace—the better to delay facing Adrian.

Even if he hadn't seen it yet, she didn't know how she could smile at him, knowing she was the antithesis of the woman he needed in his life.

Adrian took the proper seat in the carriage, on the opposite bench next to the opposite window. But he turned towards her, saying with a warmth she didn't deserve, "And so your patroness career begins."

"They were quite interesting, weren't they? I can't wait to see their work. Mr. Nadin in particular said his favorite painters are Rubens and Boucher. I love nothing more than drama in my paintings. My governess was forever scolding me because I tried to paint fairy battles into my watercolors instead of whatever simple still life she set out for me." Lisbeth looked down at her hands, folding them into her lap and trying not to fidget. "You see, I've always had trouble with obedience."

"You've always had a passionate imagination, you mean."

It was a kind thing to say. Lisbeth didn't dare look up, for she thought she might cry if she saw the same kindness on his face.

"Do you still paint watercolors?" Adrian asked.

"Of course. It is one of the acceptable activities for a well-bred young lady such as myself." Lisbeth summoned a smile to soften her sarcasm.

"Do your most recent oeuvres feature fairy battles?"

For a lone, mad moment, Lisbeth considered lying: *no, I have stamped out all such perversions from my person.* But he wouldn't believe her, if she did. "I prefer to illustrate my favorite scenes from literature. That's why *The Harrowing Adventures of Captain Urselious Bigsby* called to me so. It had the most wonderful illustration right there in the book."

"Naturally. Have you read *Captain Bigsby* yet? Was it worth the fight?"

Lisbeth still couldn't lift her eyes from her lap. She had opened the book and tried to read it earlier, but she had been too excited in triumph to concentrate. She had been too thrilled that Adrian had fought beside her. Her lips and breasts and body had thrummed from the kiss – and the way he had clasped her close to him for the tiniest second before sending her into the carriage.

She hadn't realized then what her great moment of triumph meant: that she was absolutely the wrong wife for Adrian Hathorne.

And now, she likely wouldn't ever be able to read *The Harrowing Adventures of Captain Urselious Bigsby*, not when it reminded her of her great folly.

Adrian slid down his bench to sit directly opposite her, his long legs stretching so close they would have mingled against hers had she not been the shortest woman in the world. He leaned forward, his palms stretching towards her.

"Are you feeling well, Lisbeth? You don't seem yourself."

If she were a better woman, she would confess the truth. *You'll have to annul the marriage. I can't be the wife you need. We should end this farce now.*

But she made the mistake of looking up. Adrian's green eyes were clear even in the dim street lamplight. He took her breath away with how handsome he was, and for a moment – just this moment – he was hers. Her husband. Her friend. Her man, looking after her needs.

She couldn't resist putting her hands in his. And she couldn't resist enjoying the way his fingers curled protectively around hers.

"What strikes me about painters is that it requires so much courage to devote one's life to art. For Mr. Nadin in particular, don't you think? He isn't even painting portraits to make a living. He simply paints what speaks to his heart and hopes that he will sell enough to pay his rent and buy a bowl of soup."

"Courage, yes." Adrian unfurled the words from his tongue, as if he didn't quite believe them. "Or stupidity. They both come from good families. They could have been lawyers or clerks with reliable incomes."

"It's only stupid if one gives it up for nothing. Art must be worth it to them. It must be invaluable to their souls. And Mr. Nadin won't even compromise for a commercial form of art. I don't think I would ever have that kind of courage."

Adrian's hands were warm through the kid skin of her gloves. He held her so steadily, even as the carriage swayed. "Are you trying to tell me that you wish you could throw off your life to become a painter?"

"No." Lisbeth laughed a little. "I wish I had the courage to throw off my life, if I felt so strongly about something that it was worth it. But I'm beginning to worry that I don't."

It came out more baldly than she expected it to. It was clear as day she was talking about the annulment. She looked up in terror, to see what Adrian thought of her mash of words.

He only looked at her with that solemn, unreadable green gaze. When he spoke, his voice came in a soft rasp. "You don't lack courage, Lisbeth. If anything has changed, perhaps it is that you've gained a reason to stay."

Lisbeth's stomach flipped. She didn't want to care for him if he couldn't care for her. But Adrian still held her hands. And he was still leaning towards her. The air between them suddenly wasn't the chill of a March evening; it was hot and electric like a summer storm. Lisbeth's eyes dropped to his lips, which were just a few inches from hers now. They were perfect lips for kissing, large and plump and begging for her to take a taste.

But then – right then, when Lisbeth had decided what she wanted to do – the carriage stopped. They jostled, just enough that they let go of each other's hands, and the next thing she knew, the footman had opened the door and placed the carriage steps for her to descend. Adrian leaned away to collect his hat from the bench.

She was cold again.

Chapter Fourteen

Adrian wasn't quite sure what demon seized him the next day. It happened midday, when he innocently crossed from his study to the rear drawing room in search of better daylight for reading the latest letter from his grandfather. He made the mistake of looking up as he passed the dining room – and spying Lisbeth lingering at the table, staring at nothing out the window.

She had been upset in the carriage the night before, though Adrian still wasn't sure exactly what bothered her. At dinner, she had been her sparkling, vivacious self – the Lisbeth who had so gleefully kissed him on the street – but alone with him, she had wilted like a morning glory that lost the sun.

And then, he thought she might admit something, something huge and wonderful, something that didn't explain her wilting at all.

If only the carriage hadn't stopped when it did.

If only he had kissed her anyway.

It was all of these thoughts, and the sight of his wife wilting again there at his dining table, that seized Adrian. Pushed him forward. Opened his mouth. And asked, "Would you like an adventure today?"

In the moment, it felt worth it. Lisbeth instantly lit from within, excitement leaping to her eyes, a perfect smile stealing her lips. "Oh yes, please!"

However, now that they rumbled together in the hackney cab towards the docks on the Isle of Dogs, Adrian was beginning to regret his rashness. Lisbeth practically hung out the window to see the streets, as if she had never been outside Soho before. She chattered, too, switching between exclaiming over what she saw and repeating how excited she was to go to a coffeehouse. "I shall be the envy of every bluestocking in London. A woman, patronizing a coffeehouse! Can you believe it?"

It had been a spur-of-the-moment idea. Adrian had to go meet Robert; equally, he didn't want to leave Lisbeth alone at the table with a pout on her lips.

He had thought he was above giving into impulses. Apparently not.

To make it all worse, of course, the cab was small, and Lisbeth smelled heavenly. She wore a simple beige muslin; the fabric was fine enough that, from where Adrian sat, he could see white petticoats beneath and the shape of her thighs as she leaned towards the window. How he yearned to steal her from the window and land her on his lap instead.

This was an impulse he still had the wherewithal to resist.

Robert had a window seat at Carraway's when they arrived. His friendly wave froze midair when he saw Lisbeth at Adrian's arm. Adrian couldn't blame him. Women weren't welcome in coffeehouses, unless they were serving.

But Adrian had promised his wife an adventure, and he couldn't turn back now.

The place went from the din of a hundred conversations to a flat silence as soon as they crossed the door. Standing straight as possible, Adrian nodded at his acquaintances, met the stare of strangers, and said in the direction of no one in particular, "Allow me to present my wife, Mrs. Hathorne."

Lisbeth smiled wide enough to catch every man in her net. When she beamed like that, no man stood a chance against her. At least, Adrian didn't.

He led her to Robert's table. His cousin kissed Lisbeth's hand as if it were the most natural place in the world to find her. "Mrs. Hathorne, I'm delighted you can join us this afternoon."

"Adrian is indulging me," she said, taking her seat. "I'm the cat who got killed by curiosity, so he decided he had better take me here himself before I found a way to sneak in without an escort."

She was trying to smooth things over for him. Adrian wondered if it were true, too, that she had contemplated sneaking into a coffeehouse. It was not without the realm of possibility.

He certainly had not married a fainthearted lady of the peerage.

"I hope the experience lives up to your expectations." Robert said this with a wink, earning one of those smiles from Lisbeth that sent a dagger of jealousy through

Adrian's stomach.

Mrs. Carraway, the proprietress of the coffeeshop, approached. She didn't exactly look pleased, but neither was she thundering with hands on hips to scold them. She curtsied to Robert. "Coffee for you and your guests, my lord?"

"Yes, and you had better put everyone's next round of coffee on my tab as well, in apologies for any disturbance we have caused."

No one cheered this, but it was the cue to send everyone back to their conversations. Lisbeth had to raise her voice a notch to say, after Mrs. Carraway had sashayed away, "You shouldn't have to bribe an entire coffeehouse to tolerate my presence."

"Perhaps I don't *have* to, but it is one of the perks of being a marquess, dear cousin. I enjoy throwing my money around to arrange an ideal world for myself."

"If only it would make the world ideal for everyone else," Adrian said, mostly because he was tired of Lisbeth looking at Robert.

It worked. She turned to Adrian with a glow. For a moment, he thought she might reach out and clasp his hand. Instead, she said, "Is that what you do here? Invent ways to make the world more ideal?"

There was such hope in this wife of his. She nearly vibrated with it. If only he could live up to her.

Robert scoffed. "Mostly, we invent ways for Hathorne Shipping to make more money."

And like that, the hope disappeared, replaced by something harder and darker. Lisbeth turned to Robert again. "How do you feel about your wealth coming from the blood and sweat of slaves?"

"Lisbeth," Adrian said as warning. He was all too aware of the ears around them – friendly and not – straining to hear their conversation.

Robert shrugged. "I wish it were not so, but the economy has been powered by slave labor for too long. There is no going back now."

Lisbeth pressed on. "Your family owns slaves. You could set the example and free them."

"I believe, dear cousin, you mean *our* family owns slaves." Robert leaned back in his chair, but the edge in his voice belied his casual posture. He didn't like where the conversation was going. "Furthermore, we can't simply free the slaves. First, there is the matter of our industry. Who is going to pick our sugar cane, if not slaves? Second, what would happen to the slaves? We feed them, clothe them, house them. They would not know how to survive without us. Is it not better that they have shelter and occupation than be stranded to beg in the street?"

Lisbeth opened her mouth to argue, but Robert pressed on.

"And what of our family? Were we to free the slaves, your line of the Hathornes would no longer have income. You would have to live on your savings, and once they dwindled, either rely on me for kindness or find yourself on the streets. Is that the future you envision? Raising your children poor as church mice?"

Adrian's stomach clenched. There was an anger lining Robert's voice that he hadn't heard before. An anger *he* would have to face, sooner or later.

Mrs. Carraway returned, placing clay mugs before each of them and a plate of sweet buns in the center of the table. Thanking her, Adrian decided it was time to change the subject. "Are you coming to Everly's ball tonight, Robert?"

"I think not. There's nothing at balls for me but meddling mothers trying to trap me into marriage."

But before the topic could take hold, a man sidled to their table. Adrian had seen him at Carraway's before, though they'd never been introduced. His skin was darker than Adrian's, and his clothes were the sturdy wool of a sailor. "Pardon me, sirs," he said in a broad accent that betrayed his origin from somewhere else. "I heard a discussion of slavery and thought you might be interested in my most recent pamphlet."

"Why yes, thank you!" Lisbeth said quickly. She took the parchment the man offered, which had cheap type proclaiming *The Evils of Human Bondage: First-Hand Accounts*. "And what is your name, sir?"

"Samson. I'm a free sailor, ma'am, and when I'm in London, I stay at the Friends' Society on Ewer Street to advocate for human liberation. Perhaps you would like to join us sometime. We need more volunteers to teach us to read."

He spoke rapidly, as if he knew he only had seconds to get his words out. Indeed, Adrian rose to his feet as Samson delivered his speech. There were too many eyes on them, watching as the new Mrs. Hathorne conversed with an abolitionist. All it took was for one person to report back to Everly or Brabourne or even his grandfather.

"Thank you, but Mrs. Hathorne won't be needing this." Adrian tore the pamphlet from Lisbeth's hands before she could react and handed it to Samson. "You may go."

Samson returned the set-down with large, disappointed eyes before walking away. Lisbeth, meanwhile, leapt to her feet in outrage. "How dare you! I will read what I want to read, when I want to read it, from whom I want to read it."

She took a step as if to follow Samson, but Robert stood now, too, and blocked her way. "We are in public, cousin. Control yourself."

Adrian's fists curled. Robert had no business admonishing Lisbeth, no matter how shocking her behavior. But he had too many battles to face right now, and his primary goal was to keep anyone from painting him an abolitionist.

"It is time to go," he said, as calmly and quietly as he could manage. He held out his arm to Lisbeth, praying she wouldn't make him force her out of the coffeehouse. They didn't need any more of a scene than they had already caused. Yet he would throw her over his shoulder and carry her out, if he had to.

Lisbeth glared at him for a long moment. Then she

swept past him, ignoring his arm. "You disgust me," she hissed as she headed for the door.

Adrian tried not to let her words land beyond his skin. He didn't need her approval or admiration or even tolerance. He just needed her cooperation.

That's what he told himself, anyway, though it did nothing to stop his heart from descending into his stomach.

With a bow to Robert, he followed his wife onto the street and called a hackney cab.

Chapter Fifteen

L isbeth trembled with anger. She knew Adrian didn't want scandal; she knew he wasn't an abolitionist; she knew he didn't agree with her or the way she lived her life. But she still couldn't believe he would do something so humiliating as to rip paper from her very hands. To dismiss that poor man with such short words. To let Robert scold her like she was some kind of disobedient child.

The sooner they annulled this disgrace of a marriage, the better.

Adrian didn't try to speak to her when he joined her outside. She told herself she preferred it that way. She wouldn't be able to prevent bitter words from pouring forth, and they were still in view of the coffeehouse window. Lisbeth focused on ignoring her husband, though that meant she had to inhale the stench of sea water mixed with human refuse.

This was not what she had pictured when Adrian invited her on an adventure.

She did not allow him to hand her into the hackney cab, instead grabbing the wooden doorframe in her gloved hands and hauling herself up. It was not as if she had any further dignity to salvage. Adrian had torn that to shreds in front of his friends.

For his part, Adrian pulled closed the shutters on the cab windows, plunging them into a dim, sickening light as the carriage rattled across the cobblestone road. "I'm sorry I had to be so brusque."

He said it so calmly, so quietly, as if he was guilty of something as small as spilling a drink down her dress. It soaked Lisbeth with fury.

"You had no right. You are a horrible tyrant. That man was simply spreading ideas. You had no right." She couldn't even control her own words; that was how upset she was. Lisbeth peeled off her gloves to let the anger simmer off her skin. "You should take me home to Frampton Square. I would prefer not to live with you any longer."

Adrian didn't move, yet Lisbeth could still sense how he stiffened into a statue. "Lisbeth, one can't simply speak of abolition in a coffeehouse. You don't know who was there. You don't know who they work for. You don't know whom they are going to tell."

"What do I care who hears? Everyone should hear. Slavery is evil. Your family is evil. The more people who hear it, the better."

"Our family," he corrected softly, but Lisbeth barely heard it.

"A coffeehouse is the perfect place to speak of such things, actually. Revolutions have been planned in coffeehouses before. Why not foment such a fundamental concept as human liberty in a coffeehouse?"

"It *is* fomenting there. That's why it is so dangerous.

People like Everly and Brabourne have men there, watching to see who sides with the abolitionists."

"Oh, and so I may have ruined your precious business deal? Good. Now you won't have to lick the ground where Everly walks. You should be thanking me."

"Do you know what happens once the West India lobby decides you're an abolitionist? They ruin your business. They smear your name. If you're persistent enough, they kill you, though they'll call it a sudden fatal condition of the heart." Adrian slid across the bench and suddenly she could see him in the dark. He didn't wear his mask of indifference. This Adrian was intense. He was earnest. He was serious. "Lisbeth, I want you to fight for abolition. But you must do it with your eyes open to all the people who will silence you. You must choose when, where, and with whom. You are playing chess, with men who are chess masters. You cannot simply wander into a coffeehouse and pick a fight."

The anger propping Lisbeth up, that had been balling her fists and rushing her ears, froze with her breath. Could she possibly have heard Adrian correctly? "You want me to fight for abolition."

A slow, dangerous smile spread his lips. "You do realize, don't you, that it's only one side of my family that is evil. The other half – my mother's half – were slaves. Stolen from our homeland. Forced into labor. Beaten and tortured and turned into whores. How do you think that makes me feel?"

Lisbeth had to shut her eyes when he described slavery. She had heard it all before, but she couldn't think of it with Adrian staring at her. And how could he feel, being raised by the Hathornes – the lovely, kind, funny Hathornes – while knowing the history of his mother? She whispered what she felt, just imagining it. "Confused."

His hand found hers in the dark. He still wore his gloves: they were thick, smooth leather against her bare skin. "I am not trying to be a tyrant. I am trying to play chess."

Lisbeth's body had been thrumming with fury. Now, when she opened her eyes and found his, that transfigured into a different emotion. A nameless emotion.

This was her husband. Serious eyebrows. Careful mouth. Excited eyes, watching her. Waiting for something. Planning something too terrific to be named. She had never imagined an argument like this. She had never hoped for a husband with greater dreams than hers.

The air crackled with pure, instinctive need.

She fell onto him, arms around his neck, legs straddling his hips, lips begging his. He pulled her closer with just as much intensity. His hands cupped her bum, a grasp Lisbeth had never thought to yearn for. She raked her fingers through his short, soft hair as his mouth explored hers. She wanted to touch him everywhere. She wanted to untie his cravat. She wanted to stop thinking and only feel the pure, white heat coursing over her.

His fingers trailed the length of her thighs, then up

her waist, resting just beneath her breasts. Without knowing why, Lisbeth knew she wanted him to touch them, to circle her nipples, to worship her breasts like she was the goddess Venus. Still kissing him – oh, she couldn't separate her lips from his if she wanted to – Lisbeth seized his right hand, removed the glove, and placed it on her breast. "Now the other," she murmured.

"I thought I disgusted you," he whispered, as he found her nipples with his thumbs through the layers of her bodice.

"If you're going to be a tyrant, then be one in my bed. Don't let me up until I have been slaked. Make me kiss you until neither of us can breathe. Let me lose my name while screaming yours."

Beneath her, Adrian let out a slight, delighted groan. He claimed her with his mouth again, his lips and tongue just as hungry as hers.

She was hot and wet and wouldn't have minded at all if he took her right there in the dirty hansom cab as it trotted through Soho.

But the cab had made more progress than she knew and came to a stop at Upper Norton Street. The driver let out a shout to announce their arrival. Almost before Lisbeth could separate from Adrian, their footman Newman opened the door.

He had the good training to only blush a scarlet red while stepping aside, pretending not to have seen a thing.

Lisbeth straightened her dress, stealing a proud

glance at Adrian's swollen lips and stiff trousers. She summoned herself into proper decorum. "Well, Mr. Hathorne, I shall go see about tea."

He could only look back at her with a glaze.

She hoped he would follow her upstairs, never mind that they had a ball to dress for. She hoped her skin never cooled from the excitement of his touch. She hoped her thoughts never settled enough to regret this.

Chapter Sixteen

Strictly speaking, Adrian had been to three balls before. He had danced the minuets, drunk the orange ices, and even gambled on cards with a cheroot hanging from his lips.

But those had all been at Maidenheath House. The guests had been a hodgepodge of family, close friends, and gentry from surrounding neighborhoods. His dance partners had been either Mary or his grandmother. Everyone knew him, knew what he looked like, and knew better than to be curious about it.

He had never been to a London extravaganza. He wasn't prepared at all when the hired carriage deposited them at the base of Lord Everly's white stairs.

Though it was moonlight, the house gleamed, from its marble exterior balustrades to the candlelit windows. And it was bursting with guests. The stairs themselves were clogged with finely-dressed ladies and gentlemen waiting to enter, and the broad, brightly-lit windows set on display everyone already inside, laughing and chatting and – in one case – stealing what looked like a kiss.

Then they got inside. While Lisbeth beamed at everyone around her, nodding and curtseying and acting the perfect lady, Adrian could only gulp. The sounds alone – chatter, booms of laughter, squeals of delight, strains of violin, gasps of dismay – overwhelmed. He couldn't decide what to look at, either: the walls, covered in gilt frames; the silk and muslin dresses every color of the rainbow; the diamonds and rubies and emeralds glittering in the light; the refreshment tables with ices and punches and stacks of confections on silver platters; or the servants, every one of them Black, every one of them in Lord Everly's livery with brass collars around their necks, as if they were still slaves on free English soil.

He wasn't sure anyone else noticed them.

"Ah, Hathorne, you made it after all."

Adrian snapped his attention to his host, who stood at the entrance of the ballroom, sneering. Lord Everly somehow seemed even larger surrounded by so many people, his white face powder sticking with sweat to the crevasses in his forehead.

"We thought perhaps you wouldn't come," Everly continued. Beside him, his wife didn't even try to smile, only settled suspicious brown eyes on Adrian.

Curtseying, Lisbeth glowed as if they had rolled out an elaborate welcome in her honor. "I am sure that must be my fault, for I thought to send a note but then worried that would be too familiar. Thank you so much for inviting us."

Lady Everly only gestured to the dancing, as if to bid them out of her sight.

Adrian looped Lisbeth's arm through his to calm his own nerves. That afternoon, his grandfather's man of business had been awaiting him when he returned from

Carroway's, which meant Adrian had quickly righted his senses and had *not* had a chance to follow Lisbeth upstairs. Their conversation on the way to the ball had been light and insignificant. Adrian wasn't sure if Lisbeth had forgiven him for the coffeehouse. He wasn't sure if she wanted him to try kissing her again.

But he was definitely glad she was there at his side as all eyes in the ballroom turned to him, the lone brown guest.

It was not so bad from everyone. His grandmother and Mary were delighted to see them, and Lisbeth introduced Adrian to more of her family and acquaintances. In short order, Lisbeth's male relatives had asked Lisbeth, Mary, and even Her Grace to dance the gavotte, leaving Adrian with the company of Lord Dawes and some friends from Eton.

Lisbeth, Adrian discovered, was a tidy dancer. Short as she was, she took neat steps, moved her arms gracefully through the air, and did it all with such joy that one couldn't help smiling while watching. It helped that her satin skirts caught the light every which way they turned, as did the sapphire necklace that highlighted her strong, wide carriage. He envied her the ability to flit through the world, laughing and flushed and happy, without a care as to whether it was wrong for her to be so.

Lisbeth danced two sets before returning to his side. "Do you not dance?"

"I will dance with you if I am permitted." Adrian tried

out a flirtatious smirk, and it earned him a thrilling grin from Lisbeth.

She held out her wrist so he could review her dancing card. "Alas, I've promised all the dances before supper. You'll have to find another partner until then."

Adrian penciled his name next to the quadrille after the supper break. He let his fingers linger on her bare wrist, running his thumb up from the curve of the palm as he murmured, "One dance with you will be enough dancing for me."

Her eyes widened and a pink sliver of tongue darted out to wet her lips. Adrian reveled in the reaction for as long as he could, until it bordered on inappropriate, and only then did he release her hand. Lisbeth exhaled a titter, looking about them as if to break the spell. "It is bad form to attend a ball and not dance when there are ladies who need partners."

Adrian followed her gaze to see a cadre of young debutantes in pale gowns trying not to look too bored as they awaited a gentleman's notice. "They cannot want to dance with *me*."

"And why shouldn't they?" Looping her arm through his, Lisbeth started gliding their way. Adrian had no choice but to follow. "You are the Duke of Berkwell's grandson."

"I am married."

Lisbeth didn't stop, not even as he tried to pull his arm away. "You are not proposing to them. A dance is only a dance." Then, just before they reached the debutantes, she paused, lowering her voice so no one would overhear. "If it is because you fear an unfair reaction, you must see by now that you have painted the *ton* with too broad a brush. Does not my family welcome you? Did my friends not just receive you?"

Adrian had three reactions to this speech: the first, that Lisbeth thought she was doing something kind; the second, that he wasn't sure she could ever understand the poison circling him; but thirdly, that he appreciated her trying.

Lisbeth continued, "Besides, don't you think it could be helpful to your chess game to be seen as one who fits in with society?"

"Perhaps," he conceded, though he couldn't see what a dance or two would achieve.

Smiling in triumph, Lisbeth tugged him back into action. "There's Lady Fairfax. She has always been fair-minded. I'll introduce you, and then she'll introduce you to her niece. Lady Fairfax hosts the best musicales, so you will be glad to know her in the long term as well as the short."

Lady Fairfax was a handsome woman with gray streaking through her brown pomaded hair and a dia-mond-crested lorgnette, which she held up to her eye as Lisbeth approached. "I'm so glad to see you, Lady Fairfax, as I've been married since last we met. May I introduce my husband, Mr. Hathorne?"

"*This* is Mr. Hathorne?" Lady Fairfax's eyebrow raised

as her gaze struck Adrian. He did his best to look friendly, obsequious, and calm, without being so presumptuous as to meet her eye.

Lisbeth smiled as if it were the most natural response in the world. "Does he not have the Berkwell nose? As soon as I saw him amongst his family, I saw the resemblance."

Lady Fairfax only kept staring at him.

"Mr. Hathorne would love the honor of dancing with Miss Fairfax while I am stolen away by all my friends. Could you introduce us?"

She stared for a moment longer. Then the lady – a viscountess, if Adrian remembered correctly – turned from him. To Lisbeth, she said, "My dear, I cannot." And with a swish of her skirts, she stalked away.

It was not *quite* the cut direct. No one around them seemed to notice. There were no gasps or murmurs of dismay. But it was clear enough what she meant: Adrian could not be introduced because his skin was dark.

Adrian was not surprised. He was not even hurt, which he might have expected, for it had always stung before, when these English people with their watery eyes decided he was beneath them. He felt only red-hot anger, and it burned all the worse when he saw the look on Lisbeth's face.

"Let's get some fresh air." Adrian pulled Lisbeth out the back door, where new gas lights illuminated a small garden. The cold night felt good after the heat of too many bodies sweating together.

"Perhaps she didn't hear me correctly," Lisbeth was saying. "Perhaps she thought I asked *her* to dance with you, which would certainly be unusual."

Adrian dropped his hand from Lisbeth's, letting her pace the pea-gravel path at her own rhythm. They were alone in the garden, as far as he could tell, the rest of the guests pressing against each other like animals.

He shook his head. That was his anger speaking. He needn't insult an entire building full of people simply because one of them insulted him.

"Perhaps she needed the retiring room," Lisbeth said. "I can be quite rude if I suddenly have the urge."

Adrian knew the comfort in what Lisbeth was doing. If she could somehow work it out that *she* had misunderstood, or that she had been in the wrong, then she need not face the truth.

That the people she considered kind and interesting and worthy were small-minded.

That there was nothing she could do to make Lady Fairfax look Adrian in the eye.

That Lisbeth had chosen a husband who could not even go to a ball.

"Perhaps you should like that annulment after all," Adrian said, as Lisbeth searched for the next excuse to supply Lady Fairfax.

To his great satisfaction, Lisbeth looked at him in horror. "What, because one woman was rude to you? I should like to believe I'm of stronger starch than that."

The ostrich feather atop her cap swayed at the fervor of her protest. They had marched to the back of the garden now, where a stone wall protected the Everly grounds from the riffraff of London. Yew trees pared into the shapes of animals stood between them and the ballroom, yet they could still hear the rumble of polite chatter and the breezy rhythm of a waltz.

Soon, they would have to return for the midnight supper.

"It's not just one woman, you know. I'd wager for every ten introductions you begged in there, only one would be granted, and even that one with a certain set of the lips that makes it clear it is only as a favor."

Lisbeth lifted her chin even as her eyes flicked behind him to the abandoned party. "Is it better in Kingston?"

Adrian raised his shoulders. He wanted to make her a promise that it was, but the few months he had spent in Kingston as an adult had shown him White society was even worse there. One friend hadn't even been allowed into a ball hosted by his White cousin, simply because of his mother's ancestry.

"If you're going to annul the marriage, let it be for this," he said instead. "You could have any respectable gentleman. One who could ask a young lady to do a quadrille without embarrassing you."

Now Lisbeth settled her gaze on him. In the shadows of a gas lamp, Adrian could only see her irises as dark pools of thought. Her face was milky and white and unreadable;

he couldn't tell if she was angry or sad or indifferent.

But when she spoke, her voice made it clear: anger. "It would never be for this."

Adrian should not have been comforted that she wouldn't abandon him to face London alone. He should have shaken his head at her, or walked away, or insisted that she do the sensible thing.

He didn't do any of that. He didn't *want* to do any of that. Lisbeth's words went straight to his heart, and then from there very quickly to his groin. His wife stood before him, shimmering in a light that combined the moon and gas lamps and distant chandeliers, a short, wide woman in an absurd satin dress that could never be called fashionable, and she refused to leave.

What could heat a man more quickly?

Before Adrian quite knew what he was doing, he pulled Lisbeth into his arms. It was an awkward jerk that sent her colliding with his chest, but Adrian didn't stop. He claimed her lips with his, that sweet taste of Lisbeth that had kept his mind straying all afternoon.

She kissed him back, almost immediately, her lips soft and her tongue curious. She wrapped her arms around his neck, too. Lifting her from the waist, Adrian raised her to meet his level – relishing in the little gasp that escaped her – then trapped their bodies against the garden wall to keep her there. Lisbeth's fingers roamed around his neck, tracing his jawline, playing at his tie, and Adrian heard himself growl. He wasn't thinking, wasn't quite vocalizing, was only feeling a heat unlike any he'd ever experienced before.

He wanted her naked.

And he wasn't ashamed to want it.

"Adrian," Lisbeth breathed, her words hot and soft and desperate in his ear.

"I'm here, Lisbeth," he breathed back, not sure where the words came from. His right hand was sliding up her leg now, as he traced her neck and shoulders with his lips. She slipped against the wall, and he braced her bum with his left palm to keep her in place. His righthand fingers trailed the soft cotton of her stockings, then the silk ties of her garters, and finally the soft, velvet skin of her thigh.

She wasn't wearing anything else beneath her petticoats.

"Adrian," she breathed again, and this time he couldn't find words for response. He could only slip his fingers farther, feeling everything as slowly as possible: the soft down warming her legs, the slight ridges of her inner skin, and then...

He gasped a little, his lips rising from their suckling spot at her neck in surprise as his fingers found the wiry hair. The hot, meaty, luscious skin beneath it. And – as he kept going – the wet sluice of her deep inner folds.

Lisbeth gasped now, too, one arm wrapped tight around his neck and the other braced against the wall. Her legs had curled around his waist, locking against him. Adrian shoved them both harder against the wall for leverage, cupping her bum tighter in his left palm as his right fingers relished the ocean of desire he had just discovered.

If only he knew what to do.

He started by running his index finger along the length of her folds, discovering a ridge here, a soft wall there. Towards the top, he found a little nub, and she sucked the night air as if it were her last breath. Adrian stayed there, touching it, until she hissed, "Circles."

He had never been happier to obey. He looped the nub once, twice, made the circumference wider, made it smaller, all while raising his eyes to watch Lisbeth's face. For once, she wasn't smiling. Her slim, powerful brows drew together in concentration, her eyes shut, and her mouth gaping. Her tongue darted out now and then in response to his fingers. Adrian increased the speed of his circles, and she moaned. "Keep going," she pleaded, as if he thought to stop. "Soon," she whispered, later, though Adrian had lost track of whether it was seconds or minutes or hours. Her moans were more frequent, her head rolled from one side to another, and when he stole a kiss, darting his tongue to taste her lips, she responded with ferocious, greedy gulps. He lost track of his circles, accidentally slid his finger down the length of her wet crevice, and it plunged deeper, inside of her, and that was when Lisbeth cried out, shuddering in pleasure.

Adrian waited for her to open her eyes before moving his fingers again. She was still wet, perhaps more than ever, so he stroked again, returning to the circles around her nub. "Have you ever done this before?" he asked as he did, relishing the lazy happiness in Lisbeth's eyes. She was smiling now, a dreamy, moony grin.

"Only to myself," she whispered. "Not like this."

"Shall we do it again?"

She was already writhing at his touch, closing her eyelids, frowning in that delicious concentration.

"Always," she breathed. Then she opened her eyes again. "Except I do believe it is raining."

Adrian couldn't quite bring himself to stop circling, even as he discovered the cold drizzle she mentioned. Lisbeth leaned her head against the garden wall. "We'll catch our death if you don't stop that."

"Do you want me to stop?" he growled into her neck.

"No," she sighed.

But the rain picked up, no longer just a spittle, and even with his fingers inside his wife and an erection the size of the Great Wall, Adrian had to admit they couldn't stay outside much longer. Gently, he pressed one final kiss to Lisbeth's shoulder, then returned her feet to the ground.

"I hope we haven't missed supper," he said, trying to conjure a bank of indifferent White faces to return his body to a state of boredom.

"We aren't staying," Lisbeth replied, throwing out the words with disdain. Then she cut her eyes to him with a certain fear. "Are we?"

Adrian wondered what she was frightened of. That

he would command her to stay? That he would take her home and insist they continue what they had just started? Or that he would take her home and *not* continue what they had started?

A week ago, he may not have noticed that she was scared at all. Perhaps in another week, he would be able to read her even better. For now, he merely bowed. "I am at your command, Mrs. Hathorne."

Chapter Seventeen

The household was quiet when they returned to Upper Norton Street. Ford and Mrs. Siswell had retired for the night, leaving only a few candles burning in the foyer as well as the lamps in the upper corridors. Lisbeth nearly trembled with wickedness, though there was nothing unusual about a husband and wife returning from a ball to a slumbering house. Adrian had held her the whole carriage ride, one arm around her shoulders and the other reaching into her lap to clasp her gloved hand. Now he led her up the two sets of stairs to their bedrooms, pausing on the silk carpet outside the doors.

"Perhaps you would like to sleep," he murmured, his voice low enough that no servant could hear, even were they awake.

"Perhaps I would not," she murmured back.

She saw rather than heard how his breath caught in his throat, his eyes flaring, his lips parting. How long had she waited for this, to have a man weak for *her*? Lisbeth touched his hand, a promise. "Hannah is waiting to help me undress. May I knock on your door in a quarter hour?"

He nodded, then cleared his throat. "I am at your service."

Lisbeth smiled to herself as she sashayed into her room. He had certainly been at her service in the garden.

She had not known fingers alone could be so powerful. Adrian's had not done anything so different from what Lisbeth had done to herself these past years in the dark of night, yet somehow his touch had set fire to what had only ever been an ember; her limbs still floated from the white-hot pleasure that he unleashed.

Hannah paled when she saw the state of Lisbeth's outfit: crumpled skirts, rain-stained satin, the wilted ostrich feather.

"I behaved wildly, I'm afraid," Lisbeth said by way of explanation, and something in her demeanor must have said more, because Hannah smiled a slow, wicked grin.

"Which nightdress would you like to wear, then?"

Lisbeth's trousseau – originally purchased for her marriage to an earl – included a number of French nightdresses designed to entice a husband. Her mother had recommended the one she wore on her ill-fated wedding night: white lace that revealed a shocking amount of skin.

Tonight, Lisbeth decided, she would wear what made *her* feel beautiful. The French modiste had argued that yellow silk made Lisbeth's skin look sickly, but in the candlelight, Lisbeth rather thought it set her brown eyes aglow. The lace pattern was suggestive more than it was revealing, streaming down beneath her breasts, narrowing near her navel, and then falling in soft pools from her thighs to the floor. Hannah brushed out her hair, letting it loose to reach down past her shoulder blades, then dabbed *eau d'ange* behind Lisbeth's ears before declaring her ready for the evening.

"Have a good night, Mistress," Hannah said with a smirk, and Lisbeth could only giggle.

How could she be embarrassed to have a husband who yearned for her?

Assuming, of course, that in the past fifteen minutes he had not changed his mind.

Alone in her room, Lisbeth took a moment to collect her thoughts. Neither of them had said it, but Lisbeth could feel in her bones that if she knocked on that door – if Adrian still awaited her on the other side – then their marriage would become real. No longer could she threaten to run home to Frampton Square. When he declared unilaterally that she couldn't do something, she would have to fight back without threatening annulment.

If she knocked on that door, she was accepting him, tyranny and all, for the rest of her life.

It sent a shiver down her spine, especially when she remembered her rage that very afternoon at how he silenced her in the coffeehouse.

But she knew now why he did it. Knowing that Adrian was a secret abolitionist – a careful, serious abolitionist – Lisbeth could see why he had silenced her each and every time. He was afraid of being found out. He was afraid of showing his hand too early.

And now Lisbeth had experienced it, too. From none other than Lady Fairfax, who had always been so kind and welcoming to her. She wasn't sure Adrian's extreme caution was necessary, but she certainly understood it now.

She rose, silk rustling at her ankles in delicious licks. Adrian was her husband, and he wanted her. There was no more thinking to it than that.

He answered her knock almost immediately. He wore the same robe she had seen on previous nights, but it was tied more loosely, revealing a peek beneath of bare chest and white drawers.

Her heart tripped.

"Would you like a sherry?" he asked after a long moment – a moment during which, she dared believe, he raked his eyes over her body.

She knew she should probably accept it, to set them both at ease, but she wanted nothing more than to slide that robe over his shoulders and see her husband's body once and for all.

"I'd like you to kiss me." Her voice came out a little squeaky, and she laughed at it.

Adrian smiled. He was so handsome when he smiled, so light and real and devastating. She could lose herself in it.

"I wish you would smile more," she said, reaching up to touch it. His lips were warm and soft beneath her fingertips. "It's my favorite thing in the whole world."

Adrian caught her hand, pressing her palm against his cheek. His jaw prickled with freshly-shaved hair. "I smile when I have good reason to."

"I'll have to give you more good reasons, then."

They lost words after that. Adrian's free hand came

to her waist, pulling her closer, and then he dipped his head to meet hers.

His kisses were heaven, a pillowed nirvana where Lisbeth could lose track of time and thought and simply feel. But her body burned for something more just now. Untying the sash at his waist, she tucked her thumbs beneath his robe and pulled it off one arm, then the other. She only retreated when it had fallen to the floor, roaming her eyes over the muscles defining Adrian's body. Wiry curls danced across his chest, narrowing in a trail that disappeared down his breeches.

She would have followed it right then and there if Adrian hadn't touched her in turn. His hands slipped under the bodice of her gown; his palms cupped her breasts as his thumbs drew circles around her nipples.

It was the third time that day he had touched her so, and Lisbeth hoped he would never stop.

She reached out, hooking her fingers at the rim of his breeches, tugging him closer, and then running her hand down to palm the bulge.

She loved his groan of appreciation almost as much as she loved the firmness that twitched in her hand.

"I've never been allowed to see one, you know," she murmured, running her thumb along its length the way Adrian had touched her in the garden.

"Proper ladies are supposed to faint dead away if they see it, even on their husbands," Adrian said between breaths. His hands had fallen away from her breasts, resting at her waist now as she explored him.

"I've never been very proper." If she had her way, Lisbeth would have unclothed him already.

But Adrian interrupted, lifting her into his arms and carrying her to the bed. The covers were already drawn back; he deposited her on the soft cotton sheets. He kissed her again.

"Are you sure you want to do this tonight?"

Lisbeth loved that he stared at her with those glowing green irises as he asked. "I've wanted to do it since I saw you at the altar."

He shut his eyes in shame even as he smiled. "I didn't go about it well that night. I want to do it properly now."

She anchored her hands on his neck to steal a hot, heady kiss.

Adrian trailed his fingers up her arms, clasping her palms in his. "I've heard it may hurt you."

"Yes, and I will bleed, and I may cry." Lisbeth couldn't help laughing at how horrendous the words sounded in the air. "*I've* heard that for some women, it doesn't hurt at all. Some don't bleed, even though they've protected their chastity. One friend hated it. Most of them like it. Come to think of it, I believe it is so popular an act that kings have thrown off churches in the name of sexual congress. It must not be that bad."

Adrian kissed her left palm and then her right. "May I confess I'm a little nervous?"

"That's because you're thinking too hard." Lisbeth

propelled herself onto her knees, pressing close against him so she could feel his chest on the other side of her lace. "Kiss me and then take me. If we don't get it right the first time, we'll try again."

Adrian complied. His hand plunged into her hair as he took her lips with his. Lisbeth had never felt so consumed. She loved it. Her hands went again to his breeches, and this time, he let her undo the laces, though she fumbled because she was so busy being kissed she couldn't see what she was doing. He stepped out of his pants and stood naked before her, all sinewy muscle and a strong member that nearly pulsed with desire.

Lisbeth felt her nether regions flood at just the sight of it.

He wanted *her*. There was no more evidence than this.

Adrian reached for her with his long fingers, exploring her wet folds as he had in the garden, and Lisbeth lost track of her thoughts. She wanted more this time, not with intellectual curiosity but with a deep, primal need. Her hips started bucking, and Adrian whispered against her neck, "Are you ready?"

She breathed her answer, or screamed it – she didn't have control anymore as she awaited him. Whatever she did, Adrian heard her yes. Slowly, gently, he positioned himself against her. For a moment, his tip caressed her wet nub the way his fingers just had, and Lisbeth nearly exploded. But then it descended, and next, he was plunging inside her.

It hurt. She couldn't deny that. Her muscles seized in protest, and she let out a gasp of pain. But she didn't want him to stop, didn't want to lose this experience. So she eased her hips and whispered, "Keep going, please." She focused on the feel of his thighs braced against hers, the wiry curls of hair prickling her skin. The cotton under her bum growing hot from their friction. The heat of his breath coming in quick staccato exhales on her shoulder. The pain, she realized, had evaporated, replaced by a growing, frenzied desire. Adrian was inside her, his eyes squeezed shut, his body pulsing needily in and over and around her, and Lisbeth let herself disappear into the moment.

When he came, the most beautiful smile overtook his face.

She erupted the next instant, ignited from the sight of it.

Chapter Eighteen

Adrian had never been so relaxed. So at peace. So alive.

No wonder men risked health and wealth in pursuit of sex. He had never known something more precious than this: floating beyond all problems, feeling nothing but flesh and fire, tasting the full satisfaction of desire.

Stretching onto his side, Adrian surveyed the wife beside him. Lisbeth wore a dreamy smile and nothing else; he decided it was his favorite of her outfits. Her naked body didn't match the slim Grecian statues he'd seen, nor the voluptuous cartoons passed around the Eton boarding rooms, yet Adrian couldn't imagine a landscape more erotic. The soft expanse of her skin, the muddy rose of her nipples, the rising hill of her stomach, and the silky black forest at her center.

And he was naked, too, bared for her to see in all his shy brown glory. He wondered what she made of him, whether she found him too hairy or if his cock was alarming or if she had been revolted by the constellation of moles across his shoulder.

Better not to worry about such things. Adrian sneaked a palm onto her hip to reclaim her attention. "Did you enjoy that as much as I did?"

She turned to face him, her breasts wiggling

ever-so-slightly as she did so. Adrian dragged his eyes back to meet hers as she said, "I don't think I'll mind sacrificing myself on the altar of wifely duty after all."

"Wifely duty," he repeated. "Are you to remain my wife, then?"

She trailed a finger across his lips. "Will you still have me?"

The question was so absurd, Adrian almost laughed. But for a split second, he saw the fear in her eyes. The insecurity beating in her heart. Lisbeth believed somehow that he might say no, even after this. After all they had been through together, and after all the physical joy they had given each other.

This was the woman, then, who had chosen to marry a stranger rather than stomach another Season.

He tightened his grip on her hip. "I never wanted the annulment, remember?"

It didn't seem to be quite the thing to say. Lisbeth didn't immediately burst into rapturous wonder at how romantic a husband he was, nor did she throw her arms around him and shower him with kisses – both outcomes he wouldn't have minded. She lowered her somber eyes.

"Can you tell me what your chess game is, then?" Her hand closed over his, small and soft and warm. "How do you plan to win abolition, if not by preaching it publicly?"

Adrian's blood pounded. If he told her now, the secret he had so jealously pressed to his breast all these years would be free in the world. Lisbeth need only whisper one piece of it to the wrong person and his plans would unravel. He would lose his edge of surprise; he would likely lose his father's love, too, and his inheritance and possibly all family connections.

But if he didn't tell her now, he sensed, he would lose Lisbeth.

"When the privilege bill is approved, I'll inherit Inglewilde Plantation upon my father's death. I'm going to free every last person that the Hathorne family owns. If they want to stay, I'll offer them wages to keep their positions. If they want to leave, I'll give them money to get started in their new life. Either way, I'm going to free them and support them and hopefully prove that our economy does not need to balance on slavery in order to function."

Adrian was aware, by the end of his speech, that he was no longer serene. His words flamed with the heat in his heart; his fingers at Lisbeth's hip curled into a fist.

The anger didn't feel as good, now that he had known a few moments of peace without it.

"You're the only person I've told," he continued, locking his eyes on Lisbeth's to make sure she heard him. "It means my family will lose money, friendships, respect... They'll likely disown me. They may try to sue me to take the property away from me. That's why it is so important I do things the right way. I can't give the court any extra reason to declare my inheritance illegal. And they *can't* find out what I'm planning to do."

Lisbeth threaded her fingers through his fist. "They

can't find out what *we're* planning to do."

He wasn't sure how he felt as her words linked themselves around his heart. His wife had never been more than an ivory pawn to leave in place in London.

Adrian hadn't yet reckoned with how to expect Lisbeth – the woman whose soul sparked like flint against everything she encountered – to stay in one corner of the gameboard.

For the moment, he drew her knuckles to his mouth and pressed kisses to each precious finger one by one. She would keep his secret; she might even fight for his secret. That was enough for him to know.

Her irises darkened at his kisses, which prompted him to trail his mouth farther along her arm, dotting his tongue across her wrist, inside her elbow, up her shoulder, until finally capturing her earlobe. She hissed; he was coming to love her hisses.

"Are you tired, Mrs. Hathorne?" he whispered.

She answered with a kiss, hot and eager against his lips. Earlier, their mouths had explored each other with an urgency, a prelude to how their bodies would join. Now, with his lower half still languid in satisfaction, Adrian could simply enjoy Lisbeth's lips. Her kisses were like smiles bottled into a potion, a secret elixir only for him that spread sunshine across his skin.

He couldn't believe he had wasted so much of their marriage, afraid of *this*.

"Earlier," Lisbeth said, presenting her neck as his

canvas, "I started reading *The Harrowing Adventures of Captain Urselious Bigsby.*"

Adrian laughed against her skin. Leave it to Lisbeth to introduce the topic of books while her husband nuzzled her.

"It is now evident to me why that man was so adamant that the book was for males only."

"Oh?" Adrian managed to say as he strayed from her neck to the delicate cage of her collarbone.

"Yes." Her breath hitched. "Each chapter is a different adventure, and it seems these adventures are primarily sexual in nature."

When his brain caught up to her words – some seconds later, as his focus was primarily elsewhere – Adrian finally saw the silky darkness in her eyes.

"They're rather explicit, too," she said.

"Are they?" was all he could come up with, his blood caught up on the way she looked so ready to be ravished.

She smiled, the cat who got the cream. "I'll fetch it, and you can tell me what you think."

Lisbeth – his wife – crossed into her room stark naked. Adrian soaked in the view, first of her bottom rippling with each step away and then of her breasts jiggling merrily as she returned, the book thick in her hands.

He prayed that one day he would be so confident in life that he, too, could walk around the house without a stitch of clothing.

Lisbeth leapt onto the bed with a little giggle. Adrian

pulled her close, one arm around her shoulders while his other hand crept back onto her stomach. She positioned it lower, resting his fingers on her damp curls, and then opened the book.

The first page of the chapter was illustrated, a careful watercolor of Captain Bigsby in his sailor outfit with a woman on her knees before him, her breasts spilling out of her dress, her pink lips turned upwards.

Adrian's cock stiffened. "I see what you mean."

"Would it be very wicked of us to read it together?" Lisbeth's voice lowered, but this time, Adrian sensed it was not simply from arousal. Her words tripped over each other in hesitation. "To read it and act from it?"

There it was again: the glimmer of insecurity behind her eyes. This confident, opinionated, perfect woman some-how wasn't headstrong enough to have complete faith in herself. Adrian could scarcely credit it, when just a few hours ago she had been strong enough to breeze into a coffeehouse.

He drew her in for a kiss. "Does it matter whether it is wicked when it is just you and me and it is what we want to do?"

Adrian wanted to always put such a glow on her face. He took the book from her hands.

"Shall I begin?"

Chapter Nineteen

The days disappeared in their bedroom. Oh, Adrian went off in sunshine to take care of this or that matter, and Lisbeth received visitors and attended salons, and occasionally they even returned to the theater or made appearances at dinner parties. But those all seemed like interludes between the moments when Lisbeth was truly alive: when Adrian held her in his arms.

They followed Captain Bigsby's adventures religiously. When he encountered a native woman wearing nothing but a grass skirt, Lisbeth presented herself with only a shawl hanging at her waist. When a visiting princess genuflected before the captain to take his cock in her mouth, Lisbeth dressed in her finest jewels to kneel before Adrian. When a vengeful widow imprisoned Captain Bigsby and punished him with endless intercourse, Lisbeth lashed Adrian's wrists to the bedposts and rode him until they both collapsed in exhaustion.

"Do you find it remarkable that every woman who encounters the captain is consumed with the need to fuck him?" Adrian asked after one of their exploits. The book had made them both more comfortable with the language of intercourse, too: Adrian's member was his proud and pulsing cock, Lisbeth's nether regions was her wet and dripping cunny, and the act itself was fucking.

The words alone could zip Lisbeth into a frenzy.

To Adrian's comment, she laughed. "His adventures wouldn't be very interesting if the women spurned him."

"Yes, but a man might read this and begin to think every woman wants to fuck *him*, too."

"It is a book of fantasy. No one could read this and think it is how the world actually works." Lisbeth turned onto her stomach, propping her chin on her palm to take stock of her husband. He had one arm triangled behind his head while the other hand stroked idle patterns on her skin. "Or am I to understand that you have begun thrusting your cock at every lass who crosses your path, presuming yourself to be Captain Bigsby?"

Adrian grinned. He had been doing that so much more lately, and every time, it took her breath away.

He rolled to press her into an embrace. "You're the only lass at whom I thrust my cock."

They didn't always follow Captain Bigsby's strictures. They invented their own episodes, too. In Adrian's study, with Lisbeth bent over the desk and her skirts thrown up to reveal her lily-white bum to him. Against the bookshelves, with Lisbeth suspended only by Adrian's arms as his cock moved inside her. In the carriage, every time they went anywhere. Once in the breakfast room on the servants' day off, climbing onto the gleaming polished table and feasting on each other instead of the cold meats on the buffet.

Lisbeth had imagined herself a love affair, but she had never imagined *this* – the keening desire so strong to overcome all good sense.

She devoured every second of it.

There were only three doubts that nagged her, even six weeks on. The first was that neither of them had confessed to loving the other. She did not dwell on this too much. Lisbeth knew she loved him from the way her body protested as he left the room, from the way she hung upon his every word, from the way she smiled every time she thought of him. Whether he felt the same or not, she loved the way he treated her, and so there was no reason to risk upsetting the perfect balance they had found.

Of greater concern was the fact that every day drew them closer to the inevitable summons from Bartholomew Hathorne, when Adrian would sail to Jamaica. Lisbeth had known this plan since the beginning. It was even referenced in their marriage contract, as he committed to providing her with a home in London and the English countryside equal to or better than his residences in the colonies. Before, she had yearned for that moment when her no-face husband would disappear on a sailing ship, leaving her free to an unfettered London lifestyle.

Now, she couldn't imagine drawing air into her lungs if Adrian were not within an hour's reach.

But her biggest concern were the moments that spilled between their sexual adventures. When they pressed against each other, sweaty and satisfied, Lisbeth always tried to fill the air with conversation. Sometimes it was idle chatter, but mostly, she was hungry for meaningful discussion. She wanted to know Adrian's thoughts on whether the abolition of the slave trade had been more hurtful than helpful, on how he thought they could win the fight to abolish slavery altogether. She asked his opinion on the writings of Granville Sharp and Olaudah Equiano. She wondered what his mother had been like and whether his parents had loved each other, or whether Bartholomew Hathorne had imagined himself a Captain Bigsby while Adrian's mother had in fact turned away.

Adrian was not interested in such discussions. If she asked a direct question, he batted it away with a monosyllabic reply. He changed the subject or distracted her with kisses. After a week or two, he had even learned to take charge of the conversation before she could introduce such topics. He did it well, flaming a debate about the realism of modern art with the fantasy of Baroque classics or asking what she thought of the recent play they'd attended or inquiring about what book she would read next.

Ordinarily, Lisbeth loved nothing more than a good debate about artistic endeavors, and she derived a certain erotic thrill from mingling such conversation with fiery fucking. Yet she couldn't help feeling that Adrian still didn't trust her with his true opinions, not on matters of political consequence, and every time they didn't discuss abolition, her heart bruised a little deeper.

After one particularly languorous morning, Lisbeth spiked into a particular kind of despair when Adrian rolled out of bed without so much as a by-your-leave. She simply couldn't stand the sight of him covering his majestic legs with cotton drawers. "Where are you going?"

He turned back to her in surprise. It was a sign of how he didn't sense her feelings that instead of tensing, he was almost smiling. "Robert is waiting for me at Carroway's. I told him I would be there a quarter hour from now, but it looks as though I will be late." This he laced with a wink.

A wink like that would normally erase all her thought, or at least convince her to drop the subject in favor of a dozen more kisses. But this time it didn't work. "What do you and Robert do at Carroway's all day?"

"We discuss Hathorne Shipping business." Adrian shrugged on his shirt, hiding the great expanse of his chest from her view. He tugged a finger along the collar for positioning. "I'm afraid I'll need Mr. Adkins to finish dressing."

And there he went, putting her off again. "I don't understand what Robert could find interesting about Hathorne Shipping. Surely he finds commerce beneath him."

As if part of his toilette, Adrian drew his face into the impassive mask Lisbeth had so grown to hate. "He is heavily invested in both Hathorne Shipping and Hathorne Sugar. Even lords of the realm find it interesting to track how their money is doing."

"Does he know about how you plan to run Hathorne Sugar once you inherit?"

"No." This Adrian said quickly and darkly. Then he leaned forward, stealing a kiss from her before she could back away. "What of you, Mrs. Hathorne? What do you plan to do this afternoon?"

It was so typical that he should avoid the topic. Lisbeth slid out of bed and pulled on her dressing gown. "I have my own adventure planned."

"What sort of adventure?" Adrian asked. "Music, painting, or writing?"

Any other moment of the day, Lisbeth would revel in the fact that her husband knew her so well, and that he levered the knowledge with such a gentle, almost loving smile. In the heat of his departure, however, Lisbeth only felt petulant. "Are those my only three options? How dreary."

Adrian looped a cravat around his neck and tried helplessly to tie it. "I certainly didn't mean to suggest *that*. There are no limits to your options. Let me guess: you are sneaking into White's for a game of whist."

Lisbeth drew in a breath, willing her lips to cooperate by staying in a flat line instead of twitching into a smile. "Gambling is a waste of such efforts."

"Ah." Abandoning his dressing, Adrian pulled her by the hips to stand close. "Perhaps you are sneaking into the House of Lords, then."

She narrowed her eyes. "Or into an ale house to get thoroughly swilled."

"Or into Gentleman Jackson's for a round of pugilism."

She didn't want to play this game. She didn't want to forget her anger – again – simply because Adrian was touching and teasing her. She wanted him to tell her what was in his heart. And so she said something far too heartless. "Or perhaps I am going to a courtesan's house to audition lovers for the winter."

At her waist, Adrian's fingers stiffened. For a moment, he couldn't seem to summon his disinterest, and so Lisbeth saw something – confusion? – flicker across his eyes. Then he found his composure. "In which case we both have places to be." Releasing her, he stepped backward, then across the room to his bell pull. "I had better get Mr. Adkins up here before Robert sends out a search party."

The room filled with a terrible, awkward silence as Lisbeth raced to find a way to take back her words. She couldn't think of anything, other than to follow him, wrap her arms around his perfect torso, and – when he resisted her kiss – lay her cheek against his shoulder. "I'm going to Mr. Levi's portrait exhibition on Pall Mall."

Adrian linked his arms around her. He still smelled salty of sweat and sex, and Lisbeth wished he would tumble her back onto the bed. She wished she could take back all her frustration and simply enjoy this husband who would hold her on an April afternoon.

"Will you be back for dinner?" he asked, his voice thrumming through his chest and into hers.

"Yes. We are having pigeon pie." It was one of his favorites. Lisbeth had never cared one way or the other for pigeon meat, but Adrian always ate double when Mrs. Siswell prepared it, and so Lisbeth made sure it was on the menu at least once a week.

"Then we had best get on with our afternoons, so that we can sooner rejoin for our meal." He said this softly, kindly, and dotted her head with a kiss as a final reassurance that he had forgiven her. Lisbeth would have clung to him even a moment longer, had Mr. Adkins not appeared.

"Give my best to Robert," she said instead, and then she retreated to her chambers.

The distance between them still felt too great. She could hear Mr. Adkins's incessant chatter yet had to strain to guess whether Adrian responded. By the time Hannah arrived with a bucket of hot water for Lisbeth's wash, Adrian was exiting, the corridor resounding with the sound of his door closing, and he didn't poke his head in for any final farewell. He simply descended the stairs, out of Lisbeth's earshot.

It put her in a cross mood for what was supposed to be a pleasant afternoon. Mr. Levi was displaying a collection of his more interesting portraits at the home of a well-to-do merchant; Lisbeth had been promised dozens of artists who would have nothing better to do than sip wine and tell her about their careers. She had planned on wearing one of Aunt Vivienne's gowns and spending the afternoon in a fit of tipsy giggles. Now, she dressed in a conventional muslin day dress and climbed into the carriage feeling rather like she was on her way to a funeral.

Her outlook improved only slightly when she arrived at Pall Mall. Mr. Levi himself rushed down the steps to help her out of the carriage, and he took her about the main gallery personally. It was the repurposed front drawing room of the house, with plenty of natural light to display the portraits. Yet the paintings did nothing to inspire Lisbeth; they were all giant canvasses spilling with hackneyed symbolism to display the sitter's wealth and status. For Mr. Levi's sake, she leaned into each one, admiring his brushwork or the way he drew the eye to the glittering diamond on the subject's hand. But her heart wasn't lifted or transported or any of the other transcendent reactions she so relied on from art.

She stayed anyhow, peeling away from Mr. Levi to find a glass of sherry. She met a few other artists – all portraitists hoping to find their next commission – and chatted with them about their sensibilities. All the while, however, her mind returned to Upper Norton Street. She wished she could take back her words, or even unspool time enough to hold in her questions and simply kiss Adrian goodbye.

Surely a husband had every right to spend the afternoon away from his wife. If she turned into such a shrew each time it happened, he would gasp in relief over sailing to Jamaica.

Yet even as she had the thought, Lisbeth banished it. Surely a wife had every right to know where her husband was going, when he threw off the covers as he did. It was simply a matter of asking without throwing out poisoned words while doing so.

She was just trying to focus her thoughts back on the

conversation at hand – which seemed to be a questionably appropriate story of a French portrait model – when Lord Brabourne appeared at her side.

"Mrs. Hathorne, what a pleasure to discover you here."

It was a startling place to discover the earl. For one thing, Lisbeth had never suspected Lord Brabourne the type to condescend to a mere merchant's home in order to see portraits. For another, he was so closely linked in her mind with Adrian that in the first brief instant of discovering him, Lisbeth feared she had conjured Lord Brabourne by thinking too hard about her husband.

"Lord Brabourne," she greeted. "May I introduce you to my companions?"

He dissented by bowing his head. "I would much prefer to converse with you, Madam. Permit me to escort you about the room."

He didn't frame it as a question, and therefore Lisbeth almost said no. If not for Adrian, she *would* have said no. But she remembered just before she opened her mouth to do so that Lord Brabourne was a pawn in Adrian's chess game. "How kind of you."

He offered his arm, which meant she had to hook her gloved hand through his elbow. He smelled of mustachio wax.

"I haven't seen enough of you, Mrs. Hathorne. Whenever I call upon Upper Norton Street you are away from home, and whenever I am out, you are at home."

Lisbeth had seen him visiting Adrian a few times,

spotting his carriage on her way in or shutting herself in her room when he arrived. Adrian always mentioned it with a light, never-say-care tone, yet she knew he didn't welcome Lord Brabourne's condescensions. Still, she aimed for Adrian's glibness in her response. "Had I known you were so eager to find me, my lord, I am sure we would have met much sooner."

"You are the great improvement to Mr. Hathorne's household. Why should I not want to find you?" Lord Brabourne did not wait for her reply. "Will you be staying in London when Mr. Hathorne sails for Inglewilde Plantation?"

Of course, he would touch on the one subject that felt like a dagger to Lisbeth's heart. She smiled through it. "Yes, I believe so, although Their Graces have been kind enough to invite me to winter at Maidenheath House should I so choose."

"You must let me escort you whenever you so desire. A butterfly such as you should not be at home for want of a present husband."

It was a strange response, given that a married lady could come and go as she pleased. Lisbeth wondered if there were code beneath his words, a secret meaning she was supposed to understand. "Are you not sailing for Jamaica as well, my lord? I was given to understand you prefer to spend the winter at your home there."

"Not every year. If I should be so blessed with a wife to take with me, perhaps. For now, I will stay among you beauties here in London."

Now she was sure he was flirting with her. Disgust shivered down her spine. "If you are looking for a wife, you are better off attending Almack's than escorting me to my varied interests."

This he answered with a wide, thin-lipped, wordless smile.

They had approached the front of the gallery, near to the front door, and Lisbeth suddenly couldn't stand to be anywhere except home at Upper Norton Street.

"Oh dear, I am afraid I have the most frightful headache," she said, pressing her free hand dramatically to her forehead. "My lord, would you be horribly displeased if I went home to rest?"

There was no gentleman's response other than to comply, bundle her to the butler, and wait to ensure she safely climbed into her carriage. Lord Brabourne did that, of course. But in the moments as they waited for her driver to pull up, he also said, "Do remind Mr. Hathorne that I am awaiting news from *The Rebecca*."

He didn't leave room for manners in his words. It was an order, as if she and Adrian were no more than his servants. Lisbeth stared at him, waiting for him to soften it, and when he didn't, said, "I did not know you had such interest in commerce, my lord."

His lips reared back into that false grin again. Before he had a chance to respond, the carriage arrived, and the butler opened the door silently, waiting for Lisbeth to descend the front steps. She performed a small curtsey for Lord Brabourne.

"Don't forget my message, Mrs. Hathorne," he said, as sweetly as if he were wishing her a safe journey.

Lisbeth hurried down to the carriage. She didn't know what Lord Brabourne wanted with Adrian or what news he expected from the ship, but she knew she wouldn't be his pawn. As far as Adrian needed to know, she had never seen Lord Brabourne that afternoon.

Her stomach twisted, wondering how many of Adrian's peers treated him the way Brabourne did. And worrying that every time she ignored his better judgment, she made it worse for him.

Chapter Twenty

L ooking back, Adrian could see there had been a stretch of weeks unlike any other in his life. At the time, he had simply thought: *this is marriage.* Or, *this is love.* But he could see now they had been floating along a river of clouds. By the nature of the ocean crossing, there could be no news from Jamaica yet, no pronouncement of his long-awaited inheritance, no reply from his father on the ten souls in negotiation. He and Lisbeth had been free of discord. Free of expectations. Free of everything except a wild obsession with each other.

But now April had turned into May. Three weeks had turned into six. Any day now, *The Rebecca* would dock with a belly full of sugar hogsheads and letters from Inglewilde. And every day, a little bit more silence slipped between him and Lisbeth.

They had not completely descended from the clouds – he still whisked her into dark corners of the house for kisses – yet Adrian couldn't help feeling a shift. Sometimes, Lisbeth stared in his direction without seeing him. And he knew she was thinking about what would come next.

Perhaps I'm going to a courtesan's to audition my winter lover.

Adrian pushed the echo of her words away. She hadn't meant it. There was no point dwelling on it, not when he had a stack of ledgers to examine and correspondence to answer. Lisbeth was happy, and Adrian didn't have to leave yet, and that simply had to be enough for him.

The rain tapped on his window. He arranged his papers more precisely on his blotter, refreshed the ink on his pen, and tried to focus. Even if he wanted to throw Lisbeth over his shoulder and retire to the bedroom, she was presently hosting visitors. She adored her morning calls – which were, of course, in the afternoon, for nothing London did made any sense – where most frequently she received Mr. Nadin accompanied by a fresh crop of artist friends, Lady Cecilia, and Mary. From his study, he would hear the occasional rise of laughter from across the hall or catch the heat in voices raised to intellectual debate.

He wouldn't interrupt her, no matter how it might ease his currently spiraling thoughts.

It was pure chance, then, and not a desperate need to see Lisbeth, that he strained to hear Ford announce to the sitting room, "Lord and Lady Gresham to see you, Madam."

Lisbeth's voice rang out, "How delightful! Do sit down, won't you? Ford, could you send up a plate of Mrs. Siswell's cinnamon tea cakes? Bernard, you should like these especially."

Bernard. Was it even proper to stay on a Christian name basis with one's fiancé after being jilted? Adrian tried to picture the man – a tall, strapping English lord, no doubt, who laughed easily – winking at Lisbeth in reminder of what she had almost had.

He should stay where he was. He had a steaming pot of tea at his elbow, a roaring fire, and still three more days of Hathorne Shipping activities to report to his grandfather and father.

But then he heard *Bernard* say, "I'm glad to see you looking fine as an English spring."

No, it wasn't a love sonnet, and yes, the man's wife was in the room, yet it was enough to throw Adrian from his chair. Checking that his jacket and buttons were all aligned, Adrian hastened across the hall.

The tableau he walked into was not particularly damning. Lisbeth sat in her favorite chair, the blue Episcopalian throne next to the fireplace. Nearer the window, his sister Mary bent over an embroidery hoop. The Lord and Lady Gresham perched side-by-side on the settee gifted to his household by his grandmother, a relic upon which Sir Walter Raleigh had supposedly once reposed. No one was staring at anyone with suppressed longing, nor were any hands creeping places they didn't belong.

Still, Adrian had to keep himself from glaring at their guests.

For her part, Lady Gresham was not nearly as beautiful as gossip had led him to believe. There was a certain perfection to her features, to be sure, but she was as pale as dishwater, and her costume was entirely too conventional. She belonged in a fussy painting, not in his sitting room, making his wife self-consciously adjust her ostrich plume.

And then there was Lord Gresham, the devil himself.

The earl was less than Adrian had expected. His red hair flamed like the devil, to be sure, but his face was otherwise unremarkable, his height seemed about average, and overall, there was nothing about him that screamed *handsome rake.*

Still, this was the man who had dared turn away from Lisbeth on her wedding day. She could shout from the rooftops as much as she wanted that she hadn't wanted to marry him; Adrian would never believe that Lisbeth had left that day without a gash across her heart.

"Lord Gresham, Lady Gresham, may I present to you my husband, Mr. Hathorne?"

Adrian bowed. He murmured the pleasantries and perhaps even managed a smile, once he caught Lisbeth's reminder in the form of a raised eyebrow. There being no remaining seats, he went to stand behind his wife, one hand resting on her chair.

"I'm so glad to meet you as I've heard many wonderful things of you from Mrs. Hathorne," Lady Gresham said. "How are you enjoying London?"

"Immensely." Adrian thought that quite covered it, without requiring him to elaborate on which parts of London he had or had not enjoyed. When the countess blinked, he remembered to add, "My lady."

"Have you not been before? I would have thought a man of business such as yourself would be here year-round." Lord Gresham did not aim his words with venom in his tone, yet they were arrows nonetheless. After all,

Lisbeth was the daughter of a marquess. She *should* have married a gentleman of the peer who wouldn't be caught dead lifting a finger in the name of commerce. Instead, she had married a Black businessman.

Adrian felt his cheeks flame in embarrassment.

"I am more comfortable in the country, my lord."

Lisbeth leaned forward in her chair. "Mr. Hathorne tells me he is the fastest rider at Maidenheath House, though he refuses to gallop in Hyde Park to prove it to me. Mary, is it all a boast, or does he truly always beat Robert in races through the wood?"

"He always beats Robert," Mary agreed, "but he does not always beat *me*."

"What kind of horse do you ride?" Lord Gresham asked. There was a glimmer of interest in his eye, reminding Adrian that Lisbeth had complained of the man's unending love of horses.

She had steered the conversation to a topic they could both enjoy, this clever wife of his. Adrian answered, descending into a discussion of the best racing horses, all while mourning for Lisbeth that she had been saddled with *him*. With her poise, her fire, her grace, she belonged in the drawing rooms of a duke.

Perhaps she would find her way there, once he sailed for Jamaica.

I am auditioning my winter lover.

Her words kept popping up in his mind, and as much as he tried to push it away, Adrian couldn't help himself from picking at it. Soon, he would leave Lisbeth. He *had* to; his wife was never supposed to come with him to the plantation, where diseases felled most White women within the first few months of arrival. He would hate it. Already, if he went a handful of hours without seeing her, his body ached for Lisbeth, not just in carnal need but also in a basic desire to hold her close and hear her voice.

Adrian could do it, though, because he knew it was his only choice. He could not forego his mission. He'd always known he would pay a price for his mission, and losing Lisbeth was simply the biggest one yet.

What ate at him was imagining what she would do once he left. She had told him quite plainly at the beginning of their marriage that she planned to lead a rich life. Everything Lisbeth encountered, she felt passionately about. And now that they had spent the last two months discovering every inch of physical desire, he would leave her with a hunger for intercourse.

He knew she hadn't meant it when she said she was going to a courtesan's. Yet Adrian had no doubt Lisbeth would take a lover, eventually. What he tortured himself with was who, and how many, and how soon after he sailed.

Debating Lord Gresham on who would win the York Derby, Adrian told himself to calm down. Of all the men Lisbeth would dally with, he could safely assume it would not be the one who had jilted her at the altar. He was too smitten with his own wife, and besides, he droned about horses to no end.

"I bore the ladies, I'm afraid," Lord Gresham said presently, casting an apologetic smile to Lisbeth. "Mr. Hathorne, you are always welcome to stop by my stables to continue the conversation."

"Yes, do come by when Lisbeth and Mary attend my next salon," Lady Gresham put in. "You two gentlemen may speak of horses all you like while we ladies discuss matters of importance."

Adrian looked to his sister, who blinked innocently back at him. "I didn't know you had started attending the salons too, Mary."

"I didn't suppose you needed to be informed, so long as Her Grace has given me permission." Mary said this without ire, though she raised her eyebrows as if daring him to challenge her.

Lisbeth had inspired this streak of rebellion in his sister. Adrian couldn't help but admire it. When it came to leaving his loved ones in England, he was soothed that Lisbeth and Mary were such fast friends. Mary visited almost every afternoon. When there were no other visitors, Lisbeth and Mary and her maid circled around the fireplace for hours, and he'd grown accustomed to hearing them laugh from across the corridor.

"This week, we'll be discussing divorce and annulments. I took the liberty of recommending some advanced reading." Lady Gresham tilted her head, and Adrian now saw that both Lisbeth and Mary had neatly printed pamphlets beside their teacups.

His mouth went dry. He wasn't sure he could stomach Lisbeth thinking about annulments again, even if it were only in the abstract. "What is there to discuss about divorce and annulments?"

"The wife's rights," Lisbeth answered, her ostrich feather pitching towards the mantle as she turned her face up to him. "For example, shouldn't a mother have a right to see her children, even if her husband divorces her?"

Adrian didn't have a response, other than to imagine receiving a letter from Lisbeth in six months: *I'm quite tired of this. Shall we get a divorce, then?*

It wasn't that easy. She wouldn't do it, besides. Neither of those facts made Adrian fear it less.

"An excellent debate to be had," Lord Gresham said. "Mr. Hathorne and I shall be more comfortable with a healthy ride through the park until you've sorted out the rights and wrongs of it and tell us how to proceed."

Ford interrupted, before Adrian had to decide how to respond to this overture of friendship. He approached with a silver tray carrying a single card. Adrian recognized it before picking it up: creamy paper, gilded with silver vines, and spidery writing too confident for its own good. Lord Brabourne.

The man had taken to visiting every few days or so, slinking into Adrian's study and asking questions about the plantation, about their ships, even about Lisbeth. Adrian couldn't quite figure out what Brabourne wanted, other than to establish dominance. As if Adrian worked for *him* and owed *him* daily reports.

For once, then, Adrian could show Brabourne that he wasn't intimidated by such a little thing as a title.

"Show him in here," Adrian directed Ford, then asked Lord and Lady Gresham, "Are you acquainted with Lord Brabourne?"

Lord Gresham barely concealed a wince, earning him a smidgeon of Adrian's admiration. "We have crossed paths."

Brabourne entered the room with his typical swagger. His pale hair was flattened to his head from his now-removed hat. "I have happened upon a social call. How delightful."

They conducted the proper introductions, and Brabourne bowed over Lisbeth's hand, then nodded to Mary with extra solicitousness.

"I so often visit Mr. Hathorne, but rarely do I have the pleasure of encountering his charming wife and sister. Today is a lucky day, indeed."

Mary wore the patented Hathorne mask of indifference.

Brabourne turned his beady eyes to Adrian. "I came as soon as my man informed me *The Rebecca* has docked. You have news, I assume?"

Adrian did his very best not to bristle, not against Brabourne's presumption to address him like a clerk and not against the fact that Brabourne knew about *The Rebecca* before Adrian did. Lisbeth's ostrich plume, however, twitched. "Lord Brabourne, you devil, here we are enjoying a pleasant afternoon, and you should like to ruin it with discussion of business?"

She said it in the friendly tone a marquess's daughter could use with an earl, but the rebuke was clear. Unfortunately, Ford entered again with his silver platter, this time laden with one thin note from a messenger and a second, thicker envelope, the kind that always came from Adrian's father.

The kind that Brabourne had been awaiting – and Adrian had been dreading – these past two months.

"I apologize, my dear," Adrian said to Lisbeth. "It appears there is indeed business to be handled. Will you excuse us?"

Collecting the papers from Ford, Adrian bowed to his wife, then Lady Gresham. On a whim, he added, "You are welcome to join us, Lord Gresham, if it is of interest."

He didn't know why the fellow would find it interesting. He didn't know why he should want Lisbeth's former fiancé in the study as he read his father's letter. He only knew it seemed a good idea as Lord Brabourne followed him at the heel.

Lord Gresham's blue eyes widened in surprise. For the briefest moment, he looked to his wife, as if for permission, or perhaps advice. Then he nodded and stood. "Thank you."

The walk across the corridor back to his study seemed to last forever, even though it was only a few yards. Brabourne said to Lord Gresham, "Lady Gresham is looking as enticing as I recall from her debut."

Lord Gresham fumbled his words in response. "I – yes – thank you."

Brabourne didn't feel it necessary, apparently, to comment on how splendid Lisbeth had looked with the firelight twinkling in her eye.

Adrian shoved aside the thought; it wasn't as if he wanted Brabourne coveting his wife.

And then – *oh God* – what if Lisbeth took Brabourne as a lover?

His stomach turned at the thought. And Adrian reminded himself that Lisbeth was a woman of principles as well as passion. She would never bed Brabourne, especially not when she knew he was a slaveholder who would try to stop Adrian's plan.

He needed to get ahold of himself. Fast.

Adrian had only two chairs in his study: the one behind his desk and one for a visitor. He pulled the first to the window and offered it to his guests, retreating to lean against his desk rather than take one of the chairs. "You'll excuse me while I read my father's letter."

"Read it aloud." Brabourne drawled, but it was clearly an order.

Lord Gresham didn't hide his wince this time. "Perhaps the pertinent parts. One should keep one's family news private, I've always said."

Adrian schooled his emotions into a calm, obedient farce. Cutting open the letter, he unfolded it carefully

– noting it was actually slimmer than usual – and skimmed the first page before reading aloud.

"He sends his best wishes, etcetera. There is some minutia about the cargo he has included on *The Rebecca* that would not interest you. Now: *As it pertains to the ten heads Lord Brabourne requested, we shall keep those to Inglewilde Plantation as we cannot spare them during our harvest.*"

Adrian turned the page, doing his best to hide his relief. As long as they stayed on his plantation, he could free them.

For his part, Brabourne narrowed his eyes without saying anything.

Adrian continued to read: "*I have faith Lord Brabourne will be more than happily recompensed in the dowry I bestow him upon his wedding to Mary. You will refer to my letter to the gentleman in question for the full details of the marriage contract, but I have agreed to give her hand to Lord Brabourne with a wedding as soon as possible. I trust you will work with your grandmother to make the proper introductions and solicit Mary's favorable interest in the match.*"

His lips had kept moving even as his heart stopped. Mary? Handed off to Brabourne?

Lord Brabourne beamed from his seat in Adrian's leather chair. "Excellent. My letter must be awaiting me at home. I had so hoped for this felicitous news."

Mary had never shown any interest in Lord Brabourne.

She had never shown any interest in anyone since her first fiancé, poor old Ned, had died on the battlefield.

And now their father had decided to offer her up like some sort of gambling chip to win a business deal.

Adrian could have roared with anger.

"I suppose I should go make the proposal myself, to win the fair lady's favor." Rising, Lord Brabourne headed for the door.

Adrian threw himself across the room to block the man. He took one breath, to rein his reaction to something reasonable. "There are proper ways to go about this, my lord. Let me discuss it with Her Grace to prepare Mary for your courtship."

Brabourne smirked. For a moment, Adrian thought he was going to insist, just because he knew he could.

But Lord Gresham spoke first. "That's the way of it, Brabourne. If I may speak from the wisdom of marriage, one mustn't upset a woman's delicate nature by rushing one's fences. Let her family suggest the idea first, and then you'll have her undying favors."

Brabourne's lips thinned in frustration. Then he retreated. "I suppose you'd know, since somehow you won Lady Gresham's hand when there's no rhyme or reason why she'd care for the likes of you."

The two of them laughed. Adrian could barely focus on why. He only knew his father had sacrificed his sister, and he had no idea how to make the situation right.

It was only later, after the lords had left, that Adrian

read what remained of the letter:

The Assembly has seen fit to approve the privilege bill. You are now to inherit my full fortune and property. Come home after Mary's wedding.

I rest easy knowing that whether or not I live to see you again, you are both promised a bright future.

Your loving father

Chapter Twenty-One

Lisbeth's nerves buzzed pleasantly as she changed for dinner, her mind folding over the events of the afternoon as neatly as a pair of winter gloves being tucked away for the summer. It had been a day of surprises: first Annabelle and Bernard, then Adrian, and thirdly Lord Brabourne strutting into her drawing room. Lisbeth had been visiting with Annabelle regularly, but she hadn't expected any of the three males to grace her with their presence. She wasn't sure whether she had been more surprised by Bernard's red hock of hair or the gleam of territorial prejudice in Adrian's eyes as he crossed to claim his spot behind her.

Mary had smirked with her about it, when all the other visitors had left. "From the look on Adrian's face, I'm rather surprised he didn't challenge Lord Gresham to a duel at first sight."

"That would be the most ridiculous story to grace the gossip rags in a century." Lisbeth couldn't help giggling at the thought. It was safe to imagine Adrian fighting for her honor when she knew it would never happen – and when the picture of him parrying was so delicious. For whatever reason, she conjured him in nothing but breeches, torso gleaming in the sun as his arm muscles flexed with each jab of his sword.

It was the type of fantasy best pinned to the back of her mind until her sister-in-law was safely out the door.

"I hope the two of them put Lord Brabourne in his place," Mary had continued, thankfully ignoring the blush that had crept across Lisbeth's cheeks. "One might think he owned Hathorne Shipping from the way he carried on."

Lisbeth had noticed that, too; she may even have spoken too sharply to try to muzzle the man. She hoped Adrian wouldn't be the worse off for it.

Suzy, Mary's maid, had curtsied into the room then, curtailing Lisbeth's thoughts as she presented Mary's cloak and gloves. "You asked me to make sure you left by quarter to five, Miss."

Mary visited enough that Lisbeth had grown accustomed to this dynamic of the maid shepherding the mistress to and fro. She knew by heart the way Mary beamed up at Suzy, the murmur of thanks that came from a voice Mary used on no one else: "You're too good for me, Suzy."

It wasn't something Mary felt the need to hide from Lisbeth, and therefore it wasn't something Lisbeth felt the need to interrogate. She simply enjoyed watching the glow spread across Mary's face whenever Suzy entered the room.

And here Lisbeth was again, lost in her thoughts as she changed for dinner. They were due for their weekly meal at Frampton Square, and Lady Cecilia had sent Lisbeth word that the poet Mr. Walter Scott had accepted the invitation as well. A promising evening to cap off an interesting afternoon. Lisbeth couldn't have imagined a happier spring for herself if she tried.

When she descended to the parlor, Ford informed her Adrian was still in the study. "If you don't mind me saying, Madam, I don't believe Sir has changed for the evening yet."

Lisbeth knocked lightly at the door but didn't wait for permission before pushing inside. She had grown to admire this room, even though she sometimes envied the hours Adrian spent holed up there instead of tracing kisses down her spine. Its simple decorations didn't proclaim so much as complement Adrian's personality: a sturdy oak desk, bookshelves lined with leathery economics and ship logs, a Turkish rug with yellow flowers dancing across an orange field of silk. Best of all, Adrian himself, always sitting behind that desk, one hand bracing his scalp as the other raced across the page penning whatever brilliant missive he currently worked on.

At the moment, however, he wasn't writing anything. He bent as if napping across the surface of the desk, his forehead cushioned by his palms, and when he heard the door open, he barked, "I'm not to be disturbed."

Lisbeth hesitated. "What of dinner? We'll be late if we don't leave soon."

Adrian raised his head, revealing creases across his cheeks and forehead from where his face had pressed against his hands and desk. "I didn't know it was you."

A small part of her was gratified that his harsh tone hadn't been directed specifically at her. The larger part of her, however, prickled with anxiety at what could so utterly ruffle her husband.

"Did *The Rebecca* bring bad news?"

Adrian sighed. It was more of a heave, as if he thought he could expunge whatever bothered him with a simple exhale. Yet he didn't form any words.

Lisbeth moved closer, rounding the desk to place a hand on the nape of his neck. His skin was hot to the touch, almost feverish. "Demons are worse when we refuse to name them."

"It's not that I refuse. I hate to say it aloud." Adrian leaned backwards, his head resting against her stomach. "However, it must be said. The sum of it is that my father has decided my sister should marry Lord Brabourne."

For a moment, the words didn't make any sense to Lisbeth. "Your sister Mary?"

"She is the only sister I am aware of."

"But —" Lisbeth stopped herself from finishing the thought aloud. Mary would not be the first woman who loved someone other than her husband. There was no need to call Adrian's attention to it, especially if that was what he had already been brooding over. Instead, she said, "I wasn't aware that such a match was under consideration. Is Mary amenable?"

"I don't believe she has any more idea than you do. I'm to arrange a formal call with the assistance of my grand-mother." Adrian pressed his mouth into her skirts, as if that would make his words false. "Brabourne knew what the letter would say. He struck the bargain with my father without so much as looking at Mary."

He didn't mean it literally, of course, but Lisbeth used it as an opportunity to look for a bright side. "We married without so much as a look, and it has worked out for us. Perhaps this will be best for Mary."

She wished she could believe it.

"Perhaps," Adrian said. He stood. "There's no use moping about it, I suppose. I'll go tomorrow to Berkwell House to inform my grandparents. I'm sorry, I have delayed us. Let me change, and we'll be off to dinner."

In the shadow of the news, however, Lisbeth couldn't quite summon any excitement for dinner, not even for meeting Mr. Scott. "I'll go with you tomorrow."

"No, that won't be necessary," Adrian said absently, straightening the papers on his desk. "It's a family affair."

"Am I not family?"

He looked up at her tone, as well he should. Lisbeth's stomach fizzled with tension. She didn't want to upset him further, but neither could she let such a comment settle between them, not when they had been doing so well at making their marriage real.

Adrian stepped backwards. "Of course you are. It is only that this will surprise everyone. My grandparents will want privacy. Mary will want privacy."

"Mary will want privacy, but she will need a friend. She will have so many reactions to sort through." Lisbeth resisted the urge to frame her hands on her hips. She did not want this to turn into one of their arguments of old, where neither of them won. "I am her sister-in-law. I have faced two engagements to men whom I didn't particularly want to marry. I can help her put this in perspective."

Adrian winced. Lisbeth wasn't sure why, but she didn't miss it. She couldn't; it was as visible as a sneeze. He turned away. "As you wish."

What Lisbeth *wished* was that he would clasp his arms around her and claim a kiss to end their argument. She wanted to forget their dinner engagement and retreat upstairs, where nothing mattered except each other and the count of seconds until their clothes fell to the floor.

But Adrian rounded the opposite corner of the desk. He didn't look at her again, not even when he said, "The privilege bill was approved. I am to return to Inglewilde Plantation after Mary's wedding."

He said it so easily. As if he were announcing he was off to Carroway's. As if the consequence of his words were not that he would leave her in a matter of weeks.

Lisbeth bunched her fingers into fists. If he wanted to be so cavalier about it, then she certainly wouldn't show how it made *her* feel. So she simply responded with, "We will be late for supper."

Adrian hesitated at his desk for one more, long moment. He still didn't look at her. Lisbeth thought he might say something else. But then he disappeared upstairs, and she was left standing by the embers of his fire, trembling.

Chapter Twenty-Two

Adrian knew he should be worried about Mary. Whatever fairy stories Lisbeth tried to spin, their father's decision would devastate Mary, both for how it sold her off in marriage and for the fact that their own father had done it without so much as a letter to her.

His sister deserved better. Every woman, for that matter, deserved better than to be sold off in marriage.

But all night, the more he dwelt on Mary's fate, the more he remembered Lisbeth's reaction to the news that he would be leaving in a matter of weeks:

We will be late for supper.

If she had been the one with the news, Adrian could never have responded so coldly. He would have fallen to his knees. Or broken into tears. Or said, *Don't leave me.*

Apparently, Lisbeth didn't feel the same way. He was nothing more than the pawn in her plan for an independent life. Their fucking, then, fulfilled her desire for life's experiences; it was not, as he had begun to think of it, lovemaking.

It was for the best, he reminded himself, since the news meant he would soon be at Inglewilde Plantation, and he wouldn't have room for thoughts of Lisbeth as he waited for his father to die. It was better to remember their reality, better to know that she wouldn't miss him one bit once he sailed, than to show up in Jamaica too heartsick to make a difference.

And yet, it felt the opposite of anything positive as the hackney delivered them to Berkwell House in a grim morning drizzle.

Lisbeth didn't quite look at him from her seat opposite. They had only exchanged the slightest conversation since returning from dinner the night before, when Adrian had begged exhaustion rather than face her any longer. It was the first night they had slept apart since Lord Everly's ball. He had mostly spent it staring at the canopy, alternating between convincing himself he had misunderstood her and recasting every moment they had spent together from the perspective of a woman who could never love her husband.

Which meant on this morning when Mary needed him most, Adrian was showing up exhausted and heartbroken.

Some brother he was.

They arrived at half past eleven, far too early for a social call, yet they were shown to the formal drawing room, done up in rose pink with elaborate gilt furniture and sparkling glass windows overlooking the square. Lisbeth walked slowly across the room as if evaluating every seat before taking the chair in the farthest corner. Making do on her promise of lending the family privacy, he supposed.

Adrian wished he didn't admire her so much. If he only thought of her as the generic English wife who secured his fortune, then he wouldn't feel so deeply the absence of her affection.

They waited a quarter of an hour before anyone from the family greeted them, and then it was Mary. Adrian's heart sank even further as she waltzed into the room, all rosy cheeks and smiles of delight. "We didn't expect you today. What good luck. I am dying to hear how you found Walter Scott."

She made it all the way to Lisbeth's far chair before picking up on the gloom of their moods.

"What is the matter?"

Adrian locked his hands behind his back, lest he reach out and hug his sister in a fit of helplessness. "I've something to discuss with Their Graces, I'm afraid."

Mary turned to Lisbeth with a raised eyebrow. "That sounds ominous. I should hate to have something to discuss with Their Graces. Must you stay, or shall we go for a walk in the garden?"

Lisbeth looked at him briefly before assenting. Adrian didn't know what to make of it: was she asking for permission? Attempting to whisper something with the sole power of a gaze? Or simply reminding him that she and Mary were sisters in this terrible venture of marrying a man they could never want?

He shook himself when the women had glided out of the room. He was being maudlin. He had never planned on loving his wife; this would simply make it easier to say goodbye when the time came to leave Lisbeth in London.

And he thought of a bright side of Mary's betrothal: she could live in Jamaica, just one estate away from him.

She could visit him endlessly. He could watch her children grow, dote on them as only an uncle can.

The prospect cheered Adrian. Mary had always been his closest companion. They had borne the terror of the trans-Atlantic crossing together; they had recoiled together at the cold English weather; and even as adults, when Adrian was at home with his grandparents, he and Mary spent the quiet hours of the day together. To have her with him in Jamaica, even ten miles away, would make living without Lisbeth that much more bearable.

Mary might even be able to help him transition Inglewilde Plantation into a free man's land. At the very least, she could mitigate Brabourne's reaction.

Their Graces finally descended to the drawing room. They walked in together, the duchess's arm looped through the duke's as if they were entering a formal dinner. Adrian's stomach turned again with uneasiness.

He greeted them, as he always did, with a bow, and even once they sat, he remained standing. He was there as a messenger, after all. For once, he wished he were only a servant, and not someone responsible for the mess at hand.

Their Graces took the news well. The duke didn't seem surprised. "Mary has to marry sooner or later," was his only comment. For her part, the duchess lifted her chin. "I'll tell Mary, and we shall invite Lord Brabourne to dinner tomorrow night to formally offer for her hand."

They took it so well, in fact, that Adrian felt compelled to say, "I do not think Mary will welcome this match."

His grandmother braced her lips. "Unfortunately, what is done is done."

"Surely she has the right to refuse," Adrian pursued. "She cannot be forced to marry a man she does not choose for herself."

"She has had plenty of time to select a husband for herself, and she has not done so. Lord Brabourne is wealthy, close to the family, and titled. Mary will see the wisdom in the match." His grandmother looked at him with soft, fond eyes. "We women are prepared for our lot. You'll see."

Her words echoed Lisbeth's. She had agreed to two marriages without caring for the man. Did his wife believe in love? Did *he* even believe in love, or had he confused endless lust with some fairy story?

He pushed the thoughts away. "Lisbeth is with Mary in the gardens right now. She would like to stay with Mary this afternoon, if that is amenable to Your Graces."

His grandmother grinned. "You see, you have to look no further than your own home to see how marriage works out. Already, they are more like sisters than sisters-in-law."

"Leave it to the women," the duke said, rising shakily against his cane. The man was showing his age, from the white of his hair to the constant tremble in his legs. "If you have a spare moment, come along and tell me the news of Hathorne Shipping."

Adrian followed his grandfather to the smoking room tucked in the back of the house. He took the offered cigar, obliged the duke with minute details of business, all the while trying not to listen to the triple beat of his heart. Trying not to strain his ears to catch Mary's cries of distress. Trying not to hope for Lisbeth's footfall to interrupt them.

He had placed the matter in Their Graces' hands now. He knew he should be relieved. He should set aside the strange fear churning his stomach and focus again on business. There was no room for guilt or doubt or longing in a life such as his. There was only doing what needed to be done.

Yet when he took his leave, Adrian couldn't remember what he had just discussed with his grandfather. Lisbeth leaned over the bannister of the second landing to call, "Go ahead without me. I'll be home before dark." And still, he lingered. As if his presence might make a difference. As if someone might tell him what he could do to help.

Adrian stepped outside. Without a final word to Mary. Without a kiss from Lisbeth. Even without his usual sense that he had a mission. He simply walked and hoped he was going in the right direction.

Chapter Twenty-Three

The day was too fine for bad news. The sun shone brightly on the Berkwell House private garden, and spring flowers bloomed with too much cheer. Mary chatted; Lisbeth couldn't quite focus on her words, her eyes constantly returning to the garden doors. They looped the gravel path twice, and still no one had interrupted their walk.

The time lagged such that Lisbeth began to hope she was anticipating the wrong thing. Perhaps instead of merely sharing the news, Adrian had decided to convince Their Graces not to allow the match. Or Their Graces may have refused outright without needing any persuading. It was plain as the spring sun in the sky that Lord Brabourne was not a match for Mary. Perhaps Lisbeth was distracting Mary for nothing.

She was commenting for the third time on how the yew trees were so cleverly trimmed to resemble a fox chased by hounds when Suzy collected them.

"Her Grace would like to see you in your apartment, Miss Mary. She said you could come, too, Mrs. Hathorne."

In an instant, Mary closed into the Hathorne mask. She had always dropped it more easily than Adrian; Lisbeth hated to see it return. They went inside in silence. As they climbed the great staircase, the house was so quiet that their carpeted footfalls echoed off the walls.

Lisbeth hoped Adrian had found some sort of compromise on Mary's behalf.

The duchess awaited them in Mary's sitting room. A steaming teapot sat on the table. Lisbeth tucked her hand in Mary's and pulled them both into the settee.

As Her Grace shared the news with Mary, Lisbeth couldn't help but flash back to the day Lord Gresham had offered for her. It had not been a complete shock; she had known his interest, had courted him enough to wonder whether she could learn to find the spray of freckles across his cheeks attractive. And yet, when it actually happened, when Lady Cecilia sat Lisbeth down to explain that the wedding would be New Year's Day, Lisbeth had felt faint. And nauseous. And helpless.

Now, watching the color drain from Mary's face – seeing Suzy sink onto a chair in the corner – Lisbeth felt only fury.

No one had the right to promise Mary's hand without so much as consulting her.

At first, Mary kept saying, "It can't be true." Then she demanded to see the letter, which no one could produce since Adrian had thoughtlessly left it locked in his study. It was only when the duchess asked Suzy to bring out a few of her dresses that Mary said, "But I can't marry him, Grandmama."

"Do you have a husband I don't know about?" the duchess quizzed. "Have you a fatal illness? Are you not truly Mary Hathorne, the girl I have raised since she arrived at my doorstep?"

Mary mumbled her negative response.

"Then you not only *can* marry him, you will."

Lisbeth helped Suzy lay the gowns across Mary's bed for the duchess to evaluate. They were gorgeous gowns, the best money could buy, and somehow, that made Lisbeth all the angrier. She swallowed the emotion down.

"It's not as bad as all that," she lied to the room in general. "Lord Brabourne will give you generous pin money, and you can either stay close to your family here in England or visit Adrian at Inglewilde Plantation if he takes you to Jamaica. You'll be so much more independent, you'll see."

Mary's eyes reddened with tears. "I shall have no say in that. I shall be expected to live wherever he tells me and to entertain whichever devils he befriends and to act as if every word he says is brilliant. I don't want to marry him. Why must I marry him?"

The duchess selected a green dress and directed Suzy to prepare it for the dinner the next night. "You'll not get a better offer than this, not at your age and the daughter of a second son. Your father is only looking after you as best he can in the time he has left."

Mary tried to keep in a wail, but it keened out from the back of her throat anyway. Lisbeth turned away. How she wished Adrian had been able to do *something* other than simply deliver the message. How she yearned to meet Mr. Hathorne to tell him plain and loud what she thought of his decisions, no matter that he was on his deathbed.

The duchess, however, withdrew into a straight, prim line at Mary's wail. "You're overtired. I'll leave you to rest. We'll discuss the details in the morning."

Mary glared at her grandmother's back, and Lisbeth busied herself with wetting a cloth from the bedside jug of water rather than let her own anger slip through.

The only thing worse than being furious was not being allowed to express it.

Once the door closed shut, Mary stalked to the window, arms crossed at her waist. Her apartment in Berkwell House was fit for a princess, with damask wall coverings across three rooms, fires in each hearth, and views of the leafy green square beyond. In her pose at the window, chin lifted to glare at the surroundings, she looked regal, too.

"There are worse fates, Miss," Suzy said. "Better a wealthy husband than shivering to death in a hovel."

Mary didn't look at Suzy. "Adrian would have given me an allowance. I know he would have. There's the cottage at Maidenheath House. We wouldn't have shivered to death in a hovel."

Lisbeth thought of Adrian folded over his desk in despair. He would still give his sister a living, if only the family gave her a choice to refuse Lord Brabourne. If only her father had asked her opinion before signing her fate away.

She dared to drape an arm across Mary's shoulders. "Nothing is final until you have said yes at the altar. I know that well enough. Give us some time. We'll sort this out."

"I can't marry him, Lisbeth." Mary said this in a furious, broken whisper against Lisbeth's arm. "I can't marry anyone."

"I know." Stroking her hair, Lisbeth looked to Suzy, who had retreated to the corner by the fireplace, standing straight as an arrow even though her eyes betrayed the glazed look of someone thousands of miles away.

"They don't understand. They'll never understand. They'll make me accept him tomorrow night, and then the banns will be read, and then I'll have to marry him. Grandmama will scold me for crying, but it's all I can do. I don't want to marry him and I don't want to go back to Jamaica and I don't want to live my life in fear of some husband."

Lisbeth held Mary for a while longer, letting her spill out all her fears. She wished she had a better answer for Mary than to insist that all would be well. "Why don't you come stay with us for a few days? You and Suzy. You won't have to argue with Her Grace every minute of the day, and we can come up with a plan."

Sniffling, Mary backed away in surprise. "Are you quite sure?"

"Adrian would love to have you closer," Lisbeth invented. She turned to Suzy. "What say you, Suzy? Would you like to stay with us at Upper Norton Street?"

Suzy blanched at being addressed so directly. From

the corner of her eye, Lisbeth saw that she had earned a smile from Mary.

"I go wherever Miss Hathorne goes," Suzy replied.

Mary wiped her cheeks and nose with a lace-trimmed handkerchief. "I'm lucky you married my brother."

Lisbeth didn't quite have a response. She opted for the tried-and-true English method of ignoring all sentiment. "I'll go have a chat with Her Grace to sort out your visit. Suzy, you'll start the packing?"

It was only as she shut Mary's door behind her that Lisbeth let her own cloud of emotions settle. Fury, at the family. Sorrow, for Mary. And then there was a golden thread of gratefulness she wished she could push away, for she had been lucky: she had the luxury of being married to the man she loved.

The least Lisbeth could do was try to make it possible for other people to live with their loved ones, too.

Chapter Twenty-Four

Adrian couldn't face his study that afternoon, not when every paper mocked him about Hathorne Shipping. He felt dirty from being his father's messenger. He almost wanted to burn all the records down, as if that could reverse the course of fate.

Instead, he took refuge in his bedchamber. With the curtains drawn tight against the fading gray daylight and a coal fire burning bright in the hearth, Adrian could almost pretend that the world ended with the plaster walls. From the locked cabinet beside his bed, Adrian regarded the items that anchored him in his mission. The silver locket, which kept safe the lock of his mother's hair. The worn leather-bound Bible that his mother had gifted him upon her death. Bundled in twine, collected pamphlets from Cowper, Equiano, Sancho, and Wilberforce on the evils of slavery. And a small, framed watercolor of Inglewilde Plantation that featured far too many chains.

He held each in his hands for a moment, as if touching them would give him strength. He opened his mother's Bible. It was designed to be carried around every day for consultation, with gossamer-thin pages and a durable cover. Adrian knew it had been his mother's when she was a girl; he couldn't remember whether it had belonged to anyone in her family before that, and knowing that he had lost that detail forever always made his heart break. Still, it was the only thing he possessed that retained her wide-looped handwriting. On the title page, she had written her name: *Rebecca Graham*, with *Hathorne* added later in a browner ink. Beneath it, she had listed family members:

> *Mother – Heather May Graham*
> *Brother – Henry Graham*
> *Uncle – Federico*
> *Grandmother – Calliope/Ife*

Adrian remembered studying this page with his mother when he had just begun to learn to read. She had run the pad of her thumb under each name as he sounded them out, and she added to them with stories. "How my mother hated her name. She always introduced herself as Hattie, but she made sure I knew how she was christened, just in case it ever came up as a question," and, "Uncle Federico was the handsomest man in town. Even I knew that as a little girl. It's no wonder he convinced a French woman to marry him and take him to the Continent. That's what you have to do. Find a nice woman to take you off this island." When they had gotten to Calliope, his mother had slowed, the fondness replaced in her voice with something more akin to steel. "She has two names, you see. Ife was given her by her people, and the other by the White folk who stole her. You'll never hear me talk about it again, but don't you dare forget where you came from. You are our great hope."

Now, in the damp cool of London spring, Adrian shut the Bible and returned it carefully to its resting place. He hadn't forgotten. He came from a people that had been stolen. He also came from the people that had done the stealing. If anyone could right the wrongs of the Hathornes, it was Adrian.

Which was why he had to accept Mary's marriage for what it was: a boon. In one fell swoop, his father had handed Adrian two gifts. First, he had saved ten souls from being marched to Brabourne's plantation, which meant those were ten more souls Adrian could liberate. Second, he had set up an alliance that Adrian just might be able to turn to his advantage. Brabourne would never free his slaves, no, but with Mary running the household, Adrian just might be able to find a way to offer them hope.

He locked the bedside cabinet and was just rising when Mr. Adkins stepped into the room. The man blanched. "My apologies, Sir, I didn't realize you were in here."

"I'm not usually at this time." Adrian noted the starched shirts in his valet's arms. "In any case, I'll dress for luncheon. A shave, and then the yellow waistcoat, I think."

Mr. Adkins positioned Adrian in his chair and set a hot towel about his cheeks before fussing about the room, tying open the curtains for better light and assembling the shaving accoutrement. Adrian shut his eyes, willing his thoughts not to turn to Lisbeth.

Yet he couldn't help worrying her words again:

Perhaps I'll audition my winter lover.
We'll be late to supper.
I didn't particularly want to marry you.

Of all the things she had said, the latter clanged in his head now.

There was plenty of evidence that Lisbeth enjoyed their marriage. She smiled when he entered the room. She flirted with him throughout the day and slipped into his bed at night. She directed Mrs. Siswell to prepare his favorite meals.

All this, he had thought, meant that she liked him. Perhaps even loved him. He had begun to daydream – when he dared think about a future unlikely to happen – of showing her Inglewilde Plantation and even keeping her there. She would like the constant sunshine.

And yet, Adrian knew he had not misheard her. He was one of the two men she hadn't wanted to marry.

He didn't think she could feel about him the way he felt about her and say such a thing to him. No matter if it was true at the time of the wedding. Lisbeth occupied too much of his heart for him to even remember the time before the altar. As far as he was concerned, their marriage had been fated in the stars.

Lisbeth, apparently, didn't feel the same way.

Mr. Adkins whisked away the hot towel, and Adrian shivered. "You're quiet today, Sir, if I may say so."

"Family matters on my mind. Distract me with news

from the rest of the household."

Mr. Adkins launched into his usual chatter. He was an odd duck: sometimes he spoke of his fellow servants as if they were his family, sharing little stories with a fond smile, while other occasions his words dripped superciliously, as if every other person in the household was beneath his notice. Adrian noted that it was one of those latter times as Mr. Adkins sneered through a story of how Mrs. Siswell had sold the remainders of the candles for too little money.

"If one is going to stoop to padding one's wallet with household remainders, one should do so with enough knowledge to get the maximum profit, if you ask me, Sir."

Adrian kept his eyes closed. "Perhaps she thought her buyer needed the candles more than she needed a few extra pence."

Mr. Adkins was saved the trouble of responding by a knock from the connecting door to Lisbeth's suite.

Adrian's heart jumped.

"Do you mind the interruption?" Lisbeth asked. From his position in the shaving chair facing the window, Adrian couldn't see her yet; he could only wallow in her drawl, searching each dip for the warmth he wished were there.

"Not at all." Adrian gestured her closer with a blind flap of his hand. "How is Mary?"

He smelled the mix of her perfume and powder as she drew closer, and then she leaned against the windowsill in his view. She wore the same blue dress, but her hair had frizzled out of its coiffure and her hands were bare.

Sometimes – like now – he needed only see the slender bend of her fingers to feel a spike of desire in his cock.

"She is distraught," Lisbeth answered his question. "I invited her to stay here for a few days."

The idea hadn't occurred to him, but Adrian loved it. He and Mary had never lived far from each other; even with her frequent visits to Lisbeth's drawing room, he had missed his sister.

"She can stay until the wedding if she wants," he said.

Lisbeth's eyes flicked to Mr. Adkins, then back to Adrian. "I'm not sure there should be a wedding."

The shaving knife was close to his skin, so Adrian waited until it had scraped away before responding. "Give her time to think it over. She'll see. If she were to refuse him, it would cause irreparable damage to the family and her reputation."

"Why should she care about the family reputation, when the family doesn't give a care for her preferences?"

Adrian knew Lisbeth well enough by now to recognize the particular brand of anger in her voice: she was about to expel a burning rage, and there was no holding it back. He nodded at Mr. Adkins in dismissal. The valet, well-trained man that he was, disappeared almost instantly.

To her credit, Lisbeth waited for the door to click closed before continuing. "It isn't right. It is one thing to know one must marry, and another entirely to be pledged to a man without so much as a by-your-leave."

Adrian leaned forward. "I don't disagree."

"It isn't as if Mary has never met the man. She has. She dislikes him. She can't stand the thought of him touching her. How can she be expected to accept his suit? And yet your father has left her no choice, other than scandal."

"Perhaps she hasn't given him a fair chance," Adrian heard himself say, though he couldn't forget his own shiver of abhorrence when Brabourne had bowed over Mary in the drawing room the day before. "Is there someone else she would prefer?"

Lisbeth opened her mouth as if to respond, then closed it again. She swept her eyes across his face; his stomach sucked at the evaluation. He couldn't tell if he had been found wanting.

"If there is someone else, then perhaps my grandfather can sort it out," Adrian pushed. "The man need only press his suit tomorrow, before dinner."

Bracing her bare hands against the windowsill, Lisbeth lost the anger from her voice, replacing it with something softer, something harder for Adrian to understand. "Have you noticed that Mary relies on her maid Suzy more than most ladies?"

Her question was such a pivot that for a moment, Adrian thought he must have misheard Lisbeth. "No, I haven't."

"Ah." Lisbeth twisted her lips for a moment before continuing. "She does. What's more, she lights up when Suzy enters the room. Like the sun has come out."

Adrian knew Lisbeth was trying to tell him some-thing, but his ears were pounding with his heartbeat and he couldn't quite figure it out.

Lisbeth hugged an arm self-consciously across her waist. "Mary looks at Suzy the way that I look at you."

His breath caught in his throat. He saw at once the two things Lisbeth was trying to tell him. And he couldn't help but feel joy for himself before dropping into compas-sion for his sister.

"She can't marry any man, don't you see?" Lisbeth pressed on. "She can't bear to be touched by any man."

Adrian stood. Too many thoughts – too many emo-tions – flooded his mind. He couldn't quite think clearly. "If any man is the same to her, then she might as well marry Lord Brabourne. It is the perfect arrangement. She'll be my neighbor at Inglewilde Plantation. She can soften his reaction when I free everyone."

"Every man is the devil to her!" Fury had returned to Lisbeth's words. "You don't need her for your plan. All she wants is to live quietly somewhere in a cottage with an annual allowance. Can't you give her that?"

"*I* live off my father's allowance until he dies."

Tears stained Lisbeth's eyes red. "You are her only hope."

Adrian took her hands. They were colder than he expected, and clammy. "My father offered Mary to Lord Brabourne in part as recompense for not giving him ten of our slaves. Ten souls rely on Mary to be his wife. Our family enslaved them. Can we not offer our own sacrifice in order to free them?"

"Mary didn't enslave them. Mary doesn't profit from their labor. Mary only wants to live with her love, the way you and I get to choose to live together. I refuse to deny her that in some quest to pay for the sins of your forefathers." Lisbeth said it with such righteousness that anger swirled up his throat. She didn't understand. She refused to understand.

"Every meal Mary has ever eaten; every dress she has ever worn; every fire in every hearth that has ever warmed her has been reaped from slave labor. That is as true for Mary as it is for me as it is for you. My ancestors spared no thought for family relations as they auctioned off wives and husbands and children and grandparents. Neither can I. And every second that I spend here worrying about Mary's fate is another second that I am not at Inglewilde preventing another sister from being sold away from a brother."

They still clung to each other's hands, even though Adrian clamped so hard that Lisbeth's fingers turned white as ivory. He loosened his grip. He hadn't meant to hurt her.

"I know, Adrian. I know. And yet, I cannot believe that the only way to defeat your forefathers is to act like them." Lisbeth didn't find a smile for him, but she did press a kiss to his forehead. Then she let him go. "So be it. You will do what you think best. Let me see to Mary."

Adrian didn't know what she meant by that, but he

knew he didn't want her to walk away with his anger rattling through her bones. In another moment, he might have swept her onto the bed and dissolved their argument in desire. Now, he wasn't sure he even dared kiss her. Instead, he caught her soft muslin skirt in his fingers. "I feel the same way, you know."

He waited for her to look at him in confusion before pressing on.

"When you walk in the room, the sun comes out."

Lisbeth smiled. Despite all their quarreling, she beamed. And he did dare kiss her.

Chapter Twenty-Five

Lisbeth commanded herself to stop thinking about Adrian. A little subterfuge had never killed anyone, and she would tell him what he needed to know when it was safe to do so. For the moment, her focus needed to be entirely on Mary.

Lisbeth wished she could find a way to tell Adrian that she had been wrong all those times before. Between Lady Fairfax and Lord Brabourne, Lisbeth had tasted enough of British prejudice to know she should have trusted Adrian's instincts all along. He couldn't risk scandal; he couldn't speak out; he couldn't do anything other than wait for his father to die. She understood that now. And she wanted to trust him on this matter, too. But she couldn't believe that Mary would survive a marriage to Lord Brabourne.

Perhaps it was always meant to be this way. Adrian would go to Inglewilde to battle slavery, and Lisbeth would stay in London, protecting every woman she could. Perhaps it was impossible to champion two causes at once.

Mary was looking worse for the wear as their carriage came to a stop before Lady Gresham's townhouse. Even her lips looked pale, and dark circles beneath her eyes suggested a sleepless night. Her outfit, at least, was the spectacular pink muslin of highest fashion, her hair carefully styled with pearl chains threaded in imitation of a mobcap.

Lisbeth assumed that was Suzy's doing, either as a grab at more time with Mary or a maid's stubborn pride in her work no matter the circumstances. Or both.

She didn't comment, only nudged Mary's elbow to prod her out of the carriage. As they passed through the ostentatious gate, she whispered, "I was supposed to be mistress of this house once, until I got myself out of that marriage. So you see, it isn't impossible."

Mary grimaced in response. "Would that I had your parents."

Annabelle's butler recognized Lisbeth by now and delivered them to the upstairs drawing room with the hint of a friendly smile tugging at his lips. As usual, Lisbeth had arrived a few minutes late, and the other ladies were already sipping from delicate cups of tea. Curious eyes landed on Mary, and the volume of chatter dimmed.

"Good afternoon," Lisbeth said to the room in general, dipping into a cursory curtsy of respect to all the titled women. "May I have the honor of introducing my sister, Miss Hathorne?"

Annabelle swooped over from the far corner, where she had been absorbed in discussion with Lady Pemberly. Lisbeth had written ahead of time, requesting a private word after the salon to discuss a matter pertaining to Mary, and she worried now that Annabelle would project concern to the rest of the group. But of course, Annabelle betrayed nothing except the perfect hostess's smile as she seated them on the center settee.

The discussion that week was to be around a woman's right inside a marriage. The previous night, after a near-silent supper, Lisbeth had read the tract on divorce aloud to Mary, though Mary kept interrupting with exclamations of rage that a woman should have so few rights *before* the marriage, too. Now, she watched the same anger return a healthy coloring to Mary's complexion.

Sometimes, the strong feelings governesses tried so hard to squelch from every corner of a woman were useful for finding the energy to wake up in the morning.

Most of the ladies in the room were not in favor of divorce, since it usually meant the mother lost all rights to see her children. "I cannot imagine choosing a fate that would forbid me from seeing my daughters," Lady Pemberly said.

"What if your husband were cruel? What if every time he paid a visit to your chambers, he left you bruised as a boxer?" Annabelle asked.

Mrs. Ludlow paled. "Lady Gresham, we have innocent ears present."

"Should they not be prepared for such a fate?" Lisbeth defended. "Should not unmarried women have some sort of education of what might come, so they can prepare to respond to it?"

"There is no response to such behavior," Lady Pemberly said. "One must simply submit to it and do what one can to prevent it."

"Submit?" Lisbeth could hardly believe her ears.

"Surely the proper response is to return to one's family until they can sort the man out."

Mrs. Ludlow and Lady Pemberly looked at her with the exact same pitying expression. It was the look she used to receive from married women when she ventured her opinions on matrimony, before she herself married.

Underneath her petulance at being treated as an idiot, Lisbeth was aware of a deeper horror.

Annabelle reined the conversation back towards policy. "Should the law provide protections for a wife?"

Though still heated, the debate returned to safe ground as it lost a bit of personal fire. Even as she chimed in with her opinions, Lisbeth was aware of Mary beside her, silent yet watchful. Her sister-in-law's reactions were locked behind that infuriating Hathorne mask, but Lisbeth sensed Mary would erupt with her own arguments once they were in the safety of Upper Norton Street.

The salon carried on a bit longer than usual, the topic being so close to the hearts of everyone in the room. When the butler announced Mrs. Ludlow's husband had arrived personally to accompany her home, however, the group seemed as one to decide to go. In a matter of minutes, it emptied from twenty women to three.

Annabelle turned her smile to Mary. "Now, then, shall we retire to the garden?"

It had improved considerably since Lisbeth's first visit in March. Then, she had glimpsed brown plants awaiting spring warmth. Now the flowerbeds dazzled with irises, crocuses, and daffodils. Annabelle led them to a set of delicate iron table and chairs. "I would offer something to drink, but I imagine we've all had our fill."

"I certainly have," Lisbeth said, modeling her tone after Annabelle's. Mary only twitched her lips in something that once may have resembled a smile.

Annabelle's blue eyes drifted to Lisbeth's in question. There was no point in delaying it, then. She might as well open her mouth and start speaking.

If only it didn't feel like a betrayal of Adrian to do so.

"We find ourselves in a delicate situation, and I thought you would be a sympathetic ear, if not a brilliant mind to find us a solution."

She checked on Mary, who stared at her hands, locked in white gloves and folded neatly in her lap. They had discussed this the night before. Still, Lisbeth felt a bit like she was breaking a vow of secrecy as she continued.

"Mr. Hathorne – that is Bartholomew Hathorne, Mary's father – sent word that he has promised Mary to Lord Brabourne. He expects the marriage to proceed by the end of June. The duke and duchess are both eager to oblige. Tonight, in fact, Mary is to formally accept Lord Brabourne's offer. However, Mary does not wish to marry." Lisbeth paused here. She had not quite broached the subject of Suzy with Mary, and she was reluctant to trot it out unless absolutely necessary. "She does not want to marry anyone, you see. She would like to live a quiet life in a cottage, with her maid if not any household servants.

I should like to help her do so."

Annabelle's soft gaze settled on Mary. She spent a moment in silence, perhaps weighing their story, perhaps waiting for Mary to speak. Then, she said, "I wonder if Lisbeth has told you a little of my life. I met dear Lord Gresham after my first Season. He was too young to marry, they said, and didn't have enough money anyhow. My parents married me to the Duke of Surrey, who was already past sixty and whisked me off to Europe. To marry someone you don't love, when your heart belongs to someone else, is a terrible ordeal."

Lisbeth had known the story, as told by Bernard. She had never discussed it with Annabelle. She had never imagined – not even just now in the salon, when all they thought about was marriage – what Annabelle might have experienced as the reluctant bride of an old, demanding duke.

"In the absence of assistance from the family," Lisbeth said, "the only plan I have come up with is for Mary and Suzy to run away."

"Yes." Annabelle reached out, taking Mary's gloved hand in her own. There was a flicker of hope in Mary's face as she looked up in response. "I know a little cottage outside of Lisbon that should be available."

Lisbeth's skin prickled with fear as much as it did with relief. Somehow, she hadn't imagined Annabelle would go along with what Lisbeth thought the craziest idea of her life.

When Adrian found out what she had done, would he still want anything to do with her?

Chapter Twenty-Six

A drian couldn't shake the queasy feeling from his stomach. Not after watching his sister accept Lord Brabourne's hand at dinner with the whole family looking on. Not after bringing her home to Upper Norton Street, incomparably pale and silent. And not after being forced to accompany the newly engaged couple to Lady Leighstor's afternoon at-home, as if he approved of the match.

Mary hadn't spoken to him in two days, not even a pass-the-salt-please, and Lisbeth kept glimmering with anger.

He wished he could think of a way to protect Mary without sacrificing the slaves he needed so desperately to free.

After half an hour or so of polite chitchat with the other guests, Lord Brabourne looped Mary's arm through his and suggested a visit to Lady Leighstor's hothouse. Adrian nearly yanked Lisbeth to his side as he announced they would go, too.

Lord Brabourne ushered them to the glass house where Lady Leighstor kept her favorite plant varieties growing all year long. Adrian noted the gardeners – two of them boasting darkened skin, like him – scattering upon their entrance, melting into sheds or dark corners to avoid being seen by guests. Lisbeth looked all about, her eyes dancing in delight as they passed through a bower of ivy into a lush landscape of ferns and flowers. Ahead, at Brabourne's side, Mary walked more sedately, arms tucked against her ribs, chin resolutely still.

Lady Leighstor's plants were not particularly exotic, certainly not enough to earn attention from the Royal Botanical Society. On the whole, they were English: pink roses, yellow mums, delicate orchids and swaying daffodils. A round cistern in the center of the hothouse boasted a wreath of lily pads, though no white lilies bloomed at the moment. Adrian wondered if one of the gardeners brought in buckets of bull frogs for the artificial pond; if he snuck in with Lisbeth in the quiet of moonlight, would they hear a chorus of croaks?

What a thought. Adrian shook his head, trying to focus instead on Brabourne's drone. Before his marriage, he never would have been so fanciful. And if he had been fanciful, his daydreams only included people he didn't know. He imagined the men and women on Inglewilde Plantation walking freely and joyfully. He pictured children leaping in the air at the news they were free. Occasionally, he had allowed himself to dream far ahead into the future and glimpse a warm body beside him in bed, tucked inside his arms, though he could never picture her face or laugh or even nationality.

Now here he was, ridiculously plotting to sneak into a hothouse at midnight to steal a kiss from his wife.

Said wife grabbed him – softly, familiarly – by the elbow. "Look at the morning glories! What luck they are open for us."

The flowers in question climbed a white trellis as part of the backdrop to a collection of geraniums and pansies. The blooms were small and dainty with petals eagerly spread to show off their whites and blues and purples. Lisbeth beamed. "There was a vine of morning glories that always climbed to my window every summer, no matter how much poor Mr. Trawley tried to cut them back. I would wake up with the sun and run to my window to see them open. They made me feel anything was possible."

Adrian remembered them from Maidenheath House, too; the gardeners had forever been trying to remove the morning glory vines from every fence, hedge, and haha. When the day grew too warm, the blooms closed up tight, as if to declare to the world, *You've lost the right to see me.*

He had always admired that. He had wished there were a way to do that as a person, too; pull your folds around you and stop someone from staring.

"Put us together and we're a morning glory, don't you think?" Lisbeth said this with a little laugh at the back of her throat. "I love to be on display in all my favorite colors, and you're too shy to let anyone see you."

Oh, he was in trouble. When had he handed Lisbeth his heart? When had she learned to read his mind? Who could have predicted he would love to have her there to interpret the wild thoughts beating across his brow?

If they had been alone in the hothouse, Adrian would have claimed a kiss. As it was, he pulled her close, breathing in the salty scent of her skin and lapping up the bosomy view presented by her bodice. Her eyes darkened in response, and he knew her mind was racing downwards to his body, too.

"Oh look, Adrian!" The interruption came from Mary, three yards ahead of them. "Did we not have a plant just like this growing outside our nursery?"

His sister, like him, did not wear her emotions plain for all the world to see. But for Adrian, it was as easy to read Mary as it was to read a book. The look she gave him now – wide eyes and too much breath behind her words – told him she was miserable.

His stomach twisted with guilt.

"What kind of plant is it?" Lisbeth advanced, cooperatively burrowing all her attention into the bush Mary pointed at. It was nothing particularly interesting, simply a tropical plant with wide green and pink leaves. It wasn't until Adrian stepped closer and smelled it that he remembered: playing blocks with Mary in the nursery, hoping Mama would come find him, fearing she wouldn't say goodnight.

"Jamaican Croton," Brabourne answered, launching into another lecture with more details than anyone could possibly care to know.

"You have a strong admiration for plants," Adrian observed when the man seemed to be winding down.

"I am a farmer at heart." Brabourne finally looked at Mary, his icy blue eyes crinkling just slightly. "That is why I am so thrilled to be marrying a gentlewoman who can stay by my side in Jamaica."

Mary paled. She looked down, then sideways to Lisbeth. She did not look at Adrian, her own brother.

He tried not to be hurt.

"Our families have long been intertwined," Brabourne continued. "It would bring my own father such joy to know that we are officially joining destinies. As I know it pleases your father, Miss Hathorne."

"Apparently so," Mary agreed.

Lisbeth stepped forward, a polite smile across her lips. "Lord Brabourne, seeing as how you are an expert on such things, would you be so kind as to show me the irises? And what do you know about removing slugs from the garden? Our man has such trouble with them."

Mary stayed behind, assuming Lisbeth's place at Adrian's side. She still tucked herself into a shriveled straight line, as if afraid he would reach out and grab her if she dared relax her arms.

"Are you having a good afternoon?" Adrian asked, even though he knew she wasn't. He couldn't think of anything else to say.

Mary didn't reward him with an answer.

"I know this isn't your first choice, Mary, but Brabourne will be a good husband. You won't have any worries about money; he'll leave you to your own pursuits;

and I will be your neighbor. There's not so much wrong about that, is there?"

She absorbed his words in silence. They had always had a quieter rhythm, conversations filled with pauses, compared to the rat-a-tat-tat of Robert's wit.

Adrian realized suddenly that he hadn't had a good one-on-one with Mary in far too long.

"I wouldn't expect you to understand," she said finally.

Adrian didn't like the disappointment that swelled her words. "You can take Suzy with you, too. There's nothing unusual in having a loyal lady's maid."

Mary let out a little cry. "Do you think that is enough? If you could only have Lisbeth as your personal valet while forced to bend to the whim of some other wife for your whole life, would that be enough for you?"

It was a natural situation. Most men in Adrian's class weren't lucky enough to love their wives; they married for money and gave their hearts to mistresses.

But how would it feel, if he couldn't take Lisbeth with him on this type of tedious social call? How would he cope, having to kiss another woman while thinking of Lisbeth's collection of smiles?

It would be no different than how he felt now, thinking of the 219 souls on Inglewilde Plantation. His happiness was false. His heart was incomplete.

Could life exist without a corner of despair always whispering, *This could be better*?

"How I wish I could make you happy, Mary."

It was all he could say to her. He had no more words, and he had no more time, for Brabourne had returned from the irises with Lisbeth. Adrian saw the impatience on her brow, and even a little shadow of fury in her eye.

His sister was desperate. His wife was angry. But Adrian had a mission. He couldn't possibly sacrifice his plans for anything. Not even his sister's happiness.

He truly, honest-to-god, wished he could.

Chapter Twenty-Seven

Lisbeth had to summon all of her patience to review the plan again. They had spent three days discussing nothing *but* the plan, whenever Adrian disappeared and they were out of earshot of the other staff. Still, Mary was nervous, Suzy remained unconvinced, and they had to wait another three days before they could do anything.

It was enough to drive anyone wild.

They were cloistered in Mary's chamber on the fourth floor of Upper Norton Street in the late evening. Unusually, Adrian had been called out after supper for a business meeting with Robert and Lord Brabourne. It had been on the tip of Lisbeth's tongue to beg him not to go; but it was easier to get a swath of time alone with Mary and Suzy with him out of the house. Still, he had met her eyes with a long, regretful look, and Lisbeth knew he wished he could extract himself from the clutches of the Brabourne business.

Everything would be that much more complicated in a few days when she had smuggled Mary and Suzy to safety. Including Adrian's feelings for her.

Well, let him have his principles. Lisbeth had hers, too; she didn't see why they couldn't save Mary *and* the slaves, and she certainly wasn't going to resign herself to one or the other.

"What happens once we get on the ship?" Mary asked, though Lisbeth was certain she knew the answer. She paced before the fireplace, her skirts flouncing with increasing fury at each turn. Suzy sat on a little stool in the corner of the room, having declined the proper seats in front of the hearth, and so far hadn't uttered a word.

Lisbeth picked at the embroidery in her lap, which she had brought mostly as a prop in case one of the other servants found it strange that she would seclude herself in Mary's room. Mary was supposed to be working on the other end of the tapestry, but she had begun pacing almost as soon as Suzy closed the door shut.

"You behave as if it is perfectly natural to be traveling with your maid. You chat with the other passengers about how excited you are to make the full journey to India, and how you wish there weren't so many stops along the way. If they say how glad they are to have a day to see Lisbon, you wrinkle your nose and profess to have little interest in sightseeing."

"I daresay I shan't leave the inn at all until the ship is ready," Mary practiced, pitching her voice high and haughty. Then the anxiety crept back. "Then we find Baltasar at the Café do Gelo on Praca do Comercio street."

Annabelle was behind almost the entire plot. She had spent seven years traveling Europe with her husband; she seemed to have friends tucked in every corner of the continent. Mary and Suzy would sail on a ship captained by one of Annabelle's acquaintances, under assumed names, and as far as the captain knew, they were joining Mary's husband in Calcutta. When the ship docked in Lisbon, he would believe they were changing to an East Indiaman, but in fact, they would find Annabelle's friend Baltasar. Annabelle was writing ahead to him and also arming Mary with a copy of the letter, so that Baltasar would agree to transport them in his wagon from Lisbon to the cottage a few miles outside, where a second letter would introduce them to the farm owner and secure them safe lodging.

It all made sense, and yet even Lisbeth couldn't help but tremble at the hundred things that could go wrong.

"I found a dictionary that translates Portuguese into English in my father's library," Lisbeth said. "He walked in before I could steal it, but I'll go back tomorrow."

"I'm hopeless at languages." Mary's attempted laugh came out as a bark. "My governess called me a complete failure at French, and that was after nine years."

There wasn't much to say in reply. Lisbeth threw a desperate smile at Suzy. "Then it will be Suzy's task to be your translator."

This, apparently, was not the right response. Suzy, who had been a near-silent participant all these past five days, flushed an immediate and deep red. She glared at the ground. "At what point will you realize this idea is pure folly?"

There was such acid in her tone – and such omission of propriety – that even though Lisbeth knew Suzy was more than just a maid, she still bristled at the absence of a "beg your pardon."

Mary, however, didn't flinch. "It's the only way, Suzy, and you know it. We can't stay in England or anywhere within my grandfather's reaches."

"We'll be murdered or worse before we even get to Lisbon," Suzy shot back. "Two women can't travel unaccompanied, especially if we're *not* your grandfather's wards. No more can we live alone in some strange countryside. They'll slit our throats rather than give us that cottage."

"What would you have me do?" Mary wailed. "I can't marry him. You know that. Don't you know that?"

"There are worse fates than marrying a lord, Mary!" This came out as a shout. Lisbeth had never heard any servant raise their voice to their master; she had to fight down a very unnatural response to Suzy's anguish. But it was apparently too much of a breach for Suzy, too. Almost as soon as she said it, she let out a sob and raced from the room.

Mary watched her go, taking a half-hearted step to follow. "She doesn't mean it," she mumbled, as if to apologize to Lisbeth.

"Never you mind." Lisbeth looped an arm around her sister-in-law's shoulders and guided her to the chair. "It is as scary for her as it is for you, if not more. She'll see what needs to be done."

"I should go clear this up with her."

Even as Mary said it, the hall clock chimed eleven.

Lisbeth tugged her closer. "It is too late for you to venture upstairs without sparking curiosity from the other servants. Let her have her sulk, and you have yours, and in the morning everything will look clearer."

Although Lisbeth couldn't quite speak from experience there; after her nocturnal arguments with Adrian, everything had always looked worse in the mornings.

She was so glad they had moved beyond that in their marriage. And she dreaded finding out whether it would return, once Adrian discovered his sister escaped.

Lisbeth anchored her thoughts firmly to Mary at her side, who was sniffling in a desperate attempt to keep from sobs. She needed Lisbeth's loyalty far more than Adrian did, who was currently doing god-knows-what with Lord Brabourne as if it were natural for the man to become his brother-in-law.

"Have a good cry, then," Lisbeth urged, smoothing back Mary's hair the way her mother had always done for her. "It will help."

Mary didn't need further encouragement. The clock had chimed quarter past by the time she calmed back down to a sedate sniffle, accepting Lisbeth's handkerchief since hers was soaked through.

"It did help." Mary managed a smile, though her eyes and nose were so red that it came off as pathetic.

"There, you see?" Lisbeth had resorted to murmuring platitudes. "Just wait until you see what a little sleep will do. Shall I help you into your nightgown, then?"

This brought out a few more tears, for of course Suzy was usually the one who saw Mary changed into her night things. Mary summoned her inner strength, however, and together they rustled her out of her muslin day gown and into a cozy night rail, with a nightcap tucked around her curls.

"I don't think I'll be able to fall asleep," Mary protested as Lisbeth guided her to the bed. "My mind is too full of terrible thoughts."

"Let's talk, then," Lisbeth suggested, climbing onto the mattress beside her, "but only of happy thoughts. Tell me your favorite thing about Suzy."

For the first time in days, Mary's lips curved into a real smile. "Must I choose just one? How can I? She is *Suzy*. That's what I love about her." She lifted the blankets, inviting Lisbeth to snuggle in with her. Lisbeth had already changed into her night clothes and was quite happy to tuck under the covers. "I never expected to fall for my maid, of course. I didn't even realize I didn't care for men until far too late. Ned – my fiancé, the one who died at Trafalgar – kissed me before he left, and I hated it. I thought perhaps it was only his kiss I detested. When I was reintroduced to society, I stole a few more kisses here and there." She shuddered. "Just the thought of them makes my skin crawl. It was worse than nothing; their lips were slimy and grubby and I always felt I had to slither away."

Lisbeth thought of her own stolen kiss at Vauxhall Gardens. It had not shattered the earth, but neither had it turned her stomach.

"Then my maid, Clarissa, married one of our grooms. Suzy replaced her. From the minute she walked into the room, I couldn't take my eyes off her. I jumped when she touched me. There was that much electricity. I can't explain it. I simply knew that she was the soul put on this earth for me."

The sentiment made Lisbeth's heart ache. She hadn't had the same instantaneous experience with Adrian. But she knew exactly what Mary described. That feeling that Adrian understood her. That he had been built to cradle her. He was her home.

When you walk into the room, the sun comes out.

She hoped he didn't regret those words in three days, when the household awoke to discover that Mary and Suzy had disappeared.

"Adrian is the happiest I've ever seen him when he is with you," Mary said. Her words came more slowly now, her eyes drooping.

"I'm going to miss him when he leaves for Jamaica," Lisbeth admitted. Every night she ticked the days off, each one taking them closer and closer to Adrian's departure. And each one disappearing without a conversation about what that meant for them.

She hadn't visited his bedchamber since Mary came to stay, mostly because she didn't think she could keep their plan secret if she cuddled against the warmth of his body. Suddenly, Lisbeth couldn't stand the absence. Her body burned with phantom memories of his touch, and she ached for him to come home.

She only had a few more weeks with him.

But the hall clock chimed half past eleven, and still Adrian had not returned.

As if reading her thoughts, Mary murmured, "Will you stay here a bit longer? I'm almost asleep."

"I'll stay as long as you need," Lisbeth promised. Her eyes, too, felt heavy, and as she lay in silence, listening to Mary's breathing grow steadier, she was aware, dimly, that she fell into slumber.

She awoke with a start, her eyes full of a dream image of Adrian carrying her through a green field. Blinking, she remembered she was in Mary's chamber. Yet the bed beside her was empty. When she put her palm on Mary's pillow, it was warm, and she remembered now that she had awoken from the door clicking shut. Mary must have gone up to speak to Suzy after all.

Blearily, Lisbeth rolled out of the bed. The fire glowed dim embers in the hearth, so they must have slept for a while, at least. She splashed some water on her face to wake up. She would go see if Adrian had returned yet, she decided. She wanted to taste his kiss, as if somehow that would put the world at peace.

She had just turned to the door when it opened. At first, Lisbeth thought it must be Mary returning. But the figure that approached was not female. He wore dark clothes, and his black eyes gleamed in the firelight.

A burglar.

Or worse.

She waited too long to scream. By the time her brain had processed what was happening and she opened her mouth, he was upon her. His hand clamped over her lips, his other arm snaking across her neck, and the last thing she saw was a black sack dropping over her head.

Chapter Twenty-Eight

Adrian did not want to go home. He knew what awaited him there: a silent sister, a sullen wife. Oh, Lisbeth was polite enough during the day, asking after his activities and even throwing him a smile here and there. But ever since his father's letter had arrived, the nights had stretched long and empty. He knew what to expect that night because it was the same as all of them: he would spend the night curled alone on his mattress, stealing snatches of sleep in between hoping each creak of the house was Lisbeth creeping into his room.

He could, technically, visit her room. He was her husband. He could march into her apartment and climb into her bed because that was his right.

But it did not *feel* right. Lisbeth had her reasons for keeping her distance, and Adrian could sympathize. He was not about to force his attentions upon her, even if those attentions were simply to lay by her side.

Still, there was no reason for him to return to Upper Norton Street, not even once Lord Brabourne took his slimy leave of them. Brabourne had been the one that summoned them to White's in the first place, under the pretense of discussing the minutiae of their shipping agreement. But the man had barely said a word of business, instead droning on about his recent visit to Carlton House and all the compliments Prinny had lavished upon him. Then, almost exactly at the stroke of midnight, he had excused himself, citing an appointment elsewhere.

If Adrian didn't hate the man so much, he would find it very odd. Alarming, even. As it was, he didn't have the heart to waste one more thought on sniveling Brabourne. Nor did he want to go home, which was why he found himself accepting Robert's invitation to go watch a pugilist fight at a pub in Covent Garden.

Adrian had never been out in London so late, nor had he been to a pub in Covent Garden. He expected it to be mostly lords and gentlemen like himself and Robert, and there certainly were plenty of them. However, the majority of the men packed shoulder to shoulder to watch the fight were a class or two below that, with worn jackets and cheap shoes about their feet. They spoke with broad accents and their language offended. Most surprising to Adrian was how many weren't White: he spotted a trio of Bengali sailors, a tan man in a Turkish-style turban, and a few darker men with skin close to Adrian's.

Perhaps he hadn't needed to shun London society quite as a whole. Simply the upper crust.

The fight was ugly. Adrian had never particularly enjoyed watching one man pummel another, hearing the slap of fist against flesh, watching blood spray through the air, feeling the sinister excitement of a crowd cheering for the suffering of a fellow human. Yet that night, he was the man who had betrayed his sister. He was the man who had smoked a cigar with the fiancé she didn't want. And Adrian discovered that he craved the fight and the gore and the hope that he, too, could be that vicious, if he needed to be.

It was when the back molar of one of the fighters went flying into the crowd – and when Adrian cheered with delight at it – that Robert clapped a hand on Adrian's shoulder. "Let's take a break, shall we?"

Robert maneuvered him to a table inside the pub proper, away from the fight in the back room, and somehow made two foaming tankards of ale appear. Adrian didn't hesitate to taste his.

"What is troubling you, then?" Robert asked. "You're not yourself tonight."

Adrian evaluated his cousin. He had already had three stiff brandies at White's, and his sight was a little bleary. Still, he could see Robert was more sunburned than usual, a sign that he had spent extra time at the docks recently, and that shadows hung beneath his eyes.

The two of them hadn't spoken of Mary's nuptials yet; they tolerated the subject in others' company and pretended it wasn't happening when they were alone. But perhaps Adrian had been wrong to assume that Robert agreed with Their Graces. Perhaps Robert could understand the guilt that coated every moment of every day.

"This business with Mary and Lord Brabourne," Adrian started, watching Robert for any kind of reaction, "...it doesn't sit right with me."

Robert grimaced. "He is a snake who found his way

into the garden."

"Mary doesn't want to marry him." He heard Lisbeth's belligerence in his own tone. Perhaps it was his belligerence, too, and this was the first time he'd felt safe enough to voice it.

"I wish I could call him out," Robert said, taking an angry sip of his drink. "I'm the better marksman. I would kill him in a duel without a problem. And then Mary would be free of him. If only we could catch him doing something dishonorable."

Now there was an idea. Adrian gulped down more ale, considering. Lord Brabourne was too slimy by half to be goaded into offending someone's honor, but he was exactly the kind of man who might be keeping a mistress throughout his betrothal period, or perhaps cheat at a game of cards. All they needed to do was discover how he sinned and where.

His better sense knocked through the fog of alcohol. Robert could brag, but he had no claim to marksmanship. He could just as easily be injured – or worse – in a duel as he could do the injuring.

"Lisbeth has a plan, I think," Adrian admitted. "She and Mary keep whispering when they think I don't notice. I told her I couldn't help, though."

He hoped she would forgive him one day.

Robert frowned. "They could get themselves hurt."

"Mary is already hurt."

"Not physically." Robert shook his head at Adrian

now. "Whatever plan they come up with, it will only make things worse. You had better put a stop to it."

Adrian heard his own thoughts in Robert's words. Was this not what he had said to Lisbeth just a few days ago?

And yet, he couldn't agree with Robert. Whatever Lisbeth and Mary were planning may be terrible. But if it were Mary's idea, it couldn't be *worse* than marrying Lord Brabourne. Not from her perspective, and wasn't hers the only one that mattered?

Sighing, Adrian helped himself to another gulp of ale. "I would pay for Mary to live in her cottage myself, if it didn't complicate the other matter."

"What other matter?"

Adrian's stomach turned. He had never come so terribly close to coming out with his secret. He shook his head, unsettled. "Nothing. I'm in my cups."

Robert pulled out that easy, good-natured smile that made him so amiable. "First time in years, then. Cheers."

They clinked their tankards, and Adrian drained his in two greedy swallows. Might as well hang for the sheep as the lamb, as his grandmother was so fond of saying.

But when he thudded his cup back to the tabletop, he discovered his cousin was watching him with bright, alert eyes. "This other matter. What does it have to do with Mary?"

Adrian suppressed a groan. "It doesn't. Except that if I help Mary, I can't help…this other matter."

"Why not?"

"Because…" But Adrian couldn't find any good reason, no matter how vague. What reason was there? He was prioritizing ten people he had never met over his own sister. He knew he was right to value those ten people; he knew Mary had more hope than they did, even married to a man she couldn't stand. Still, there was no way to explain it to Robert. There was no way to explain it to Lisbeth, and there was certainly no way to explain it to Mary.

Either way one cut it, he was a heartless, hopeless bastard.

"Is it Lisbeth?" Robert asked.

They were interrupted before Adrian could respond. He saw the man angling for their table, and his brain flared with recognition, but it wasn't until the man started speaking that Adrian recognized his silver hair and ruddy cheeks and careful vowels. It was his valet, Mr. Adkins. "Begging your pardon, Sir, but Miss Hathorne has been kidnapped."

At first, Adrian couldn't tell whether he said Miss or Mrs, and he was so hung up on that detail that he missed the part about being kidnapped.

Robert jumped to his feet first. "Kidnapped? When? Where? By whom?"

"An hour or so ago, my lord. We've been searching for Mr. Hathorne. I'd say it was Lord Brabourne who ordered it, if you ask my opinion, and he'll be headed to Scotland. Rumblings are that he heard Miss Hathorne wasn't keen to marry him, and he wants to elope to make sure she doesn't disappear."

Rage soared through Adrian's veins. Lisbeth and Mary had been right. Lord Brabourne wasn't fit to live, so much as touch Mary. Adrian would have to find some other way to save his slaves. For now, he would settle for saving his sister.

Chapter Twenty-Nine

L isbeth couldn't tell how much time had passed. She had lost track of how many turns the carriage had taken. She couldn't quite feel her fingers anymore. She did know the carriage was cold. There were two men inside with her, yet neither had offered her a cloak or blanket; they let her lie there in her thin night rail. At first, when the second man had lifted her ankles while the first man held her silent in Mary's bedroom, Lisbeth had thought they would violate her. But so far, they had done nothing more than smuggle her out of the house and into a carriage that stank of manure.

The gag in her mouth grew more suffocating every second. By the time she had stopped counting the carriages turns, she had started fearing that she would die from whatever cotton they'd stuffed in her mouth. She tried to slow her spiking heart rate. She focused on breathing through her nose, no matter that it suddenly felt blocked to all air. To calm down, she shut her eyes against the darkness of the sack and pictured Adrian. She traced the sharp plane of his cheeks, touched the stubble shadowing his jawline, imagined those green eyes warm with a smile meant only for her.

Her breathing grew a little easier, at least for the few moments when she could focus.

It must have been hours before the horses slowed. The carriage humped over a bump, then rolled across rougher pitch than whatever road they had been on. Her two kidnappers exchanged words, and Lisbeth caught their accents, Cockney and something northern she couldn't quite place. They opened the carriage door; cold morning air rushed in, raising goosepimples across Lisbeth's skin.

Outside, she could hear muffled voices. Her captors were both out of the carriage. If she could move her feet, she might be able to get herself out the other door and crawl away.

But her ankles were still tied together, her wrists still bound behind her back, and when Lisbeth tried to heave herself into a sitting position, she only wriggled against the hard wooden bench.

She refused to admit the despair flailing inside her. One way or another, she was going to escape.

Lisbeth was the daughter of the Marquess of Ipswich. She was the granddaughter-in-law of the Duke of Berkwell. And her husband loved her. She would not allow herself to be felled by some common kidnappers.

Still, she shrieked through her gag when one of the men hooked her beneath the shoulders. Her feet thudded against the carriage body as he dragged her out. Her heels landed on soft ground; even through her stockings, she felt chilled, dewy grass. Lisbeth vaulted herself one way and then the other, but the man didn't lose his grip on her. Someone else grabbed her ankles, and suddenly she was hefted through the air.

She landed on her side on a cushion that smelled vaguely of hay. A door shut with a wooden click. Then everything started moving again, and Lisbeth realized she was in another carriage.

A better carriage.

"Now, my dear, let us see what we can do to make you more comfortable. Why, they treated you no better than some common fishwife."

The voice was baritone, silky, and instantly sent a shudder down Lisbeth's spine. A second later, she realized whose it was: Lord Brabourne.

He leaned closer, the air filling with the smell of mustachio wax, and gloved hands sat her upright. Lisbeth suddenly remembered that she wore nothing but her white muslin night rail over a chemise. Had he heard what she was planning with Mary? Did he mean to extract revenge by compromising Lisbeth?

She had been afraid before. But now – now fear tasted like bad fish on her tongue.

"It is most unfortunate that things have come to this, but you'll see I protect my own. Do you promise to behave, if I remove a few of your bindings?"

Lisbeth summoned a vigorous nod. The instant he untied her hands, she would claw his eyes out.

He did not, unfortunately, loosen either the ropes at her wrists or at her ankles. Instead, he lifted the sack from her head and pulled the handkerchief from her mouth.

She blinked against the sudden brightness; early morning sunshine filtered through the carriage curtains, and her eyes fizzled in pain for a moment before she could make out Lord Brabourne beside her.

He stared at her with wide, horrified eyes. Lisbeth realized she wasn't who he had expected.

Despite herself, she smiled. "Your cronies kidnapped the wrong woman, didn't they, Brabourne?"

He launched himself to the opposite carriage bench, as if he couldn't stand to be within inches of her.

Triumph surged through her. "I'm glad. You don't deserve to look at Mary, so much as touch her. What, did you think you would take her to Gretna Green?"

Anger heated Lord Brabourne's gaze. "It is my right. Her father signed the marriage contract. I was only looking after my interests, after I heard *you* were whispering in her ear about scarpering out of the marriage."

"Who told you that?"

"You didn't truly think servants would be loyal to a half-breed master, did you?" Lord Brabourne sneered.

Lisbeth stifled her natural flinch. Let him be hateful; he was clearly insane.

"Hathorne's valet is friendly with mine," he added. "He told us your plans, and he let us into the house last night. Apparently, he described the wrong bedchamber."

Lisbeth didn't see the need to explain that *she* was the one in the wrong bed. "Why marry a woman who would rather run away than be your wife? Surely you could find a fiancée who doesn't vomit every time your name comes up."

"None has what Miss Hathorne does."

"Good taste?" Lisbeth pushed against the restraints on her wrists. They were too tight.

"A claim to Inglewilde," Brabourne sneered.

It was so absurd, Lisbeth actually scoffed. "Mary has no more claim to Inglewilde than I to my father's title."

"We shall see what the law thinks when I sue for inheritance on her behalf. After all, your husband is nothing more than an octaroon with pretensions. He has no right to inherit property. I think my peers on the Jamaican Assembly will agree that the plantation should go to Mary instead."

Lisbeth was already terrified and angry, but now, a new horror spread like ice across her skin. Brabourne would not only ruin Mary; he would keep the slaves at Inglewilde in hell, too.

She squared her shoulders. "A fine plan, perhaps. Except you will never marry Mary now. No matter what Mr. Hathorne promised you. The family would never marry her to a known kidnapper."

She caught her words just after they left her mouth. After all, the Hathorne fortune was built on kidnapping people from Africa. Her stomach twisted.

Lord Brabourne didn't notice her error. "You make an excellent point, Mrs. Hathorne. What am I to do with you?" Reaching under his bench, he withdrew a wooden case, opened it, and lifted out a dueling pistol. "I could kill you and leave your body to rot in the woods."

She had to bite down on her lip to keep herself from reacting.

"However, I am no murderer. A man must have his principles." In spite of his words, Brabourne pointed the pistol with her as he talked. "You were so eager for my Mary to set sail. It seems to me you should take the journey in her stead."

With his free hand, he slammed on the ceiling of the carriage. "Driver, turn back to London. We're going to the docks."

He sealed his words with a thin, pale smile that made Lisbeth shiver. "What do you think will happen to you when I leave you on a cargo clipper to Bangkok?"

The image settled between them for a moment. Then Lisbeth screamed as loud as she could, pistol be damned, and launched herself at him.

Chapter Thirty

I t took too much time to get on the road north. Adrian and Robert had to trek to the duke's stables and rouse a groom to get their horses. Mr. Adkins tagged along, offering this and that useless advice, until Adrian realized the man was hanging on in hopes of a tip, as if the news that Mary had been kidnapped were the same as reporting a ship had come to dock.

"To bed, Mr. Adkins," he snapped. "I will need you when I return."

The man scampered away in the direction of Upper Norton Street, and Adrian allowed himself one moment of indecision on whether to follow him. Lisbeth would be awake, beside herself with worry; he pictured her pacing across the new carpet in the drawing room and knew she would prefer to see him before he raced off after Mary.

But he had already lost so much time to Brabourne. He couldn't risk the half hour it would take to check in at Upper Norton Street.

Adrian spurred his horse in the direction of the highway. He would just have to earn Lisbeth's forgiveness for this along with her forgiveness for all the other ways he had already failed her.

Even pre-dawn, the London streets weren't quiet, with lamplighters and watchmen and prostitutes and flower girls and fishermen and bakers all going about their days. The cold air pricked Adrian's senses, sobering him up as he set his focus on saving Mary. He should never have gone along with his father's wishes. All he had to do was pretend that letter never came. He should have thrown Brabourne out of his study, burned his father's note, and let Mary carry on as she had been. Happy. Carefree. Unburdened.

Or once the letter had been read, he should have put up a fight. Lisbeth had needed no convincing to shelter Mary in their home; she didn't ask his permission to plot whatever she was planning. Adrian should have done that and more. He should have spoken for Mary to His Grace and their father and Lord Brabourne. He should have listened to his sister.

He hoped it wasn't too late to make it up to her.

The sun rose in a spectacular show of pinks above farm fields as they cantered along the highway. Robert periodically let out bursts of speech, but for the most part, they rode in silence, contemplating what awaited them. They passed a black hackney cab heading back to London and a few farm wagons carrying wares towards a market town; other than that, they had the highway to themselves.

It set Adrian's nerves on edge.

They spotted the carriage half a mile away. It was clearly a noble equipage, wide and painted a black polish that gleamed in the early morning light. When it followed the curve of the road, Adrian glimpsed the Brabourne family crest emblazoned in gold and red on the side of its door.

New, hot rage surged through Adrian. The man wasn't even trying to hide. He and Robert wordlessly spurred their horses into gallops.

Just as they approached the carriage, it rocked onto its right side. Its four horses startled; one reared onto its hind legs, and for a terrible moment, Adrian thought the whole coach was going to roll over. It righted itself, coming to a stop, only for the door to swing open. Two stockinged feet shot out.

Mary.

"Let her go, Brabourne!" Adrian shouted. He pulled his horse beside the carriage and jumped off. He had gotten his hand on the door when Brabourne responded.

"Don't come any closer, or I'll shoot her."

Brabourne held her against his chest, one arm looped across her waist. The other held a silver pistol to her temple.

And it wasn't Mary.

It was Lisbeth.

Adrian's heart stopped.

"Adrian!" Of all things, Lisbeth smiled. She wore nothing but her night rail. Its hem and her stockings were muddy, and her hair frizzed out of its braid. And still, she found it appropriate to put on a smile.

Adrian was going to kill Brabourne.

"Let her go."

Brabourne only tightened his hold on her waist. "I'll let her go if you promise to march your sister down the aisle yourself. Only fair, since this little tart has been try-ing to keep my rightful wife from me."

Robert had stayed on his horse behind the carriage, out of Brabourne's line of sight. He'd had the foresight to grab a hunting rifle from their grandfather's stable, whereas Adrian only had his own fists.

"Mary isn't your rightful wife," Adrian said, more to distract Brabourne while he strategized. If he could some-how pull Brabourne onto the road, then he and Robert would have the advantage. But he had to do it without risk-ing Brabourne pulling the trigger against Lisbeth's head.

"What would you know about rightful?" Brabourne spat. "Your mother was a quadroon slut. Anything you have isn't rightfully yours."

Adrian had long since stopped hearing such slurs. They weren't worth listening to, much less responding to.

But Lisbeth – lovely, ferocious Lisbeth – hadn't become immune. With a cry of outrage, she slammed her elbow directly into Brabourne's gut. He cowered, the pistol leaving her temple, and Adrian grabbed her hips, pulling her from Brabourne's grasp.

No sooner had he set her to the ground did Brabourne jump from the carriage directly onto Adrian. His weight hit Adrian's shoulders, and Adrian fell to his knees before he could land a punch against Brabourne's arm. Robert leapt into the fray, wresting away the pistol. Adrian levered his feet to flip Brabourne onto his back. Dust erupted, cloud-ing Adrian's eyes and mouth for a moment. Brabourne flailed forward, trying to land hits against them. Adrian pummeled him, one punch in the face and the rest at his midsection.

No hit was enough for Adrian's fury. He jabbed at Brabourne's stomach over and over, as if each punch could leach away the earl's sins against Adrian. Manhandling Lisbeth. Daring to look at Mary. Weaseling his way into Hathorne Shipping. Trying to steal ten of the 219 souls from Inglewilde Plantation. Treating Adrian like a lackey. Over and over and over again.

Until suddenly, his energy disappeared. Brabourne lay limp, blood pooling in the dust beneath him. Robert kicked his gut, and the man's whole body shook like a bag of cotton.

Adrian didn't have the stomach to do anything more. And he suddenly remembered Lisbeth, lying in the dirt where she had fallen from the carriage.

He rushed to her. "Are you all right? Did he hurt you?"

Her hands and ankles were still tied. His fingers – numb and sore from punches – fumbled over the ropes.

"He was about to before you arrived. They were supposed to kidnap Mary, but they took me accidentally. He had just decided he needed to dispose of me one way or another." Lisbeth's arms fell forward once he released her bindings, and she wrapped herself around him.

Even after everything, her hair smelled of cinnamon. "Lisbeth." He couldn't find any other words.

She kissed just below his ear, where her lips landed

278

naturally. "I am fine. Mary is fine. You are fine."

He wanted them to be more than fine. He wanted them to have never been threatened in the first place.

Lisbeth handed him the ropes he had just untied. "Here, truss him up."

Robert helped bind Brabourne's feet and hands together. Then – huffing – Adrian and Robert carried Brabourne and the driver into the ditch. Justice would begin by leaving him to the mercy of the countryside; from there, the Duke of Berkwell would need to lobby for charges as an exception to Brabourne's immunity as a peer of the realm.

Adrian's heart stammered again when he turned and saw Lisbeth standing by the carriage, exhaustion lacing her whole body.

She was his everything. He didn't understand yet how she ended up in the carriage and not Mary, but he sensed it had everything to do with Lisbeth refusing to accept reality. If not for her, Mary would be married to that monster. If not for her, Adrian would be the brother that didn't fight for his sister.

How could he ever leave her behind?

Chapter Thirty-One

Somehow, Lisbeth slept the whole ride back to London. She didn't think she would, alone on the Brabourne carriage bench swaddled in Adrian's cloak while he and Robert drove the carriage and two horses, but almost as soon as the coach rolled into motion, she fell into a dreamless sleep. When she awoke, they were turning the corner onto Upper Norton Street.

Adrian opened the carriage door himself. She flashed back to the moment only hours earlier, when Brabourne had dangled her before Adrian like some sort of doll he could toss away at any moment. Lisbeth wasn't sure Brabourne would truly have shot her, but she had worried he would turn the gun on Adrian.

It was all behind them now, she reminded herself, and instead of terror, there was relief on Adrian's face. He smiled at her. "Did you rest?"

"As if we had done nothing more exciting than attend a ball." Lisbeth put her hand – bare – in Adrian's gloved palm to step down. She had hardly landed on the cobblestones when he scooped her into his arms. "I can walk!" she protested, but without much conviction. Even though he stank of sweaty horses, she felt better wrapped against him.

Robert followed them up the stairs with amusement wreathed about his face.

Ford opened the front door in his usual, serene manner. It was only when he saw Lisbeth in Adrian's arms that he blanched. "Should I call for a doctor?"

"That won't be necessary." Adrian placed Lisbeth on her feet in the parlor. The household didn't feel any different than any other day. For the first time since Adrian and Robert had left Brabourne in the ditch, her skin crawled again with unease.

"Where is Miss Hathorne?" Lisbeth asked. Almost as soon as she did, Mary came down the stairs herself.

"Lisbeth! Where on earth have you been?" Her tone was cavalier until she got close enough to spy the mud on Lisbeth's nightgown. "What happened to you?"

Adrian's hand flew to the small of Lisbeth's back. "You didn't know Lisbeth was missing?"

"Missing?" Any color drained from Mary's cheeks. "I thought it strange you didn't come down for breakfast, but I thought perhaps you were overtired. Hannah only just told me she hasn't seen you this morning."

"What about you? Did you disappear at all last night?" Adrian might as well have heaved the question at Mary, with all the intensity in his voice, and she backed up as if he had.

"I…"

Lisbeth knew what Mary did not want to admit: she had snuck up to Suzy's quarters. Lisbeth tugged on Adrian's arm, both for his attention and to silently beg him to calm down. "They thought they had Mary because I was in her bed. We were awake late talking, and she wanted my company as she fell asleep. I fell asleep too. When I woke, Mary had just left...for a snack in the kitchen, I suppose... and then the men entered and took me."

"Took you?" Mary whispered. "You were kidnapped?"

Lisbeth wished she could spare Mary the truth, but it was the least her sister-in-law deserved. "Lord Brabourne wanted to take you to Gretna Green for an elopement."

Mary wrapped her arms around herself. "Where is he now?"

"Lost in the countryside, I presume," Adrian said. Dropping his hand from Lisbeth's waist, he approached Mary. Slowly – almost as if afraid – he drew her into a hug. "I'm sorry, Mary. I should have listened to you."

From behind Lisbeth, Robert asked, "If Mary didn't know anything had happened, how did Adkins come to know that someone had been kidnapped, and why did he think it was Mary?"

Lisbeth wished she could spare them all from this next truth. "Mr. Adkins informed Brabourne that Mary did not want to marry him. Brabourne told me himself. Adkins provided him with how to get into the house and which bedroom to go into."

"He wanted a tip for telling us." Adrian's voice shook with a dangerous anger. "He thought he could work both sides for money."

Ford, who had been standing by the door the whole time, let out a discreet ahem. "Permit me to mention that

Mr. Adkins removed himself from the household this morning. I suspect you will find him at the Horseman's Arms on Cortland Street."

Lisbeth felt the look between Adrian and Robert, the one forged in steel. Adrian touched his hand to her shoulder. "Do you mind if I go?"

For once, she didn't mind not being involved. "Go. I'll have Mrs. Siswell fix a breakfast for when you get back."

Adrian gave her one last smile – just a twitch of the lips, really – before charging off with Robert. Lisbeth whispered a little prayer to safeguard them before allowing Mary to draw her upstairs.

"You must be exhausted," Mary chattered, leading Lisbeth to her proper bedchamber. "How horrifying. It makes my stomach turn. Kidnapped out of your own house! Were you terrified? I'll call for Hannah. You'll want a hot bath, won't you? Perhaps some chocolate, too."

"I rested in the carriage." Except now that Lisbeth stood still in the cocoon of her rooms, her every muscle trembled with exhaustion. Mary sat her near the fireplace and rang the velvet bellpull for Hannah.

"Let Hannah see to you. She knows best. I expect her to report that you followed her every order."

"Yes, Your Grace," Lisbeth teased. That seemed to be the last of her energy. Through fuzzy eyes, she watched Hannah approach with a fresh nightgown. A hot towel scrubbed her skin, followed by creamy rose-scented lotion. Then someone guided her to the bed and tucked her under the heavenly-soft sheets.

This wasn't a dreamless sleep. First, Lord Brabourne leered at her with that gleaming pistol held to his own jaw. Then, she had transformed into Mary, and she couldn't free her hand from something, and when she looked down, she saw her wrist clenched in an iron shackle emblazoned in raised, red letters: Hathorne. Now it was her own hand again, and the cuff melted from iron to gold, but it still read Hathorne. She tugged and tugged at it, but it wouldn't come off. She was about to scream when two slender fingers pressed the seam of the shackle, and it slid off like discarded silk.

Still foggy from the dream, Lisbeth batted her eyes open to see Adrian standing above her. His knuckles drifted across her exposed arm. "I didn't mean to wake you."

"Did you find Adkins?" Her voice came out scratchy from sleep.

"Yes, and he is now safely tucked away in Newgate Prison." Adrian slipped his fingers between hers. His skin was cool. "We need to tell His Grace what happened. I wanted to make sure you had not perished of shock."

Lisbeth sat up. "I want to go with you. It is a family discussion."

Adrian was silent for a moment. His expression was shuttered with his mask, but Lisbeth spied a little emotion in his eyes as they looked at every part of her face but her own gaze. Six weeks ago, she would have raged at him for being so reluctant to respond. Now, knowing that a thousand calculations of fear were stopping him, her heart swelled.

"If you think it wise," she edited herself. "I will do whatever you need. You know best."

Tipping onto her knees, Lisbeth linked her fingers around the back of his neck and kissed him. They hadn't kissed in days. She had almost forgotten the way he tasted, always of Ceylon tea.

Adrian palmed her bum, locking her hips against his stomach. He growled, a back of the throat exhalation that vibrated all the way through her tongue. His hands roved upwards, claiming her breasts with rough kneads, and then down to catch the hem of her nightdress. He backed away from her kiss long enough to pull the gown over her head.

Lisbeth had not yet grown inured to being naked before her husband. Her skin tingled with delicious, hot desire as she watched his green eyes rake over every inch of bared flesh. She lay back on the mattress, spreading her legs, and relished how eagerly he climbed on top of her.

They kissed with more urgency now, as if the energy behind their locking lips would save the world. Lisbeth pushed off Adrian's jacket, untied his cravat, unbuttoned his waistcoat and then his shirt, all while tasting the heat of his tongue. He raised away from her for another moment, discarding the rest of his clothes, and then she saw nothing but the muscles rippling beneath his skin and the proud, thick cock twitching in anticipation.

Oh, she had missed this.

Adrian rested on his elbows above her. His breath was hot and fast against her neck. He stared at her, still, until she thought he would never move again. Now she was the one to growl, launching her legs to wrap around his waist, pulling him inside her with a slick, satisfying jerk.

He gasped a little. Lisbeth laughed, rocking her hips faster and faster. Adrian joined in too, so she could feel him deep inside in hot, swift, teasing strokes. They usually lingered over sex, stretching it into an hour of orgasms, but now they fucked as if they were stealing time. Their bodies fused in sweat and desire. Their rhythm increased to a frenzy. The bed creaked in chorus. And then Adrian cried out in release. Watching his face puddle with satisfaction – knowing that she was the reason he felt such ecstasy – rushed Lisbeth to her own climax, a rolling happiness that pulled him even closer.

They curled against each other. Lisbeth had missed disappearing into the cave of Adrian's embrace, where nothing mattered but him. Where nothing threatened except the idea that they might not do this again soon enough.

A pang of sorrow shot through her heart. "What am I going to do when you go to Jamaica?"

She hadn't even realized she spoke it aloud until Adrian responded, "What am I going to do when you stay in London?"

He held her for a moment longer, but the air between

them had changed. His arms were more tense, and Lisbeth almost held her breath, not sure what to say next. Then Adrian rolled away. He started collecting his clothes. "Of course you should come with us to tell Their Graces what happened last night. Will you be ready within the hour?"

Lisbeth felt she was agreeing to something more than a timeline when she said yes. But she watched Adrian disappear into his bedchamber, and she couldn't think of anything to say that would call him back.

Chapter Thirty-Two

Adrian had spent almost the whole day out of doors, yet he didn't notice the sunshine or the summery warmth to the air until his grandparents received them in the garden. They sat amidst the duchess's prize tulips, on chairs carried out by the servants along with trays of cold meats, warm scones, and lemonade from freshly-arrived Sicilian lemons. A fat bumblebee buzzed about their glasses until the duke shooed it away.

Adrian placed himself between Mary and Lisbeth. When he'd left Lisbeth in her bedroom, she had looked a woman thoroughly rutted, with hair frizzing in every direction and delicious red swelling about her lips. Now she looked almost virginal in a pale muslin day dress frothing with lace about the hem. Her hair had been tamed and curled into a perfectly respectable coiffure.

Adrian wished they hadn't had to cut short their interlude that afternoon. He wished he had a better answer than matching his own fears to hers.

For her part, Mary wore a long-sleeved gown that looked far too warm for the afternoon. She sat almost perfectly still, and even her lips were pale.

"Now, what is this all about?" his grandfather asked, looking first at Robert and then at Adrian.

Robert, as always, spoke first. "It's about Lord

Brabourne. I'm afraid he has revealed himself to be unsuitable for marriage."

"Unsuitable for marriage!" Adrian couldn't help but balk at the phrasing. "He is unsuitable for honorable life. He kidnapped Lisbeth, thinking she was Mary, to elope in Gretna Green. It is only because my valet – who instigated the whole plot – alerted Robert and me that we were able to stop him from…" Adrian hadn't yet let himself contemplate what Brabourne would have done had they not interrupted.

"He had just decided to place me on a tea clipper to Bangkok," Lisbeth volunteered. She almost smiled after, as if it were funny.

Adrian's grandparents had two opposite reactions: the duchess paled while the duke turned red as a lobster. "Why should he need to elope?" the duke growled. "The wedding is scheduled for June. The invitations have already been sent."

Adrian looked to Mary, who was staring at the ground. Then he sensed Lisbeth opening her mouth, and he placed a hand over hers to silence her. "Mary does not wish to marry Lord Brabourne. We have been making plans for an alternative."

His grandmother wilted further into her chair. The duke's knuckles went white from gripping his cane. "What alternative could there be? The marriage contract is signed."

Adrian studied his grandfather. He had spent so much energy molding himself into the perfect grandson, memorizing every appropriate response and wearing the best outfits and never placing a foot out of line. But the duke had yet to react to the fact that Adrian's wife had been kidnapped from her own house.

"Mary will always be welcome in my household," Adrian said. "In England or Jamaica or wherever else. She need not marry anyone."

The duchess had collected herself enough to sit up, and she placed a palm on her husband's arm as if to reel him in. "Of course she won't marry Lord Brabourne now. We will cut all ties with him."

His grandfather still glared at him. "The Hathorne name will be dragged through the scandal sheets."

"A small sacrifice for my sister to be safe from a monster."

Mary stirred beside him. "What upsets Your Grace? That your family was threatened, or that Adrian and I dared disagree with you?"

"If you had not disagreed with me, the family would not have been threatened!" The duke knocked his cane against the flagstone terrace to emphasize his point.

"I beg to differ, Your Grace." Lisbeth somehow managed to make this sound demure as a debutante refusing a dance. "If we had not disagreed, Mary would be wedded forever to a man who stoops to kidnapping and murder."

Robert had been silent this whole time. Now, he leaned forward. "Grandpapa, I'm sure you can see it is better this way. Let Adrian care for Mary. Every family deserves a little scandal, and if that is our only one, I'd say we're getting away lucky."

The duke shook his head. "You are being naïve, Robert. Only one scandal?"

Adrian didn't know what his grandfather referred to until his grandmother said sharply, "Adrian is our beloved grandson."

"That doesn't stop him from being a scandal, any more than if he'd been born on the wrong side of the blanket." The duke looked at Adrian now with the soft, watery blue eyes that Adrian had so long associated with kindness. "This will make things worse for you, not better."

Too much had been said already. Too much had happened. Adrian didn't know how to sort his heart from his brain from his gut reactions. But something crystallized for him that made it easy to decide what to say next.

"This is nothing compared to what I plan to do once I inherit Inglewilde Plantation. I'm going to free all our slaves."

Mary gasped. Robert swiveled to stare at him as if he'd sprouted two heads. And his grandparents – his grandparents didn't look as if they'd heard.

"This is your secret plan? Are you mad?" Robert might as well have shouted this. "We will lose all our profits if we have to pay for labor."

"Perhaps."

"You'll start an insurrection," Robert continued. "All the slaves on the island will want their freedom. They'll revolt, like they did in Haiti, and all our friends will lose their livelihoods, if not their lives."

Adrian lifted his shoulders. "Slaves are human souls no different from me or you. They deserve their freedom, no matter the consequences to us."

He looked to his grandfather, bracing for a reaction. He might be thrown out. He might be expelled from the family. They might even write to his father to take his inheritance away. Adrian might have risked everything by confessing his heart.

He didn't regret it, not yet.

The duke sank back in his chair. "You will be the most hated man in the British Empire."

"A small price to pay."

"Your children..." The duchess's eyes darted to Lisbeth. Even when she didn't finish her sentence, Adrian knew what she meant. He was cutting his children from any future in the higher echelons of English society.

Lisbeth smiled. She was gorgeous in the sun, beaming with pride. "If we are blessed with children, they will know the pride of choosing the right action over the expedient or greedy one."

It was in that moment, watching Lisbeth say the most extraordinary things in the tone of an ordinary wife, that Adrian knew he could never leave her behind. He couldn't spend his life on one side of an ocean knowing she was on the other, charming everyone but him. He couldn't exist a single day without seeing her, without basking in her determination and her empathy and her plucky cheer. He loved her.

"Will you come with me to Jamaica?" he asked, even though he knew the conversation was better saved for a moment alone. He couldn't last another second without knowing her answer.

Lisbeth blinked at him, her brown eyes bright and her pink lips suspended in surprise. Then she smiled, teeth and all. She tucked her gloved hand in his. "I thought you would never ask."

Adrian almost kissed her. Instead, he stood. "Your Graces, Robert, I should take my leave. Please know you are my cherished family, and you always will be. Mary, if you would like, you are welcome to stay with us indefinitely, but I also understand if you prefer to stay here."

Mary rose. She was beaming almost as much as Lisbeth. "I'm coming with you."

And so, with his wife and his sister on either arm, Adrian strolled out of Berkwell House on a perfect, sunny afternoon.

Chapter Thirty-Three

In the summer heat, Lisbeth could smell the docks a mile before the carriage deposited her at the wharf. The July sun had been shining at full intensity for almost two weeks already, heating every cobblestone within an inch of its life and liberating every stench of sewage, seaweed, and sweat. She couldn't imagine a more suffocating heat, yet she knew at the other end of her voyage, she would be introduced to a climate where this would be considered winter.

The past few months had disappeared in a flurry at Upper Norton Street. After Adrian had declared his intentions to his family, he had decided they should sail to Jamaica sooner rather than later. That meant ordering new clothes, packing trunks of books, writing letters of recommendation for the staff, and soaking up as much time with her parents as she could. She and Mrs. Siswell had only just finished closing up the house an hour before Lisbeth climbed into the last English carriage she would see for the next few years.

They were sailing on the newest pride of Hathorne Shipping. They had christened it at a small ceremony the previous week, where the only Hathornes in attendance were Adrian, Mary, and Lisbeth. It was a majestic three-masted sailing ship with a painted mermaid rising on its helm. Mary had been given the honor of naming it, and now it bore *The Suzy* in carved, gilded letters.

Standing on the wharf, Lisbeth's stomach flipped in anticipation. She had never been on a ship for a single day, so much as the seventy days the captain predicted for their journey to Kingston. Since May, all she had read were travelogues: Captain Cook's journals from the Far East, Lady Craven's record of her trip to Crimea, and George Forester's *A Voyage Around the World*. She expected sub-par food, hammocks for beds, and surprise storms. Then, too, there might be fevers or bowel cramps that swept the ship. Or, once she got to Jamaica, she might catch one of the hundred swamp diseases that infamously killed White women as soon as they docked.

Whatever she was about to embark upon was beyond anything she had ever imagined, and Lisbeth could hardly wait.

Two sailors in freshly starched uniforms waited at the bottom of the gangplank to help her board the ship. Lisbeth refused their hands. After all, she wore sensible travel boots instead of slippers, and if she couldn't climb a slanted board, she would have a hard journey ahead of her indeed. She almost lost her footing at the very top, but she managed to land on the deck with steady feet.

The farewell party welcomed her with a little round of applause. Lisbeth had invited her parents to see her off, as well as the painter Mr. Nadin, Annabelle and Bernard, a few other friends from Annabelle's salons, and, of course,

Mary. Adrian had invited Mary and Suzy to travel to Inglewilde Hall, but they had decided to stay in England and were moving into a cottage Adrian had procured for them in a bucolic Surrey town.

Lisbeth went to her parents first, pulling them each into a hug, propriety be damned.

"Are you quite sure about this?" her father asked. "I went to great trouble in that marriage contract to keep you from going to Jamaica."

"Yes, what of your life as patroness to every artist in London?" Her mother tucked an errant curl of Lisbeth's back into place. "The life you dreamed of will be hard to find in Jamaica."

"Dreams change." Lisbeth squeezed her parents' hands. "I've never been more certain of anything in my life. Adrian and I are going to change as much of the world as we can. Besides, art does exist outside of England."

As if hearing his name called, Adrian appeared at her side with a flute of imported champagne. "This is your last chance to stay in London for your own set of adventures."

Her husband was always handsome, but Lisbeth took a moment to appreciate how he was especially so in the summer sun, a glimmer of excitement in his eyes and a perfect, contented smile on his lips. If it wouldn't make her mother swoon, she would kiss him then and there.

Instead, she accepted the champagne with a tease. "This is your last chance to order me to stay behind so you can carry on your own adventures in Jamaica."

"*Order* you? Me? I'm sure I've never dreamed of doing such a thing."

They lingered in each other's smiles for a moment longer before turning to their guests. Everyone kept the chatter pleasant and focused on the exciting parts of travel, which Lisbeth appreciated because seeing her family and friends on the ship – knowing in just a quarter hour they would disembark and she wouldn't see them for years – put a lump of regret in her throat. When Annabelle said, "My salons won't be the same without you there to tell Mrs. Ludlow exactly how stupid she is," Lisbeth's eyes stung with tears.

"I've never said that," Lisbeth defended herself, fluttering her fan to distract from emotion.

"Not in so many words, anyway," Annabelle agreed.

Bernard, as usual not at all in tune with Lisbeth, cleared his throat and dived straight into the territory she wished to avoid. "It is hard to believe that it was only the beginning of this year when you so tactfully told me to shove off. I cannot tell you how glad I am to see you happily married."

Now Lisbeth had to look away to keep them from seeing the tears flooding her eyes. "Indeed. I hope you will not take it poorly when I declare I am *so* glad I did not marry you, Lord Gresham."

It may well have turned into a terrible display of emotions, but they were interrupted by the arrival of more guests. Over the gangplank came not only Robert but also the Duke and Duchess of Berkwell. Lisbeth looked to Adrian – she wasn't sure if her blood should run cold or warm at the unexpected guests.

The Hathornes had been absolutely silent since that afternoon in May. They had not so much as written a note acknowledging Adrian and Lisbeth's plans. Nor had they taken any action to stop them, though Adrian still mentioned almost every day that they could very well keep him from inheriting.

Now, the duke and duchess walked directly to Adrian. Robert trailed behind them. He was so uncertain that he hardly looked like himself.

"My dear," the duchess began, taking Adrian's hands into her own. "We would not have you sail away with unpleasant words between us. Would we, Your Grace?"

The duke, leaning on his jeweled cane, did not quite look at either Adrian or Lisbeth. Still, he said, "I have given your proposal much thought. While it is a huge risk, the Hathorne family has made our name for taking risks. After all, Charles II would not have granted us the duchy if we had not risked life and limb to put him back on the throne. Nor would Hathorne Shipping be prosperous if it were not for your father's risks. You have my permission to proceed." Then, more gruffly, he added, "Scandal be damned."

Lisbeth watched surprise play behind Adrian's emotionless mask. He bowed his head. "Thank you, Your Grace."

"You may name your firstborn after me in thanks,"

the duchess said, winking at Lisbeth.

Lisbeth willed her hand to remain at her side instead of flying to her stomach. She wasn't sure she was with child, and if she *was,* she wasn't sure how the two-month journey to Jamaica would impact her. Still, she and Adrian would be together. If not now, then soon.

Not that she would take the duchess's suggestion. The duke was the one who had furnished Mr. Hathorne with the money to purchase slaves in the first place, and now he offered his permission as if he were a kindly king. Lisbeth would not reward Adrian's family for agreeing to decency.

Robert stepped forward, offering his hand for Adrian to shake. "You will have a hell of a challenge on your hands. I'll be here to smooth feathers however I can."

Adrian grinned, the boyish smile that Lisbeth liked to imagine had been a constant presence before he had been shipped to England, and shook Robert's hand. "I wouldn't want life to grow boring for you, after all."

The duchess turned to Mary. "I have heard you plan to move to some unknown town in Surrey. You silly girl. You will move to the dowager cottage at Maidenheath, and there you shall stay as long as you want."

Lisbeth saw tears spring to Mary's eyes and had to bat away her own. She hadn't known she had been holding her breath these three long months. She must have, though, because all of a sudden, she felt she could inhale again – even if they were deep, healthy gulps of London stink.

Her mother stepped forward, raising a glass in toast.

"To the happy and healthy Hathornes!" She meant Lisbeth and Adrian, but Lisbeth celebrated the broader, newly repaired family. How much easier it was to sail across the ocean knowing Adrian hadn't lost the relationships he had so jealously protected all those years.

Their guests remained another quarter of an hour. Then, in a flurry of unprecedented embraces, Lisbeth said goodbye to her parents, her friends, and the Hathornes. Sailors raised the gangplank. Lisbeth and Adrian were sealed into their voyage.

Adrian took her hand. They dodged sailors throwing ropes, hauling sails, and swearing blue streaks, until Lisbeth found herself at the prow, just behind the mermaid's head. Adrian leaned against the wood railing, his arms framing her. The ship was sailing down the Thames now; Lisbeth waved to the wharves, the sailors on the quays, the marshlands beyond. The breeze turned into a wind, catching her hair and swirling her skirts.

She turned to face Adrian. She had ordered a purple traveling suit for precisely this purpose. Now she removed the jacket, so that her bare arms caught the sunlight as they wrapped around his neck.

"Well, Captain Bigsby, I suppose it is time to discover what adventure awaits."

Adrian – careful, wonderful Adrian – grinned and leaned down to claim his kiss.

Five Years Later

Adrian could never find Lisbeth when he needed her. The thick letter was growing damp from his sweat as he searched Inglewilde Hall. She wasn't in the sitting room, nor the nursery, nor their bedchamber. Neither was she in the schoolroom, the gallery, or at the harpsichord. Finally, when he checked in the communal kitchen, Mrs. Plummer told him Lisbeth was running wild through the gardens with the children.

He couldn't help but smile. As much as Lisbeth played the proper English lady for the benefit of Kingston society, whenever no judgmental eyes were looking, she loved to play on her hands and knees with their children, no matter if she was wearing her Sunday best. Their neighbors – the freed slaves who had decided to stay on the land Adrian offered – laughed with her and sometimes even joined her. Sure enough, he found Lisbeth in the ornamental garden, crouching behind a rose bush with the toddler in her arms while their four-year-old counted to ten across the path.

"Papa!" Rebecca squealed when she opened her eyes. She had Lisbeth's wide brow and easy smile, but his own green irises. Now she raced to catch his legs, forgetting her game entirely.

Adrian lifted her in the air, spinning her the way she loved, and smacked a kiss on her cheek before setting her back down. "I have missed you, Miss Rebecca!"

"It has only been since luncheon, Papa." This from Lisbeth, who rose and handed him Oliver for a kiss, too.

Adrian obliged, happily, then asked Rebecca, "Have you not missed me, even though it has only been since luncheon?"

She giggled. "Of course I have!"

Lisbeth rose to her tiptoes to claim her own kiss. "I have, too."

"Good." Adrian held up the letter. "We have news from Aunt Mary."

"From England?" Squinting, Rebecca made it sound as dubious as if the letter had come from Heaven itself. Adrian could just imagine how the lords of London would purse their lips at the suggestion that England did not, in fact, exist.

He led them to the stone bench nestled between hibiscus trees. Lisbeth settled on his one side, Rebecca on the other, and Oliver wriggled in his lap. Making great ceremony out of it to elicit every reaction from Rebecca that he could, Adrian opened the letter and unfolded the four square sheets. After a dramatic clearing of the throat, he began to read:

Dearest Adrian, Lisbeth, Rebecca, and Oliver,

How happy I am every time the post includes a letter from you! Your most recent missive made me tear up like a sentimental fool as I remembered Easters at Inglewilde as a child. I am glad that your family is happy there.

Easter has passed here, and now we are in the season of summer house parties. Rebecca and Oliver, can you imagine a passel of adults invading Inglewilde Hall for weeks on end?

Here, Rebecca obliged with a wrinkled nose. For want of a better reaction, Oliver imitated his sister.

It has been great fun. Suzy and I go up to Maidenheath House to participate in afternoon picnics, games of croquet, swims in Fairy Pond, and of course charades after supper. Most recently, our guests included friends of yours: the Duke and Duchess of Harrodshire with their two children, Lord and Lady Windemere with their three children, and Lord and Lady Gresham with their little girl. Suzy and I pronounced ourselves headmistresses of the children. Between those six and our own Jules, Polly, and Nat, it was pure chaos – and pure joy – for three weeks straight.

Our guests asked me to remember them to you, Lisbeth, directly. Margot and Annabelle are hard at work on your most recent directive; I believe the Ladies' Society for Liberated Labor now numbers forty members (including myself and Suzy, of course). For her part, Alice gets positively feral with passion when discussing the Yorkshire school that you brought to her attention. I cannot believe any patron of a school has ever been so involved, nor so committed to providing the students a better opportunity.

Rebecca let out a wide yawn. "I don't know these people, Papa. Where is the news of Uncle Robert?"

"*I* know these people." Lisbeth laced this with the newest from her arsenal of smiles, the one that communicated admonishment only one degree more than it expressed love. "These were some of my dearest friends when I lived in London, before I met Papa."

"Anyhow, if you had been patient instead of interrupting, we have come to the news of Uncle Robert." Adrian resumed his narration:

Uncle Robert is a gracious host, as always, but he continues to avoid matrimony despite every guest's best efforts to introduce him to such-and-such friend. He says that as this was the first Season of putting off mourning for Their Graces, he is entitled to fun, and perhaps next year he will choose a wife. I am not holding my breath. After all, he loves to crow that should he fail to produce an heir, Oliver will inherit. He quite likes the idea of our branch of Hathornes running the roost.

"What do you think of that?" Lisbeth teased Rebecca. "How would you feel if Oliver became the Duke of Berkwell?"

"Could I be duchess?"

This was perhaps Adrian's favorite thing about his daughter: she had her mother's eternal optimism, and the sense that the world would always right itself to give her a fair shake. He hated to betray her with the truth. "That isn't how it works, but perhaps Oliver will change the rules for you."

"I want to be a princess."

But she said this with much less conviction, and her eyelids were beginning to droop. Lisbeth stood. "It is time for your nap. We will read the rest of the letter before bed."

Rebecca protested, but barely. Cradling Oliver against his chest, Adrian followed Lisbeth to the cool, dark nursery. He had all but banished his memories of waiting for his mother to come visit; at present day, the chambers were strewn with toys, and he and Lisbeth were more frequently with the children than they were anywhere else. Now, they tucked them into their beds, cajoled them to sleep, and shut the door.

Adrian rested a moment against the wall, breathing in Lisbeth. They each of them had five more years of life on their bodies. He had grown a bit of a gut, and he kept his hair shorn short to hide the fact that he was already balding. Lisbeth, meanwhile, seemed only to grow more beautiful with each year and each baby. Her cheeks were a little plumper, her figure a little softer, her aura a little more irresistible. Now, he admired the way the breeze ruffled her coiffure – already frizzed from the constant humidity – as she asked, "Was there much more to the letter?"

"A few more lines about the children." Suzy and Mary had informally adopted three orphaned siblings from the nearby town when they lost their entire family in a sweep of typhoid. Mary's letters had always been cheerful, but they had picked up a new sheen of joy since she took the children in. "Jules is almost old enough to learn to dance, so Mary is considering bringing in a governess."

Smiling, Lisbeth turned down the corridor toward their bedchamber. "Did Mr. White find you? He had something to discuss about their goats."

"No. I'll stop by before supper." Adrian looked forward to it, too. Thurber White was one of the freed people he felt was a true friend, which was mostly because the man was so gregarious. When Adrian had settled everyone's freedom, he had offered them fifty pounds and ten acres of land. The majority of souls had chosen to stay at Inglewilde, which meant mass confusion if they had all chosen the surname Hathorne. Lisbeth had pulled out her copy of Debrett's to offer up more English names, but Thurber had simply laughed and said he wanted to be White.

Adrian's experiment had, for the most part, worked. Those that had stayed at Inglewilde could choose to grow whatever they wanted, but Adrian paid them handsomely to produce sugar at the same rate as before. He had furnished them with supplies both for farming and to build houses, and a neighborhood now dotted the Inglewilde fields. The house slaves were offered their same positions for a wage, and Inglewilde Hall turned into a community center, with a communal kitchen, a schoolroom, a library, a sick room, and – for Lisbeth – a gallery dedicated to art of all forms.

A few of the 219 souls he freed had chosen to leave. More stayed, but remained silent whenever he visited, leaving Adrian to rely on allies like Mr. White to tell him where he might help. Worst, the neighboring plantations didn't take Adrian's actions kindly. Every few months, something new and terrible happened: fields catching fire, livestock let loose, people disappearing.

If all Mr. White had to discuss that afternoon was a goat, then Adrian was in for a visit of rum, jokes, and a little ordinary animal husbandry.

Lisbeth had started running through the laundry list of what she had to do before supper. She turned into their bedchambers, going directly to her dressing room. "All this, and Mrs. Hatchley sent a note that she plans to call this afternoon! Perhaps our money isn't too tainted to contribute to the church roof after all."

Adrian caught her waist in his hands. "Did you ever imagine your life of adventures would include battling with the vicar's wife over whether or not you are allowed to contribute money?"

Lisbeth looped her hands behind his neck. "My imagination was not vast enough. It has gotten bigger over the years."

"Oh really?" Adrian traced his fingers up her bodice. "What are you imagining this very moment?"

Her cheeks flamed red even as she smiled naughtily. "I'm sure I haven't the time to imagine anything this very moment."

"Ah, I see. I mustn't leave anything up to your

imagination."

Lisbeth protested – "I *really* must dress for Mrs. Hatchley" – but Adrian wasn't deterred. He placed kisses along the curve of her neck as he freed her of dress and chemise in one or two practiced moves. Moving his lips to taste hers, he disrobed, too. Lisbeth ran her fingertips across his chest, down his stomach, around his thighs. He pushed her against the wall. His face buried in her halo of hair, he suddenly remembered that March night so long ago, when he had accidentally kissed her hair instead of her lips.

What a fool he had been. How glad he was Lisbeth asked for an annulment and jolted him into discovering her for who she was.

Adrian paused the frenzy of the moment to take a long, slow kiss. Lisbeth blinked up at him, dazed. "What was that for?"

He couldn't quite answer. "Are you happy?"

"I'd be happier if you were inside me," she breathed, tilting her hips towards him.

"In life, I mean. Are you happy?"

She responded with an equally long, slow kiss. "I have two wonderful children, a husband who does right by everyone he meets, a fine house and reliable income, a hundred and one projects to improve our little patch of the world. Oh, and my own salon of Jamaican painters and musicians. And let me not forget I am currently being fucked by the love of my life." Placing each palm on his ass, she sheathed herself onto his cock in one, easy thrust. "Yes, I am happy. Are you?"

Mrs. Hatchley may have been kept waiting, but Lisbeth got her answer a hundred times over.

Historical Note

When I first conjured Lisbeth Dawes in *The Ideal Countess*, I knew that her love story would be unique. She is too spirited to settle with any old lord, so I wrote all the other installments of *The Countess Chronicles* worrying that I wouldn't find the right hero for Lisbeth. Then I started digging into the question of race – would Lisbeth have encountered non-White people in her sphere? – and stumbled upon Adrian, whose family had put him in an impossible position. From there, the novel got written.

Much of my inspiration for this book came from two research sources: *Staying Power: The History of Black People in Britain* by Peter Fryer and *Children of Uncertain Fortune: Mixed-Race Jamaicans in Britain and the Atlantic Family, 1733-1833* by Daniel Livesay.

Staying Power traces Black people in Britain from their first visits in pre-Elizabethan times through to the 1970s. If your first reaction to the presence of a Black character in Regency England is, "that's unrealistic," then I highly recommend this research book to open your eyes. Since Britain was the center of a global empire, there is a rich history of non-White people in all parts of the country (yes, even tiny farm towns!). Fryer shares the overarching history of communities, the history of concepts such as racism, and individual life stories to paint an incredibly helpful picture. I turned to this research multiple times to understand how Lisbeth and Adrian would understand race, where Adrian might encounter other people of color, and what they might read about abolition. I did take the artistic liberty of introducing a Black actor a decade earlier than the real Ira Aldridge.

I turned to *Children of Uncertain Fortune* to inform Adrian's life story. Daniel Livesay and his research team pored through centuries of Jamaican wills to paint a picture of how race informed family in Jamaica as well as Britain. Since the Jamaican economy was labor-intensive sugar plantations, the British relied on slavery. Until 1807, they kidnapped hundreds of thousands of people a year from Africa and forced them into slavery. Although the slave trade was abolished in 1807, slavery itself remained legal until 1834, and it took an additional four years before all slaves in the British Empire were emancipated (plus massive payouts to slave owners that stretched into the twenty-first century).

Wealthy White planters in Jamaica commonly had mixed race children (in or out of wedlock). However, non-White people in Jamaica had limited rights, such as not being able to testify against Whites in court and (as of 1761) an inheritance cap of two thousand pounds. While this was a substantial amount of money in those days, it was only a small percentage of what wealthy sugar plantation owners were worth. Many White fathers objected to this, so they petitioned the Assembly for privilege bills, which were used to grant mixed race people "White" legal status. White fathers bolstered their case by sending their mixed-race children to England for schooling or marriage. While privilege bills were common in the late eighteenth century, between 1803 and 1813, the Assembly only agreed to listen to three of these petitions, apparently because member Mr. George Crawford Ricketts blocked them to preserve his own inheritance from a mixed-race "rival." That's why Adrian needs Lord Everly to apply pressure to Ricketts.

However, Livesay also points out several instances of White relations suing their mixed-race kin over rightful inheritances. In cases such as the Morse family, these suits were between siblings, lasted decades, and were followed closely in the newspapers. This introduces a fair amount of anxiety for Adrian that his plan won't even work.

Children of Uncertain Fortune also shows that many mixed-race children were sent to schools in Scotland and Yorkshire (because many of the Jamaican colonists were Scottish). While I didn't explore this much, I do imagine Alice and Hugh have taken to reforming one of these schools, since they live nearby.

One takeaway from both these books is that the concept of race is a social invention that made it easier for White British and Americans to subjugate the non-Europeans they encountered around the world. By the Regency period, British wealth came from exploiting people and economies across the globe, and so it was in the British power bloc's best interest to dehumanize as much as possible. This includes the racial classification system Adrian is subjected to, where his "Blackness" is defined by how long ago an ancestor was Black. I included that terminology because it informs so much of Adrian's life and motivation, but I want to be clear that it is the product of a racist system.

Speaking of terminology, I wrote this in the second half of 2020, as style guides are updating their conventions for capitalizing races. The AP style guide capitalizes Black but not white, declining to do the former because they claim the White community is not homogenous and because the capitalization is closely linked with White supremacy. I disagree with this style choice: no racial group is a homogenous community, so I want to give the word White the same treatment as other race words. And hopefully, if we all start doing that, we take away some power from White supremacy. (Thanks to Jen Trinh for talking through these nuances with me.)

Other research that has informed this book include:

- The Last Great Great House blog
- The Saint Lauretia Project
- Museum of London Dockyards
- *The History of White's* by the Honorable Algernon Burke
- *The Mirror of the Graces; Or, The English Lady's Costume* by a Lady of Distinction
- *The Coffee-House: A Cultural History* by Markman Ellis

This book is also inspired by other historical romance novels. For example, I was about 30% through my first draft when I realized I had chosen the name Adrian because of Courtney Milan's Adrian in *After the Wedding*. (By then, I was too connected to the name to change it, though I did try out Adam and Aaron as alternatives.)

The bookstore scene was inspired by Julia Quinn's *The Secret Diaries of Miss Miranda Cheever*. In that book, the heroine is denied a book purchase based on her gender. However, as a reader, I was disappointed that the hero only reinforced this and "solved" the problem by buying the book for her himself. I wanted him to help the heroine stick it to the Man! So I decided to write my own version. (I haven't found any evidence that there were actually gender-exclusive bookstores, which is why I made it a gentleman's club that purveys books.)

Finally, it is worth noting that I am a White, straight American twenty-first century author writing about British people in the nineteenth century who are different genders, races, class, religion, and sexual orientation than me. I have done my best to avoid character stereotypes and narrative archetypes in the interest of writing an emotionally honest story, but I am sure I got something about their experiences (or your experience as a reader identifying with them) wrong. If you have the energy, please let me know because I would like to learn to do better.

Thank you for reading!

Acknowledgments

For this book, I tried out a larger beta read process than before, so a huge thank you to everyone who gave me feedback. This includes my husband, parents, and sister (PhD). In addition, I would like to thank: Amy Lorowitz, Sophia Lynn Hamilton, Sydney Bixter, Jen Trinh (contemporary romance author extraordinaire with clutch steam advice – go check out her books!), and Carole B. from Romance Refined, who gave me expert sensitivity reader feedback.

I am incredibly grateful to the two talented designers who put together the final product in your hands. Julia Gerbach designed the cover and Asya Blue designed the layout.

I struggled with whether, as a White author, I should write this novel or not, and that translated into a lot of anxiety about everything. Thanks to my therapist for helping work through various issues. Thank you to my husband, Michael, for refusing to let me give in to that feeling of failure. His only plot is to make me so happy I could plotz.

Writing is my dream job, so most of all I want to thank everyone who makes this possible: my husband, my family, and you!

About the Author

Katherine Grant writes Regency Romance novels with smart women, sensitive men, and a healthy tablespoon of history. She published her debut novel, *The Ideal Countess*, in 2020. If you love ballgowns, secret kisses, and social commentary, a book hangover is coming your way.

While studying creative writing at Northwestern University, Katherine worked as a developmental editor for several small presses before moving to New York. Her short stories have been featured in several literary magazines, and she was nominated for a Pushcart Prize in 2018.

Her ideal day includes a cup of tea, a good book, and a board game with her patient husband. Find out more at www.katherinegrantromance.com

Stay in touch!

Don't forget to subscribe to my newsletter to read my free short story, *The Spinster!*

Plus, you'll get updates on my upcoming books directly to your inbox. Such as when my brand-spanking new series, The Prestons, releases.

Sign up at www.katherinegrantromance.com to get started!

www.ingramcontent.com/pod-product-compliance
Lightning Source LLC
Chambersburg PA
CBHW031620100726
47898CB00006B/1874